## A FAMILY AFFAIR

Born just two years apart, sisters Kathy and Maisie Bates couldn't be more different. Kathy has a good job and a handsome fiancé, but her parents despair of younger daughter Maisie. Pretty and fun-loving, Maisie has one thing on her mind: men. The arrival of hundreds of troops and handsome GIs means Southampton is the perfect place to meet them, but Maisie has no idea that servicemen are not always gentlemen. She takes too many chances, but it is Kathy who pays a horrific price, and when Maisie gets involved with a notorious local racketeer, Kathy finds herself in danger again.

# A FAMILY AFFAIR

# A FAMILY AFFAIR

*by*

June Tate

**Magna Large Print Books**
Long Preston, North Yorkshire,
BD23 4ND, England.

British Library Cataloguing in Publication Data.

---

Tate, June
A family affair.

A catalogue record of this book is available from the British Library

ISBN 978-0-7505-3099-6

First published in Great Britain in 2008
by Headline Publishing Group



Published in Large Print 2009 by arrangement with
Headline Publishing Group Ltd.



Magna Large Print is an imprint of Library Magna Books Ltd.

Printed and bound in Great Britain by
T.J. (International) Ltd., Cornwall, PL28 8RW

For my dear friend, Sylvia Brooks. We met when we were young and dangerous, working as hairdressers on the *Queen Mary*, and our friendship has not diminished with the passing years. It is something very special.

I also send my love and a hug to her gorgeous daughter, Tracy.

My love and gratitude as always to my
two daughters, Beverley and Maxine,
who make me proud to be their mother,
and to my son-in-law, Ronnie,
who has a lovely pair of knees!

# PROLOGUE

Saturday, 3 June 1944 was a dull day with occasional bright periods, but the weather was the last thing on the minds of the thousands of troops marching towards the Southampton docks. Hundreds of landing craft were waiting to take them across the English Channel to the beaches of Normandy, to face the enemy.

'Poor devils,' remarked Kathy Bates, standing watching with her younger sister Maisie. 'Who knows how many of them will come back alive?'

'Oh, for heaven's sake,' snapped her sister, 'do you have to be quite so miserable?' She smiled and waved at the troops as they passed. Maisie was a pretty girl with blonde hair cascading down her back, and shining blue eyes. At nineteen she was thrilled when she received catcalls and whistles of appreciation.

'Will you behave!' Kathy said.

'I'm just doing my bit for the war effort!' retorted Maisie.

'No doubt that was what you were doing last night. You came home very late. You woke me up.'

'I was out with a very nice army captain, if you must know. He took me to dinner.'

'A captain? Well, you seem to be working your way up the ranks. First it was a gunner, then a sergeant and now an officer.'

'And tonight I'm seeing a flight lieutenant in the RAF!' Maisie grinned at her sibling. 'Thought I'd like a change.'

Kathy couldn't help but smile. Her sister was outrageous. It wasn't that she minded Maisie enjoying her youth. After all, she was only twenty-one herself, but being engaged to Jimmy Greene, an engineer who was now in the army, had made her more settled in her ways. Her concern was that her flighty sister would get herself into, trouble, but whenever she tried to advise her, Maisie would fly off the handle.

As they started to walk away, Kathy said quietly, 'I suppose Jimmy will soon be on his way to France too.'

Maisie tucked her arm through her sister's. 'Try not to worry,' she said, 'I'm sure he'll be just fine. He's too good-looking to be wasted on the field of battle!' But as Maisie spoke, she knew that she too was anxious about her sister's fiancé. She had lusted after the handsome boy from the time he had started courting Kathy four years earlier. She was only fifteen at the time and Jimmy had treated her like a fractious teenager, but just lately, when he came home on leave, she knew that she made him uncomfortable when she flirted with him. And she was sure that he had felt a flicker of interest.

At night she fantasised about him. She longed to feel his arms about her, his mouth on hers, and she was certain that if she could get him to kiss her, just once, her fantasies might became a reality. The fact that he was engaged to her sister bothered her not one bit.

# CHAPTER ONE

***Four years earlier***

As the air raid siren blared, Annie Bates ordered her daughters to the Anderson shelter in the garden.

'Come along, you two, hurry up!'

'Do we have to, Mum?' moaned fifteen-year-old Maisie. 'I want to listen to the wireless. It's time for *Paul Temple*.'

'Don't be difficult,' Kathy admonished her.

'Every time the siren goes we bury ourselves in that dreadful dugout and nothing happens. It's a waste of time!'

Annie ignored her younger daughter's petulance and bundled her into the garden.

'Now get in there and don't give me any more trouble. If your dad was here you wouldn't argue.'

Wilfred Bates, at forty-one, was a part-time ARP warden, out on fire watch until the morning. It was he who had dug deeply to build the Anderson shelter. Inside were two pairs of bunk beds, a Primus stove, several blankets and a bare electric light bulb, which only seemed to add to the dreariness of the place.

'It's so damned depressing in there.' Maisie was not to be silenced, it seemed, until the drone of planes overhead and the sound of gunfire in the distance could be heard.

'Come on, for goodness' sake!' Kathy prodded her sister in the back.

Before long there was the whine of bombs being dropped, followed by loud explosions. The three women huddled together. Tonight's raid was different from previous ones and the seriousness of the threat became apparent as the explosions sounded nearer and nearer.

'God, I hope Wilf's all right,' Annie muttered more to herself than to the girls.

Putting a comforting arm round her mother, Kathy said, 'I'm sure he's fine, Mum.'

'We should have gone to Chandlers Ford with Mrs Bennett next door,' said Maisie nervously. 'She said her sister would put us up.'

'I'm not leaving my house for any bloody

German!' her mother declared. 'Your dad built this shelter for our safety and here we'll stay!'

After what seemed an eternity, the all-clear sounded and the three women gratefully returned to the house. Shortly afterwards, Jimmy Greene, Kathy's new boyfriend, called round to make sure that all was well with the family.

As he entered the sitting room, Maisie hurled herself at him. She flung her arms round him and clung on.

'Oh, Jimmy, I was so scared,' she cried. 'I wish you'd been with us, then I'd have felt safe.'

The young man extricated himself from her hold. 'Rubbish! You scared? I don't believe it.' And to the young girl's annoyance he crossed to her sister and kissed her on the cheek. 'You all right, love?'

'I'm fine,' Kathy said. 'It sounded as if someone really got it tonight, though.'

'Yes, but I don't know where. I came straight round here when I heard the all-clear.' His voice was filled with warm affection as he hugged Kathy and added, 'I had to know my favourite girl was all right, didn't I?'

'Thanks very much!' snapped Maisie. 'Never mind the rest of us.'

'Don't be so childish,' Kathy told her. 'You know what Jimmy meant.'

Maisie went off in a huff.

Annie looked at the young man and shrugged. 'Teenagers, eh? Bloody pain in the neck!'

He laughed. 'Oh, she'll grow up soon enough.'

'That's what I'm afraid of,' Annie muttered. 'I'm off to bed to read my book. Don't you be too late, Kathy.'

Left alone, the two of them settled on the old but comfortable settee and snuggled up together.

'You realise that Maisie has a crush on you, don't you?' said Kathy.

'She'll have to queue up with all the others, I'm afraid,' he teased her. 'I hope you fully understand what a catch I am?'

'Oh, you!' She punched him playfully. 'But be serious for a minute, Jimmy. Our Maisie is at a vulnerable age. You'll have to be careful how you handle her. You could hurt her deeply.'

'You worry far too much about your little sister. She's as tough as old boots under all that simpering. She may have you fooled, but she hasn't pulled the wool over my eyes.'

'Whatever do you mean?'

'Young Maisie is a calculating, conniving little minx and she plays you and her mother like a couple of fine fiddles and neither of you can see it!'

'That's not true!'

'Now don't get a cob on with me because I'm being honest. Sometimes the person on the outside can see things more clearly. You'll see – eventually I'll be proved right. Anyway, why on earth are we wasting time? Come here!' And he pulled her closer and kissed her.

Meanwhile, on the roof of the Supermarine buildings in Woolston, Wilf Bates and his fellow fire-watcher, Betty Langdon, settled down with a flask of tea and a sandwich once the all-clear had sounded. Below them in the factory, men worked on the night shift, building and repairing Spitfires. It was thought to be a prime target for the German bombers, and the raid had filled both the wardens with some trepidation, so it was with great relief that they had come through the raid unscathed.

They sat among the sand-filled fire buckets, stirrup pumps and scoops designed to pick up incendiary bombs, and lit cigarettes.

'That was a bit bloody hairy for a while,' Wilf remarked.

'Too right,' agreed Betty. 'I must admit I had few bad moments when the planes flew over.'

Putting an arm around her shoulder he said, 'You'll be all right with me, lass. You're a brave woman. Many a female would have gone home screaming during that raid.'

She gave him a coy look. 'I always feel safe with you, Wilf. Nothing seems to faze you.'

He suddenly felt ten feet tall. 'Well, you just have to get on with it, don't you?' He gazed at the soot-covered face of his companion, and taking a handkerchief from his pocket he said, 'Here, love, you dampen this under the tap and wipe your dirty face.'

'Oh, goodness, I must look a sight!'

'Not at all,' he said softly. 'You look lovely in the moonlight, honest.'

She gave him a grateful smile and took the handkerchief from him. 'Thanks.'

'Heard from your old man lately?'

Shaking her head, she said, 'No, but he warned me this would happen. I'll probably get several letters all at the same time. I'm not sure where he is. His regiment was sent somewhere in France, I believe. They can't tell you a thing, of course.'

'It must be difficult for those chaps to get mail home – and to receive it, too. When a man's away from home, letters from the family are a lifeline.'

Betty didn't answer as she rubbed the soot from her face and brushed her hair, flattened by the tin hat she'd worn during the raid. She supposed she and her husband had what people would call a happy marriage. Fred was a solid sort of bloke but not very exciting. The war had brought more excitement into her life than the six years of marriage ever had. She had wed at twenty-four, and Fred was a year older. Now, at thirty, she felt she had blossomed as a woman ever since she had joined the ARP and had been partnered with Wilf Bates. She had started wearing make-up, which Fred didn't much like. A smudge of lipstick was all he thought appropriate. But Betty had bought rouge, mascara and a box of Coty powder. Sometimes she even wore Coty's L'Aimant perfume, which made her feel really daring.

'I could kill a gin and tonic right now,' she said.

'You'll have to make do with coffee, I'm afraid. Tomorrow I'll bring a nip of brandy to pep us up.'

The following morning, Southampton returned to normal for most, except those unfortunate people whose houses had been bombed the previous night. There had been fatalities, and firemen and wardens were still digging through the rubble trying to find anyone who was still alive.

Surrounding houses had all suffered bomb damage: windows were smashed despite the sticky brown paper that criss-crossed them to prevent flying glass, and roof tiles had been blown off. A cluster of neighbours who had escaped with their lives studied a bomb crater.

'Bloody Germans!' swore one man. 'They think they're the master race. Well, I'll show the buggers if ever I get my hands on one!'

'Poor Mrs Harrison bought it last night,' remarked another. 'She would never go down to the shelter, you know. She said no German was going to rob her of a good night's sleep.'

'Well, the poor old duck can sleep as long as she likes now,' said the man beside him.

'Shush!' called a fireman and everyone was quiet. A whimpering could be heard from among the pile of masonry. The firemen dug quickly. After some time, a very frightened dog was dug out. As the fireman who had rescued him held the quivering animal to his chest, the poor mutt licked his face.

'I wonder if his owners are down there?' said an onlooker.

'If they are, I don't reckon they stood a chance,' said another. 'Bloody war! When will men ever learn? That crazed paper-hanger wants power and will stop at nothing. I hope the RAF drop a bomb on him!'

Maisie was in seventh heaven now that her schooldays were over. During her final break time she had regaled her friends with her future plans.

'I shall find a job that pays me enough to buy my own grown-up clothes. I'm sick of Mum dressing me like a child!'

'What sort of clothes?' asked one girl.

'The sort that women wear. And I'll buy a decent bra, one that shows off my bust. The ones Mum buys are awful. I want ones with lots of lace.'

'Clothes with lace are restricted now, silly, and what about clothing coupons?' queried another.

'I'll get mine to myself. I intend to have a good time, I can tell you.'

'What, going out with boys?'

'Boys, are you mad? The town is full of uniforms. I shall go dancing and meet real men.'

As she strutted away, pushing out her chest, one of the girls said, 'She'll end up in trouble, that's for sure.'

'Nah, she's living in a dream world. Her mum won't let her go dancing, not at fifteen.'

'She'll find a way, mark my words.'

A few weeks later, Maisie stood in front of the wardrobe mirror and looked at her reflection with glee. This morning she was starting her first job and had insisted on buying a new skirt and blouse for the occasion.

'You can't expect me to wear my school uniform,' she had told her mother.

'Of course I don't,' said Annie. 'I know you have to wear a black skirt, but you do already have a couple of white blouses that would do.'

'Do! Honestly, Mum, they are so childish, I had to wear them to school, but I wouldn't be seen dead in them now. I want something more feminine. I am a working girl, or soon will be, so I must dress accordingly.' She had secured a job in the local Woolworth's on the jewellery counter, which suited her perfectly. She liked to be surrounded by pretty things.

And so precious clothing coupons had been spent on new clothes.

Kathy Bates was working at the British American Tobacco Company, doing shift work. The money was better than shop work, but in any case she'd had no choice. Unmarried women of her age were now expected by the government to do their share towards the war effort, and anyway, she was saving for the future. Like most young women, she dreamed of a home of her own, a happy marriage like her parents' – and children. Jimmy Greene was the man she'd fallen in love with and she hoped that eventually they would get married. Not that things had progressed that far, but a girl had to be prepared, she thought. The shortages due to the war had meant that collecting for her bottom drawer had become difficult. Her mother had given her a couple of lace-edged tablecloths, and she had spent clothing coupons on a pretty nightdress from old stock that she couldn't resist. After all, a girl needed to look glamorous in the bedroom.

Brides of today had a tough time, she mused. Wedding dresses were in short supply and took too many clothing coupons. Many a bride was married in a borrowed dress or a smart costume. She wondered if her relationship with Jimmy would be permanent. Should they wait until after the war? But God alone knew how long that would last. 'Over by Christmas,' had been the cry in the beginning, but that hope had been dashed. As she worked at her machine, she wondered how her sister was doing on her first day at work.

Maisie was in her element. The manager of the store, Mr Bell, had shown her the goods on display and how to work the till, and left her with Jane, a married woman who already worked on the counter, to instruct her on other issues.

'Mr Bell insists on politeness to the customers,' Jane warned. 'He's a stickler for rules, but as long as you follow those you'll be all right.'

'He's getting on a bit, isn't he?' Maisie remarked.

'Well, dearie, all the young blokes are off fighting the Hun. Mr Bell was due to retire but the firm asked him to stay on. Here comes a customer. Off you go – let's see what you can do.'

A pair of fake pearl earrings was her first sale and she persuaded the woman to buy a matching necklace.

Jane stood watching and as the woman walked away she said, 'Well done. I can see you are a born saleswoman. Keep it up and Mr Bell will be delighted.'

Shortly afterwards, a young soldier lingered in front of the counter looking pensively at the display of jewellery.

Going up to him, Maisie smiled. 'Can I help you?' she asked, batting her eyelashes at him.

'I'm looking for a gift for an aunt of mine.'

'Do you mind if I ask how old she is?'

'She's middle-aged, and I'm really not sure what to buy her.'

'We have some really pretty brooches,' Maisie suggested. 'Ladies do like them, I know, because my mum wears them.' She showed him several. 'This one is particularly pretty,' she said as she picked up a delicate filigree circle decorated with different-coloured glass stones. 'It's so dainty, and I think it looks really expensive.'

The soldier took it from her. 'You're right, it is pretty. I'm sure my aunt would love it.'

'I'll wrap it in tissue paper for you if you like.'

'Thanks, you've been very helpful.'

She beamed at him. 'My pleasure.'

'I know it's a bit of a cheek, but would you let me take you to the pictures tomorrow evening as a way of thanking you for your help?'

Without hesitation she said, 'How kind. I'd love to.'

'I believe there is a good film showing at the Forum. I'll meet you outside at six thirty. By the way, my name's Robert – known as Bob.'

'I'm Maisie,' she said, 'and I'll be there.'

As the soldier walked away, Jane came over. 'Well, you don't waste any time, do you?'

'Why miss an opportunity? He seems a nice chap and I intend to enjoy myself. School is over, and I'm grown up now!'

'I'm not so sure of that,' said Jane. 'Just make sure you don't grow up too quickly. It can be dangerous!'

## CHAPTER TWO

War brought hardship to many, but for others it was a way to make money, even if it was by nefarious means. Sonny Nolan was one such person, in no way as innocent as his name implied. Aged thirty-two, he was a ruthless, hard-nosed racketeer, feared by others who lived in his murky world.

Before the war, he'd made a living by selling second-hand goods from his small shop in the Ditches, but as soon as war broke out he foresaw opportunities ahead to make a great deal of money and he was not going to miss the chance to feather his nest. He fronted his activities by continuing in the second-hand business, which in itself took a decent turn-round, with so many needing furniture, kitchenware and clothes after they had been bombed during the air raids. But in the room behind the shop, hidden behind a false bookcase, he dealt in stolen books of clothing coupons, petrol coupons, and any black market goods he could manage to buy, like fresh eggs, tinned fruit, blankets, silk stockings and make-up. In fact, anything that was in short supply. He also loaned money at extortionate rates. Anyone having difficulty in making repayments knew they were likely to be visited by his bully boys, once as a warning, then with a severe beating and confiscation of goods far and above the value that was owed.

Sonny was always well turned out in his bespoke suits, silk ties and fedora. He was attractive in a coarse kind of way. His features were strong if a little heavy; he was tall with broad powerful shoulders but a trim taut body. He took care of himself, going to a boxing gym in London when he had the time. It was a way of keeping fit and meeting members of the London underworld who kept him supplied with goods. He was there today, sparring with a well-built boxer who had seen better days but nevertheless could still pack a punch.

As the gloved fist of the boxer caught Sonny on the side of his face, his head snapped back at the force of the blow.

'Bastard!' he muttered through his gum-shield. 'I'll show you.' And he feinted, pretending to throw a punch and catching the man unawares as he ducked then straightened up to meet a punch on the chin, followed by a low blow to the stomach. As the man doubled up in pain, Sonny smiled with satisfaction and climbed out of the ring.

'That wasn't on!' the trainer chided him. 'You did that deliberately.'

'Serves him right!' Sonny retorted, removing his gum shield and taking a drink of water. 'He didn't pull his punches.'

'And you do, of course?'

'Don't be bloody stupid!'

'You don't fight fair,' the man accused him.

'What the hell's got into you? Fair? What's fair in this day and age? Have you found religion or something?' And he walked away to take a cold shower in the back of the gym.

Harry the Dip, one of London's cleverest pickpockets, entered the room. Harry worked the markets, especially Petticoat Lane, and always had goods to offer.

'Wotcher, Sonny. Want to buy some watches?'

'How many?'

'Twenty, and a couple of women's lockets. I've also got a fine diamond ring.'

'How did you get that?' Sonny asked.

'Well, this flash bird stepped out of a taxi and tripped over.'

'And you helped her to her feet, I suppose?'

'Of course I did. I'm a gentleman, after all.' Harry smirked.

'You, my friend, are a bloody shark. Let's take a look.'

A little later the two men emerged from the gym, Harry with money in his pocket and Sonny with goods to sell.

Another member of the London underworld sidled up to Sonny. 'Can you do with two rolls of gents' suiting?' he asked. 'It's good quality – came from Burton's. One navy, pinstriped, the other dark grey.'

'You got it here?'

'Nah,' said the man, 'but I've got to come to Southampton at the weekend. I can drop it into your shop if you like.'

'That's fine,' Sonny said, and the two men shook hands on the deal.

After several such encounters, he took himself off to the West End for a meal and on to the Windmill Theatre to see a show before catching a late train home.

Letting himself into his flat in Archers Road, he looked with great satisfaction at the goods he'd bought. They would make a healthy profit, as would the material due at the end of the week, which he would sell on to a Jewish tailor he knew who would be delighted with it. The trip had been very worthwhile. He smiled slowly, wondering how the boxer was feeling. Somewhat sore, he mused as he poured himself a drink and lit a cigarette.

Slowly removing his tie and undoing the top buttons of his shirt, he sat back on his plush velvet sofa and pondered his life. He was content, he thought. Business was brisk; he was never short of money or women. The female sex loved the good time he was able to give them; in return they offered their bodies for his gratification. He laughed as he thought about marriage – it definitely wasn't for him. He never allowed his lady friends to hang around too long and get the idea that they could share his life permanently. He'd never met a woman he'd loved. Not even his mother. She'd never shown him a moment's affection. As for his father, he'd beaten him all his childhood, until Sonny grew up and one day fulfilled a long-held promise to himself, when he'd turned on the old man and given him the hiding of his life.

Stubbing out his cigarette in the ashtray,

he went to the bathroom, swilled his face, cleaned his teeth and went to bed.

After meeting Bob outside the cinema, Maisie was disappointed when the soldier bought tickets for the back stalls. Secretly she had been hoping to be taken up to the circle, the most expensive seats, although she did realise that being an ordinary soldier he could probably only afford the two shillings and sixpence for the back stalls. At least he offered her a cigarette and bought her an ice cream during the interval.

The programme at the cinema was fortunately not interrupted by an air raid, but as they started to walk home the warning sirens began and Bob hustled her into a concrete shelter near the park.

Maisie was very nervous. These shelters were above ground and she never felt that they were as safe as their Anderson in the garden. The sound of gunfire echoed as the ack-ack guns blazed. Bombs could be heard exploding and the ground beneath them began to shake. Maisie gripped her companion with a scream at the last bomb, which sounded far too near.

Putting an arm round her he said softly, 'It's fine. Just try and keep calm, or you'll panic the others in here. It'll all be over soon, you'll see.'

She buried her head in his chest and

covered her ears with her hands, until the all-clear sounded. 'Thank God for that!' she cried, and hurriedly began to follow the others out into the street.

Bob kept his arm round her as they walked through the darkness of the park with only a small torch to show them the way. She couldn't remember the last time there had been any street lighting. Gone were the days when the town centre was bright and cheerful. The few cars that were on the road had their headlights covered with just a narrow strip left open to show the way and consequently there had been several accidents.

'It was a great film, wasn't it?' Maisie remarked, clutching Bob's arm as they made their way home. 'Clark Gable is so handsome. That Scarlett O'Hara was a fool.'

'I'm glad you enjoyed it,' he said. 'So tell me, who would be your ideal man?'

'Well, I love Errol Flynn. He's so dashing.'

'Not much chance for me then,' he chortled.

'I expect you have film stars you admire,' she said.

'Of course. Rita Hayworth with her lovely red hair, or Veronica Lake – the way she wears her blonde hair falling over one eye is very appealing. You should wear yours like that.'

'Do you think so?' Maisie was flattered. 'Perhaps I will.'

When they arrived at her house, Bob stopped and in the darkness pulled her into his arms. 'Thanks for coming out tonight. I really enjoyed being with you.'

'Me too.' Holding her breath, Maisie wondered hopefully if he was going to kiss her goodnight. She wasn't disappointed as he lowered his mouth to hers.

In the living room of their home, Annie and Wilf were sitting listening to Radio Luxembourg and the music of Glenn Miller.

'I hope our Maisie is all right,' Annie muttered. 'She promised me she'd go to the shelter if there was a raid. She should be home by now,' she added, looking at the clock on the mantelpiece.

Wilf, who was enjoying a night off from fire-watching, said, 'I'll just take a look outside and see if she's coming.'

He put out the hall light before opening the door and stepping outside, where he was shocked to see his younger daughter in the arms of a soldier.

'Maisie! Inside, now!' He caught her by the arm and dragged her away, pushing her into the hallway. 'And you, young man, you be on your way. My girl is only fifteen. You should be ashamed of yourself!'

Bob, completely flustered, tried to pacify Wilf, but when the older man took a step towards him with balled fists, he fled.

Closing the door behind him, Wilf walked into the living room and glared at Maisie, whose face was puce with rage. 'What the bloody hell do you think you're playing at, behaving no better than a woman of the streets?'

'I've never been so embarrassed in all my life!' she retorted. 'You had no right to do that, Dad.'

'I had every right,' he stormed. 'You're just a child. That's how girls get into trouble. How dare you be seen out with a serviceman at your age? I won't have it, do you hear?'

Maisie burst into tears. 'You're beastly!' she cried as she ran to the stairs and up to her room. Wilf turned to his wife.

'I've never seen the like,' he said. 'You should have seen the two of them, wrapped around each other. You would have thought they hadn't had a meal in days!'

'She really worries me,' Annie said. 'She's so flighty. She flirts with anything in trousers, always has done from the day she was born.'

'Then it's time you had a chat with her. Tell her about the birds and the bees, about getting pregnant. I don't want her bringing trouble to this house, because if she does, she's out on her ear!'

At that moment, Kathy walked through the door. 'Whatever is going on?'

'Your sister is what's going on!' Wilf

snapped. 'I caught her outside, snogging a soldier. I soon sent him on his way, I can tell you.'

'Oh, dear,' said Kathy. 'I bet that didn't please her. She would have been mortified.'

'She's only fifteen, for God's sake! Just out of school. Bloody jailbait is what she is!'

'I'm going to have a talk to her tomorrow,' said Annie.

That won't make a scrap of difference, thought Kathy, but she kept such feelings to herself. 'I'm off to bed then,' she said, kissing her parents goodnight.

When she opened the door to the bedroom she shared with Maisie, her sister was sitting on her bed in tears.

With a sigh, Kathy sat beside her and, putting an arm round her shoulders, said, 'It's no good crying. Dad was only trying to protect you.'

'I've never been so embarrassed in my life! God knows what Bob will think.'

'That's the soldier, I presume? Where did you meet him?'

'He came into Woolworth's to buy a present for his aunt.' She looked to Kathy for understanding. 'I wasn't doing anything wrong!'

'I know that, and so does Dad, but you have got to realise that this is wartime; men are waiting to be sent to face the enemy. They want a good time while they can. Morals fly out of the window during such days, so a girl has to be careful. You should stick to boys of your own age. It's safer.'

Maisie stood up and with an arrogant air declared, 'I don't want to go out with boys. I want to be with a real man!'

'You've seen too many films, my girl. It's time to keep your feet firmly on the ground.'

'Like you, I suppose!'

The note of disdain in her sister's voice riled Kathy. 'And what's so wrong with that?'

'You think you're so clever, don't you, Kathy? Life is sorted, you think. A job and a good-looking boyfriend who you hope and pray will want to marry you so you can settle down to cooking, cleaning and hordes of bloody kids.'

'Is that such a bad thing?'

'It's all so dull. Jimmy is the only good thing about it, but he's so good-looking you had better mind someone more exciting doesn't tempt him away from you. Someone sexy!'

'Oh, thanks!' Kathy laughed at her sister. 'You may not think so, but Jimmy is perfectly happy with me as I am.' Turning back the bed sheets, she said, 'The trouble with you is that you are in too much of a hurry to grow up! Now, get into bed or we'll both look awful in the morning.'

Maisie climbed into bed, thinking, I'm not in a hurry – I *am* grown up. Why doesn't anyone realise that?

## CHAPTER THREE

The Bates family, along with the rest of Southampton, continued to struggle on, but the air raids increased as the month of August progressed. The lower end of Canal Walk, better known as the Ditches, was severely bombed. Sonny Nolan was thankful that his shop, situated at the other end of the Ditches, was still intact. He shuddered at the thought that all his dodgy stock might have been blown up or, worse, might have been uncovered and brought the local police force snapping at his heels.

Houses in Woolston were obliterated and, in September, the Supermarine works were destroyed in a daylight raid. Annie Bates thanked God fervently as she washed up, because her Wilf was at his day job as a welder, instead of being on fire watch on the factory roof. Had he been, the consequences didnt bear thinking about. She would perhaps have felt somewhat differently had she seen Wilf and Betty Langdon together in a local pub, celebrating their lucky escape.

With tears brimming her eyes, Betty gazed at Wilf and said, 'Just imagine, we could have been killed!'

'Now then, lass,' he said, leaning forward to take her hand in his, 'we weren't, so there's no need to fret.'

'I don't know what I would do without you, Wilf,' she murmured. 'Will we be given another duty together, do you think? I don't want to work with anyone else.'

'I'll see if it can be arranged,' he said, with a fond look.

During the next weeks, 'trekking' was much in evidence as droves of people walked or cycled out to the country to sleep under bushes or trees, to get away from the danger areas. Some moved out altogether to stay with relatives, which was wise of them because at the end of November, and the beginning of December, the German planes came back night after night to devastate the town. Children were killed when a bomb landed on the art gallery, and later that month the High Street and Above Bar was a scene of pure destruction. The king himself came to Southampton to see how the town had suffered under the Blitz.

Shopkeepers struggled to stay open in difficult circumstances. Some businesses closed temporarily. Woolworth's was able to remain open so Maisie was still in employment, to her great relief.

Kathy Bates was the mainstay of her family during this time, trying to calm her mother, who was worried about Wilf's safety every night, and to curb her sister's love of dancing, knowing how Annie worried when Maisie too was out of the house during the evening. This of course did not sit well with Maisie, who accused Kathy of being jealous.

'What do you mean, jealous?'

'Well,' Maisie retorted, 'I'm enjoying myself when all you do is wait for Jimmy to come round. Then what do you do? You sit with Mum and listen to the wireless. What sort of life is that?'

'We go out for a drink occasionally and to a film, but other than that we keep Mum company. I'd be worried to death about her if I was out and the siren went – but not you, you're just selfish. All you think about is your own pleasure.'

'That's not the case at all,' Maisie protested. 'I want to enjoy my life. If I'm going to be killed in a raid, I want to feel I have lived a little.'

'You're impossible!' Kathy walked away, knowing she was wasting her breath. But she wasn't a fool. She had noticed how Maisie would wait until Jimmy arrived before she left the house. How she would hover round him, fluttering her eyelashes, flirting with him, teasing him, before she went off to enjoy her evenings. Kathy seethed inside, but kept her anger hidden as Jimmy just laughed at her sibling's antics.

Annie did draw rein on some of her daughter's outings, but she felt it was only fair to let Maisie have some fun. She was allowed to go to the Guildhall to dance every Saturday and to the films once a week with a girlfriend. What Annie didn't realise was that instead of going to the cinema, Maisie would turn the corner of the street, put on her lipstick, pile up her hair to make herself look older, and go off with her friends Milly and Hazel to another dance hall, where she met servicemen who treated her to drinks and danced with her. She was cunning enough to come home at the time she would have had she been to the pictures. Maisie was enjoying the war. For her it meant freedom and a good time.

One evening when Jimmy arrived early, before Kathy had finished her shift, Maisie sidled up to him and said, 'Kathy will be tired when she gets home. Why don't you come with me to the cinema? *The Outlaw* with Jane Russell is on.' She stroked his arm. 'We could snuggle up in the back row.'

Jimmy glared at her and brushed her arm away. 'For a kid you play a dangerous game, and one day it will get you into trouble.'

'What on earth do you mean?'

'You know what I mean. Coming on to me like that – me of all people! What's the matter, Maisie? Are you jealous of your sister?'

Her face flushed with anger. 'Jealous? Why

on earth would I be jealous of Kathy?'

'Because she has me for a start, because she's a much nicer person.' He continued without sparing her. 'I have seen through your tricks from the first time I met you. You are a spoilt brat who always wants to be the centre of attention. You can't bear it when I come in and make a fuss of Kathy ... you want me to make a fuss of you instead. You're pathetic! It's time you grew up.'

Maisie ran for the stairs and up to her bedroom.

Annie came in from the back yard with a basket full of washing. 'Don't want to leave these out all night,' she said. 'If there's a raid they'll get filthy again.'

At that moment, Kathy arrived home just as the sirens started wailing. Maisie came down the stairs, coat on, ready to leave.

'You're not going anywhere,' said Annie.

'But Mum...'

'Don't you argue with me. Take these blankets down to the shelter and I'll make a flask of tea. Now go on!' She piled the blankets into her daughter's arms and pushed her towards the door.

Jimmy took the flask from her. 'You all carry on,' he insisted. 'I'll do this – it will only take a minute.'

The raid seemed to last for hours. Looking out through the doorway of the shelter, they watched as searchlights lit the sky, sometimes trapping an enemy aircraft in their beams. Explosions seemed to surround them, and the noise of broken glass and shrapnel landing on the concrete of the garden path kept them inside and out of danger. An incendiary bomb landed in the garden and Jimmy rushed out to cover it with sand from a nearby bucket. It was a long night.

Dawn brought the sound of the all-clear. They all climbed from the dugout to find windows smashed, roof tiles on the ground – but the house intact. Going out at the front to check for more damage, they were met by devastation. All the houses had had their windows blown out, as theirs had, and the smell of smoke from further down the road where one had received a direct hit filled the air. Firemen were busy trying to put out the fire, but the top floor of the house was no longer there. The front wall had been blown away; a bed seemed to hang at a crazy angle clinging to what was left of the floor. Clothing, torn by the blast, was strewn across the road.

'Oh, my God!' exclaimed Annie.

'Come on, Mrs Bates,' Jimmy said, 'let's go back inside. There's nothing we can do here, and we have plenty to clear up, so let's make a start.'

As they worked, Wilf arrived home, face blackened with soot, uniform covered with dust from falling masonry. Taking off his tin helmet, he sank into a chair.

'What a bloody awful night,' he said as he lit a cigarette. Looking round the room he saw the broken windows, the pile of glass swept up to be disposed of. 'At least we have a house still in one piece,' he said. 'You all right, Annie?'

'Fine,' she said as she passed him a cup of tea. 'Jimmy has been marvellous. He's helped us to clear up a bit, tacked blackout curtains across the windows until we can replace the glass, and he put out an incendiary in the garden.'

Wilf raised his cup in Jimmy's direction. 'Thanks, lad.'

'I was only too pleased that I was here,' he said, 'but I must get home and see how Mum and Dad are.' He kissed Kathy on the cheek. 'I'll see you as soon as I can.' He ignored Maisie.

That morning, Kathy was the first to leave the house as she had an early shift. As she walked to work, she eyed the devastation caused by the previous night's raid, wondering where it would all end. After she clocked on and made her way to her place on the assembly line, the raid was the main topic of conversation.

'There's a bloody great crater at the end of our road,' cried one of the women. 'I thought we were goners last night. When the bomb dropped my front windows blew in, and I wet my knickers I was so scared. I felt a right fool, I can tell you.'

Tales were exchanged amid the noise of the machines until lunchtime when the workforce went to the canteen for their break. *Workers' Playtime* was on the wireless and everyone started singing along to cheer themselves up after such a night.

'How's your Maisie?' asked Kathy's friend Joyce. 'I saw her with a soldier at the Saturday dance; she knows how to have a good time. She had her hair piled on top of her head. I didn't recognise her for a bit, she looked so much older.'

Nodding, Kathy said, 'She's heading for trouble and she doesn't realise it. I've stopped wasting my time trying to talk to her.' A frown creased her brow.

'What's the matter?' asked Joyce.

'She's such a little devil. You should see how she plays up to Jimmy when he calls for me. She does it deliberately, I swear.'

'What does he do when she's mucking about?'

'He just laughs at her, but I want to slap her, to be honest.'

'Well, I wouldn't bloody well put up with it!' Joyce retorted. 'I'd kick her up her arse!'

At home, Kathy helped her mother with the laundry before washing her hair and changing ready to go out with Jimmy that evening, but when she opened the door and saw the expression on his face her heart sank.

'Whatever is the matter?'

'I've got my call-up papers,' he said grimly. 'I have to report on Monday morning.'

'Oh, Jimmy!' Kathy was devastated.

Putting an arm round her he said, 'Well, we knew it would happen soon, but I have to say my heart sank when the brown envelope arrived.'

'They could send you over to France,' she said, voicing her fears.

'It's possible, but they'll have to train us first. No doubt we will be doing a fair amount of square-bashing, and they'll have to instruct us in the use of weapons.'

It was the day Kathy had been dreading ever since they had met.

'Come on, love let's go and drown our sorrows. It's no good sitting around worrying. After all, there is a war on!'

But beneath the bravado, Kathy recognised the worried expression behind the smile. She knew how she felt about Jimmy's going away, but for him it had to be so much worse. Each and every man who joined up had to wonder if they would come through the war unscathed. The only way she could help him was to be cheerful.

'Come on then, I'll treat you to your first pint.'

'Bloody hell, a kept man! I think I quite like the sound of that.'

'I said the first pint, that's all. Don't get carried away!'

Later, as they sat in the saloon bar of the local pub, sipping their drinks, Jimmy gazed at Kathy and said, 'Look, I don't know how long this damned war is going on for, but I would like us to get engaged before I go away.'

Kathy was speechless.

'I know it's a bit sudden, but when a man is away fighting for his country he wants something to live for. A wife, a fiancée, someone he can picture in his mind when things get bad.'

Kathy could feel the tears brimming her eyes. 'Oh, Jimmy,' was all she could say.

'I love you, Kathy, and when the war is finally over I want us to be married, have children, grow old together. I hope you feel the same?'

'Of course I do! I love you too.'

His smile lit up his eyes. 'Wonderful! Tomorrow we'll go and buy a ring.' He leaned forward and kissed her.

There were a few ribald cries as the other customers watched this display of affection. But neither of them cared.

When they returned to the house, they held

hands as they walked into the living room. Annie and Wilf were sitting by the fire, Maisie was doing some ironing.

'We've got something to tell you,' said Kathy. 'Jimmy and I got engaged tonight!'

'If that's all right with you, Mr Bates?' said Jimmy. 'Only I've been called up.'

Annie rose from her seat and embraced her daughter and kissed Jimmy. 'Congratulations! I couldn't be more pleased.'

Wilf got up and shook Jimmy by the hand. 'It's more than all right, lad. Welcome to the family!'

Kathy glanced over to her sister, who was looking thunderous. 'I can see that you're happy for us too, Maisie,' she said sarcastically. 'But I'll take your good wishes for granted, shall I?'

'Congratulations,' Maisie said, somewhat reluctantly, but as she gazed at Jimmy her expression crumpled. She looked shattered. She put down the flat iron, standing it on its end, picked up her clothes and left the room.

'Don't take any notice of her,' said Wilf, going to a cupboard and producing half a bottle of sherry. 'Let's all drink to this happy event.'

Afterwards, the two men sat and talked whilst Annie and Kathy made some Spam sandwiches. 'So you've been called up, lad?'

'Yes, my papers came today. How long do you think the war will last, Mr Bates?'

'I wish I knew, Jimmy. These are bad times and none of us know what lies ahead. We just have to grit our teeth and get on with it. You take good care of yourself. I want to walk my daughter down that aisle,' Wilf said, patting the young man on the shoulder.

'I'll certainly do my best,' Jimmy promised.

## CHAPTER FOUR

It was the beginning of June 1944 and the war raged on in Europe. For the citizens of Southampton, at last there was a respite from the constant air raids. Debris from many of the bombed buildings was cleared and temporary single-storey shops had been built in Above Bar to replace those that had been blitzed. There had been an influx of American soldiers once America had entered the war, and they were now an accepted part of the local scene. With their offers of gum, candy and sometimes nylon stockings, they were welcomed by the children and many young women who were enjoying the licence that the troubled times offered them.

Troops entered the town by their thousands. Tented camps were set up all over the countryside to hold them until they were finally marched through the streets to the docks, where they waited to board ships to take them across the Channel to join the battle for supremacy.

Apart from the English Tommies, there were battalions of Canadians as well as the GIs. French sailors were a common sight with their sailor hats decorated with red pompoms. There was an air of expectation and fear as anticipation of the invasion loomed.

Kathy continued working on the factory line as decreed by the government for women aged twenty and over. Maisie, not old enough to meet this criterion, had moved from Woolworth's and was working on the jewellery counter in Tyrell & Green's. The intervening years had brought a sort of truce between the sisters as Maisie matured. But she had not lost the crush she had on Jimmy, Kathy's fiancé, although she was wise enough now to hide her feelings from her sister.

Wilfred Bates had eventually succumbed to the wiles of Betty Langdon. Their affair had started after a really bad air raid when Betty had lost her nerve and had dissolved into tears. Wilf had gathered her into his arms to comfort her.

'Come along, Betty, lass, have a good cry and get it out of your system,' he said.

'I was so scared,' she said, trying to control her sobs. 'I thought we were going to die and I wouldn't have had the chance to tell you that I loved you.'

Wilf was at a loss for words. He had been well aware of the chemistry between them from the very beginning, but had pushed it to the back of his mind; after all, they were both married. Trying to be sensible, he had put it down to their long hours spent together in extreme circumstances, and had not let himself acknowledge the fact that he was attracted to the young lady who was so different from his wife. Betty was vulnerable and needy, whereas Annie was solid and stoic, coping with the difficulties of life during wartime without complaint or need of his comfort.

And now, looking down at the tear-stained face of the frightened younger woman in his arms, he lost all sense of propriety and, leaning forward, kissed her.

She clung to him, returning his kisses with a hunger. 'Oh, Wilf, it's been so long since a man gave me any affection.' She caressed his face. 'And no one has ever kissed me like that,' she said as she covered his mouth with hers.

He was lost, overcome with sexual longing. 'Let me take you home,' he said.

Betty unlocked the door of her house and, holding Wilf tightly by the hand, led him inside and upstairs to her bedroom, where they undressed with indecent haste.

'Oh, Betty,' he murmured as he took her in his arms, feeling her bare flesh beneath his fingers. They lay on the bed together, caressing and kissing each other, each fuelled by lust and longing.

'Love me, Wilf,' she cried as she lay on her back and spread her legs.

From then on, he'd been lost to the thrill of a new woman in his life.

Their affair had progressed. With Betty's husband away, it was simple for Wilf to call for her early when they were due at their post and snatch precious moments of lovemaking before going on duty.

'We're not hurting anyone,' he told her. 'This is not serious for both of us, you understand, we are just giving comfort to each other. There is no way either of us would jeopardise our marriages.'

She had agreed. And so it had carried on.

When Kathy left the factory after her shift, to her surprise she saw Jimmy waiting for her. As she walked towards him she saw his grim expression and her heart sank.

'What is it?' she asked.

Putting his arm round her he said, 'I can't stay, but I've come to tell you the company is being shipped out. From tomorrow, all leave has been cancelled, but I managed to slip away as I had to deliver some papers for one of the officers. I'll be round tonight to see you.'

Kathy clung to him for a moment and then, with tears streaming down her face, she watched him walk away.

Her friend Joyce, who was on the same shift, had watched the moving scene and now walked over to Kathy. 'Bad news?'

Nodding, Kathy said, 'His company is being shipped out. Tonight will be our last time together until God knows when.'

Joyce tucked her arm through Kathy's. 'Come on, love, we both need a stiff drink,' she said, and marched her off to the nearest pub.

As they sat with their gin and tonics, Kathy asked, 'How do you manage when your man goes to war?'

Joyce, whose husband was in the Navy, said, 'You get on with life, knit socks and scarves, write letters and look forward to the day they come home. That's what a million women are doing.'

'And if they don't come back?'

'I never want to hear you say that again!' said her friend. 'Always believe you'll see them again or you'll be a basket case.'

'I'm sorry,' Kathy said, fingering her engagement ring. 'I'm just scared.'

'Look, love, we all think that at least once. After that you put it to the back of your mind and carry on.' She laughed. 'Some women carry on in a very different way. I know lots of women who are having the time of their lives, especially with the Yanks. What some women will do for a pair of nylons would make our hair curl!' She then proceeded to tell her friend some juicy gossip about a few of the co-workers until she had Kathy laughing.

Annie Bates had been persuaded by Beryl, a friend of hers, to join the WVS. As she said, 'The government are asking married women to try and help the war effort too. It's great to feel useful instead of sitting at home trying to cope with the rationing, cooking Lord Woolton's pies. Thank God for Marguerite Patten, I say.' She smiled at Annie. 'Several of my friends have joined us and of my neighbours is an ARP warden. One is even driving ambulances! We've all got to do our bit.'

It wasn't long before Annie was making tea for the troops waiting at the dockside, serving them from a mobile canteen. They all looked young to her, and she found herself talking to them like a mother.

'Here you are, son,' she said as she handed one young soldier a scalding cup of tea. 'Take care not to burn your mouth; it's a fresh brew. Do you want a piece of cake?'

'Thanks, missus,' he said, and taking an envelope from his pocket he asked, 'Would you mind very much posting this letter to me mum? I don't have a stamp, I'm afraid.'

'Of course I will. Don't worry about the stamp, I'll get one from the post office.' She refused his money.

The times she worked for the WVS seemed to add another dimension to her life. At home all day or queuing for food, trying to make ends meet, left her feeling dissatisfied. Wilf was a good husband but she didn't see very much of him these days. He'd come home from work, have a meal, get changed and leave again to do his stint as a warden. It seemed to her they almost didn't share a life any more. Now she had other things to think about and she felt more fulfilled.

When she wasn't serving tea to the troops, she helped behind the counter in a shop where second-hand clothes could be bought or exchanged, which was a boon to all women. Not only was there a shortage of good clothing, but any that could be had took a chunk out of the clothing coupon allowance. She herself had bought a couple of summer dresses there, which helped to cheer her up, and of course there were other women to chat to. In all it was quite a social time for Annie, and she blossomed. She had her hair cut and permed, bought a lipstick and started using mascara. After all, there were quite a few women working with her who looked after themselves and she didn't want to appear frumpish.

Wilf noticed the difference and it unsettled him. Annie was changing from the woman with whom he'd shared over twenty years of marriage. With her new hairdo she looked younger and more attractive. She was lighter of spirit, and these days there seemed to be a spring in her step. It made him feel a certain amount of guilt about his affair with Betty, but he was so enamoured with the younger woman that he couldn't bring himself to end their adulterous relationship. It made him feel manly to think that a girl so many years his junior could desire him. After living as a devoted husband for so long, this was heady stuff. It boosted his ego so much, he didn't want it to stop. Not yet, anyway.

But when Annie looked at him one day and asked, somewhat coyly for her, 'How about us going out for a drink when you have your night off, perhaps go for a meal somewhere?' he felt awkward.

'Yes, all right, love,' he said.

'Well, we haven't been out together for an age, have we? I just thought it would be nice. Like courting all over again.'

With some embarrassment, he said, 'What's come over you, talking about courting?'

'Well, some of us were talking at the WVS and saying that with the war we all have so much to worry about, what with rationing, clothing coupons, air raids and so on, that the romance has gone out of marriage, at least for those of us with our husbands still at home.'

'Don't be daft, Annie. We've been married for years.'

'Exactly! And we take each other for granted. I'm just saying let's try to get out of the rut, that's all.'

Now he was completely flustered. He was out of the rut! He had another woman. He had romance in his life, but unfortunately not with the woman he had married. He didn't know how to cope with this demand from his wife.

'I think it would be lovely to go for a drink and a meal somewhere,' he said. What else could he say?

Maisie Bates wasn't finding life dull at all. For her it was exciting. She was earning her own money and was free to live her life. At nineteen there were no longer restrictions from her parents on her coming and going and she took full advantage of the fact.

She and her girlfriends were off dancing most evenings, either to the Guildhall, where Bert Osborne and his band played, or to hear Gil Hume and his music at a different venue. She had a friend who was a nurse, so sometimes she was invited to hospital dances where they invited men from the local RAF station. But the best times were when the Americans held a dance, like the one Maisie went to a couple of days before Jimmy dropped his bombshell. There was a buffet which owed nothing to rationing. The sandwiches were made with fresh egg mayonnaise; a treat in times when one was only allowed two eggs a week. There was real ham in others. Cream cakes and doughnuts too.

One of her friends said, 'If only we could sneak some of these in our handbags to take home to the family!'

Maisie, not daunted at all, asked one of the men, as she danced with him, if that would be possible. He was only too pleased to agree ... if she let him see her again. She said yes at once. Especially when he told her he could get her a pair of nylon stockings as well. She was determined to buy a new frock for her date with him, so, having heard that a man called Sonny Nolan sold clothing coupons, she went to the Ditches next day and walked into his shop.

A voice called from the back, 'I won't be a minute!'

She looked around at the myriad things on sale. There were pieces of furniture, kitchenware, table lamps, rugs, curtains and jewellery in a locked case by the counter; hats and dresses on a clothing rack which she riffled through as she waited. Finding a frock in a delicate floral material in her size she removed it from its hanger and held it in front of her, looking in a full-length mirror propped up nearby.

'That suits you.'

She spun round at the sound of the voice.

A handsome dark-haired man was standing watching her. 'That dress will look good on you. You should buy it.'

'How much is it?' she asked warily.

'As it isn't new, ten bob. After all, it is quality stuff.'

'What if it doesn't fit me?'

He gazed at her and said, 'You could come through the back and try it on if you like.'

Maisie didn't like. She'd heard various stories about the man standing before her. Sonny Nolan was supposed to be a hard man who was involved with criminals and London gangs – a person who could be dangerous if crossed. Looking at him, she believed it. Although he was attractive, his eyes were watchful and cold as he waited for her reply.

'Can I take it home and try it on? I promise to bring it back tomorrow if it isn't any good.'

'Sure, why not? Is there anything else?'

Normally Maisie could be brash when she wanted something, but the man standing in front of her was intimidating and she hesitated.

'Well?'

'I need to buy some new clothes,' she said,

'and I don't have enough clothing coupons. Someone told me you might be able to help.'

His steady gaze held hers. 'Really? In what way?'

Had she made a mistake, she wondered? Was the information wrong? Would she be in trouble if she asked? But the thought of new dresses made her brave.

'I wondered if you knew where I could possibly buy some clothing coupons? Of course, I realise that this would be confidential.' For a moment she saw his mouth twitch as he suppressed a smile. 'Please say you can help me,' she begged.

'And why would you need these clothes?'

She smiled at him, thinking she would try to charm him. 'Well, Mr Nolan, a girl likes to look her best. I like to go dancing, you see. I have only two good dresses and I can't just keep wearing the same old thing, can I?'

He chuckled and, looking at the pretty girl before him, said, 'I can see that for you that would be difficult. I'll see what I can do. Come back tomorrow.'

'Oh, thank you.' Maisie was delighted. 'It will have to be in my lunch hour. Is that all right, will you be open?'

'Yes, I'll be here. You can let me know if that dress fits you, can't you?'

Maisie paid for the garment and said, 'Yes. And thank you so much.'

Sonny stood at the door of his shop, watching her hips swinging as she walked away, and thought, I bet she's a load of trouble to her parents.

The next day during her lunch hour, Maisie returned to the shop, as promised.

'The dress was perfect,' she told Sonny Nolan. 'I shall be the belle of the ball!'

With a knowing look he said, 'You'll like that, won't you?'

'Absolutely!' She hesitated and then asked, 'The clothing coupons?'

'Twenty be enough?'

She nearly fainted with delight. 'That's wonderful!'

'You want anything else that's scarce, you come and see me, girlie,' he told her. 'We have to help each other in such bad times. Maybe one day you'll be able to return the favour.'

Maisie didn't really like the sound of that and wondered what he had in mind ... but twenty coupons! She laughed. 'Who knows?'

Much later that day, Maisie took her dinner out of the oven and sat at the table with Kathy to eat. Annie was off somewhere with the WVS and Wilf had left to go on duty just as she arrived home. Looking at her sister, Maisie asked, 'What's wrong? You look really miserable.'

'It's Jimmy. His company is being shipped out soon. Tonight is the last time I'll be seeing him for some time.'

Maisie dropped her knife with a clatter. Jimmy going away! He'd been lucky enough to be billeted near home for so long she'd taken his presence for granted. Now he was leaving. She was devastated. He was such an important part of her life. Every time he was near her she wanted to hold him – be held by him – and now he wouldn't be there. He could be killed! She pushed her plate away.

'Oh, Kathy, that's terrible news.'

Filled with her own despair, Kathy misunderstood Maisie's concern. 'I'm shattered at the thought. What would I do if anything happened to him?'

'Now stop that!' Maisie didn't want to hear such things even if they were in her own mind. She had to get out of the house, be alone. She couldn't be here when he arrived, knowing he was leaving. It was more than she could bear.

'I'm going to get changed,' she told Kathy.

'When you've finished I'll do the same. Jimmy and I will probably go for a walk and a drink somewhere.'

Maisie felt the tears on her cheeks as she changed her clothes. She brushed them angrily away. How could life be so cruel? The one man who meant anything to her wouldn't be around for much longer. She idolised him, had done so for four long years. She loved him even when he was cross with her and told her off. In her eyes he could do no wrong.

When she came down the stairs, ready to leave for an evening's entertainment, Kathy left the table to go to the bedroom and get ready. And so it was Maisie who answered the knock on the front door. Opening it, she saw Jimmy standing there.

She gazed at him. Her eyes filled with tears. As they trickled down her cheeks she said, her voice choked with emotion, 'Oh, Jimmy.'

He could see the genuine despair on her face and asked, 'What's the matter?'

She stepped back to let him enter the hallway. 'You're being sent away to fight. I can't bear it.' And she started sobbing.

He took her into his arms to comfort her. 'There, there,' he said, trying to lighten her mood, 'thousands of soldiers are being sent to France, you know. There's a war on!'

'Please don't joke about it,' she cried, looking up at him.

He was overcome by her raw emotion and it moved him. 'I do believe you really care about me.'

'I've always cared about you,' she cried, 'even when you told me off when I was a kid. I love you, Jimmy.' She reached up and, pulling his head down, she kissed him. It was a kiss full of passion and desperation – four years of longing for this to happen.

It was so unexpected that for just a moment Jimmy returned her kiss. But almost at once, realising what was happening, he reached for her arms round his neck and released her hold.

'Now then, Maisie, pull yourself together.'

But she had felt his response and with shining eyes she said, 'Just for a moment you liked it. Go on, admit it!'

'Stop it! You're just being dramatic. You took me by surprise, that's all.'

'Surprise or not, there was passion in that kiss and you can't deny it!' she said with great delight. Then, hearing Kathy's footsteps on the stairs, she opened the door, but before she left she said, 'You take care, Jimmy, my love, because like it or not, you want me, and I can't wait to see you again.' And laughing with sheer happiness, she walked out of the house.

## CHAPTER FIVE

'Is that you, Jimmy?' Kathy called, peering along the hallway. She smiled when she saw him. 'I was sure I heard a knock on the door.'

'Maisie let me in,' he said, trying to push what had happened to the back of his mind.

Kathy embraced him. 'What do you want to do on your last night home?'

'Let's go for a walk, so we can have a chat,' he suggested. 'Then we'll call into a pub for a drink.'

'I'll get my coat,' she said.

The weather had been cloudy and dull most of the day but the evening had brightened. The sky, however, looked threatening and Kathy took an umbrella with them, just in case it was needed. They strolled through the park and eventually sat together on a bench beneath overhanging beech trees.

Jimmy gazed about him, filling his mind with the familiar scene. He wanted to be able to remember it, carry it with him when he left it behind. He put an arm round Kathy and kissed her softly.

'As soon as I can I'll send you an address so that you can write to me.'

She was trying hard not to let her emotions surface and said, 'Yes, please do.' Cuddling in to him she said, 'I'll write a bit every day. Tell you all the gossip. No doubt Maisie will provide plenty of that!'

'No doubt,' he agreed. 'Look, darling, I don't want you to sit at home and mope. I want you to go out and enjoy yourself, but make sure you keep away from the bloody Yanks.' He was teasing her, trying to make light of the situation.

'Oh, Jimmy!' Kathy's resolve had disappeared and tears brimmed her eyes. The two of them clung together. Kathy stroked his cheek, gazing into the handsome face with its piercing blue eyes, and brushed back a wayward strand of his dark hair. How she was going to miss him, she thought.

Eventually, taking a deep breath, Jimmy said, 'Now come on, love. This won't do, we've got to be brave. This war can't go on for much longer and in no time at all I'll be home and we'll be planning our wedding.'

Wiping her nose and trying to smile, Kathy said, 'Of course you're right. Before you know it we'll be celebrating an end to all this. Meanwhile, you watch out for those ATS girls too! A good-looking chap like you will have to fight them off, and you make damned sure you do.'

Laughing, he said, 'I'll tell them I'm spoken for.'

'Did Maisie say goodbye to you?'

'Yes, when she let me in. Why?'

'It's just that when I told her you were leaving she was genuinely upset.'

'She told me to take care of myself, then she left,' he lied. 'You don't have to worry about your sister. She'll survive the war better than any of us.'

'You're probably right,' Kathy agreed, 'but I do worry about her. She's hell-bent on having a good time, but she's so headstrong and impulsive. She doesn't seem to realise that these are dangerous times and that, for many, morals fly out of the window.'

'You mean the men who are leaving to fight, I suppose?'

'Yes, I do. They want to sow their wild oats while they can.'

Maisie was the last person that Jimmy wanted to talk about. 'Does that mean you and I can ... well, you know. I might want to sow my wild oats tonight too. How about it?'

'Jimmy Greene! Are you making immoral suggestions to me?'

Pulling her closer he said, 'Damned right I am.' Tilting her chin, he gazed into Kathy's eyes. 'At this very moment, I want you so much it's unbearable.' His passionate kisses were filled with longing as his mouth explored hers, his hand caressing her breast.

Eventually, Kathy broke away from his embrace, breathless and aroused. 'We had better stop this now, before it gets completely out of hand, but just you come home soon for good, that's all.'

'Come on, love, let's go and have a stiff drink,' Jimmy said. 'We can both use one.'

In the pub they talked about everything but the war and Jimmy's departure, going over old times, the laughs they'd had together, storing memories for both of them to draw on during the long months ahead.

Kathy gave him a snap he'd taken of her on the pier earlier that year. In it she was laughing, her hair blown by the sea breeze.

Jimmy gazed at it and smiled softly. 'That was a good day, wasn't it? You won sixpence on one of those machines where the ball bearings run round.'

'Yes, that's right. I'd forgotten.'

He took her hand in his and said, 'You make sure you don't forget me when I'm away.'

She gazed fondly at him. 'As if I could. I'm wearing your ring, aren't I? You're the only man I want, now and for ever.'

They walked slowly home. When they arrived at her door, Jimmy said, 'I won't come in, darling. I hate goodbyes. Saying it to you is bad enough; I couldn't face your parents too.'

'I understand,' she said. Putting her arms round his neck she whispered, 'You take care. I love you, so keep safe.' He couldn't speak. He kissed her long and hard, then abruptly walked away.

She watched him go with a heavy heart, knowing that all round the country women were feeling as she did and that there were thousands who had already been through the same scenario. She pushed to the back of her mind the thought that many of those women had opened their doors to see a telegraph boy standing there with a yellow envelope bringing the news they dreaded to hear. She uttered a little prayer under her breath asking for Jimmy's safe deliverance. Then she went inside and upstairs to her room, where she sat on the bed and wept.

Jimmy Greene was never far from Maisie's thoughts either that night. Although she wasn't without a dancing partner throughout the evening, her mind was elsewhere, reliving the moment when she had kissed Jimmy – and he had responded. No matter what excuses he made, she knew that there was passion in the lips that had covered hers. A hunger, which she recognised and enjoyed. He might deny it to himself, but she had felt it. The fact that he was engaged to her sister gave the whole experience a frisson of excitement. After all, she was like forbidden fruit. If Adam could be tempted in the Garden of Eden, well ... the possibilities were thrilling. What a pity he was going away just at this moment. But she could wait.

Wilf Bates and his mistress were lying side by side on her bed, smoking a cigarette, after enjoying a passionate hour of sex. Slowly blowing a circle of smoke, Wilf sighed contentedly.

'Oh my, Betty love, you do know how to make a man feel good.'

She turned on her side and snuggled in to him, running her fingers over his chest, kissing his neck, nibbling his earlobes and pushing her full breasts against him until eventually she sat astride him, moving sensually.

Wilf moaned softly. 'What are you trying to do, kill me? A man can only take so much, you know.'

'Not you, Wilf, darling. My God, I never knew men could make love so often in one night. My Fred didn't have your stamina.'

Caressing her soft breasts above him, he said softly, 'Then he didn't know what he was missing.'

'For him it was the missionary position on a Saturday night, but you ... you're like a tiger. I didn't know you could make love in so many different ways.'

Chuckling softly, Wilf said, 'You really do like to experiment, don't you?'

She threw back her head and laughed with delight. 'I've never had so much fun in my life.' Gazing at him, she asked, 'Do you make love to your wife the way you do to me?'

Although Wilf didn't mind discussing Fred with his lover, it made him uncomfortable to mention Annie when he was enjoying his extramarital relations. He put his cigarette in the ashtray on the bedside table, and pulling Betty's head down he kissed her and said, 'You talk too much. Come here.'

Later, as he walked home, he thought about Betty's question. In fact he wasn't nearly as exciting a lover where his wife was concerned. Somehow it didn't seem quite right. Not respectful. With Betty he didn't feel in any way constrained. It wasn't that he didn't respect her, he did, but there was a certain freedom about an adulterous liaison that he hadn't felt within the bounds of marriage. And now when he and Annie had sex his guilt seemed to inhibit him even more, and he knew that he left his wife feeling disappointed. Not that she ever complained: that wasn't her style. Sometimes he wished she were more like Betty, without reserve of any kind. Yet he loved and admired her for her fortitude in all things. If only she would show a sign of feminine weakness sometimes, then he could rush to her side, be a hero, as he seemed to Betty.

The evening he'd taken Annie out for a drink and dinner, she had seemed to become softer, almost flirtatious, as she had been before they were married, but he had been so filled with guilt over his affair that he hadn't been able to respond, and the evening had fallen flat. He regretted that: it hadn't been fair to her.

In his heart he knew that he should put a stop to his relationship with Betty Langdon. Despite the fact that they had agreed it could not be permanent, the longer it continued the harder it was to end and the more dangerous it became. He sighed as he put his key into the lock of the front door and entered the hallway.

Upstairs, in bed, Annie heard her husband's footsteps. Turning on the table lamp she looked at the time. He was late. No doubt as he climbed into bed beside her he would smell of L'Aimant perfume again.

## CHAPTER SIX

At the WVS shop the following morning, the three women on duty carefully poured some Camp coffee into three cups and took a break. D-Day had started and a constant drone of planes could be heard as they flew overhead towards France. The massed troops marching towards the docks were the topic of the day.

'I was woken up at the crack of dawn,' said Martha. 'When I looked out of the window, it was like a plague of locusts in the sky.'

'Poor devils,' Annie's friend Beryl muttered. 'God knows what's ahead of those boys. They look no more than teenagers, some of them.'

Sipping her coffee, Annie told them about Jimmy. 'My future son-in-law will soon be off too. My poor Kathy walks around looking so sad these days.'

'I thank God my husband is too old to join up,' Martha said, sipping her coffee. 'He's in the Home Guard, playing at soldiers.'

The others laughed, but one chipped in, 'We all think that's funny, but who knows, if the Germans do land here or parachute in, the Home Guard will be needed.'

They stood by the shop window watching the troops march past, whistling 'We're going to hang out the washing on the Siegfried Line'.

'They won't be whistling when they land in France, poor souls,' Annie remarked. 'I'm glad I'm a woman. I wouldn't like to have to go into battle.'

'Me neither,' agreed Beryl. 'Mind you, we have our own battles, ladies! Queuing for food – digging for victory. My back garden is thriving. We've got plenty of vegetables and the chickens are laying so we have extra eggs.'

‘If you get stuck, there’s always Sonny Norton,’ Martha suggested. ‘I bought some tinned pineapple from him the other day and some corned beef. Under the counter, of course.’

The other two looked shocked. ‘That’s black market!’

‘So what? My grocer hasn’t got anything worth having and I’ve got a family to feed, so I’m not too fussy where it comes from. Besides, my hubby likes his corned beef hash!’ She glared at the others in defiance. ‘That Sonny sells some smart clothes too. I bought a lovely dress there for seven and six. He’s got some very stylish stuff.’

‘I’ve never been inside his shop,’ Annie admitted. ‘I’ve heard he’s a dodgy character ... but I could do with another dress,’ she added, looking somewhat guilty.

‘Well, go and have a peek. It isn’t going to hurt anyone. After all, we sell second-hand clothes, don’t we, so what’s the harm? That’s nothing to do with the black market.’

In the army barracks at Andover, Jimmy Greene and his company were in training. They had been moved out to Salisbury Plain where they were using live ammunition in their manoeuvres.

‘This is bloody hairy,’ said one man as he aimed his machine gun at the supposed enemy, firing over their heads. ‘What if some bleeder is exceptionally tall and stands up? I could take his friggin' head off!'

'Would you stand up, knowing that there were real bullets flying around?' asked Jimmy. 'I know I bloody well wouldn't!'

'Let's hope you're right, mate.'

There was a strong camaraderie among the men, all of them wondering when they would be sent across the Channel. Reports kept coming in about the Normandy landings, about the gains and the losses. High winds had caused havoc for the 6th Airborne division and the Red Berets had been blown all over the place. Jimmy hoped to God that when it was their turn it would not be quite so chaotic.

After lights out in the barrack room, each man was alone with his thoughts as the day when they would leave drew ever nearer. Jimmy's thoughts were mixed. He was worried about his parents. He was an only child and as such was the one who fixed things when they went wrong, since his father was hopeless in the house. His mind was filled with thoughts of Kathy too. Their future as man and wife ... if he pulled through the conflict ahead. However hard he tried to put such doubts to the back of his mind, he had to face the possibility. He dearly wanted that future. A home, children – to grow old.

Try as he could, he found it hard to forget

the raw emotion he had seen on Maisie's face when she sobbed in his arms, crying because he was leaving, and her declaration of her love for him. She meant every word and it had touched him deeply and that was why, he told himself, he had found himself returning her passionate kisses. But in his heart he knew this wasn't strictly true.

Sonny Nolan stood outside a pub near the docks and watched the troops march past. Hard man as he was, he felt sorry for the young soldiers. He took out a cigar from the top pocket of his jacket and lit it. Well, it was an ill wind, he mused. War wasn't all bad for those who had a few brains. He intended to make as much money as he could whilst he had the chance. He glanced at his watch, then made his way to the Lord Roberts in the Ditches.

As he walked towards the pub he saw some of the local prostitutes walking up and down, accosting any likely punters. He knew most of them by name and many of them were regular customers of his. They'd come in and buy dresses and tins of food, if they'd had a good day's business; sometimes they would bring in a punter who wanted to buy them a gift, then later they would sell it back to Sonny at a lower price. This way they both made a profit. They were a decent bunch on the whole and knew better than to cause him any aggravation.

One of them greeted him. 'Hello, Sonny. You skiving off then, darlin'?'

'No, Gerry's looking after things for me.'

Gerry Middleton worked for him in many capacities. He was an ex-wrestler with arms of steel. He could break a man's back if he had a mind to and had done so in the past. He was utterly trustworthy and had worked for Sonny for years. Watched *his* back, when the occasion arose. Gerry was known as Sonny's bodyguard, and Sonny supposed in a way he was. If ever Sonny knew he was going into a dodgy situation, Gerry was always with him.

He entered the bar and ordered a half of bitter. Whilst he waited he glanced around the bar and saw the man he was supposed to meet sitting alone in a corner. Picking up his beer, he walked over to him and sat down.

'Got the stuff?' he asked quietly.

'Yes, it's in the car down the road,' the man answered.

'Make sure there's no one around when you bring it to the shop,' Sonny told him. 'How many cases?'

'Two. Best malt whisky.'

Sonny gave a satisfied smile. 'Good. I'll take as much as you can get.'

'It's like gold dust,' said the man, 'but I'll see what I can do.'

'Can you get me some nylons?'

'Yes, I've got a nice connection with a Yank who looks after the PX stores on the camps. Want any boxes of chocolates?'

'I told you, anything you can get your hands on I can sell.' He rose to his feet and left the pub.

He walked a few yards along the Ditches to his shop on the opposite side. As he opened the door the bell above it jingled, but Gerry was already standing behind the counter reading the daily paper.

'Hello, guv,' he said. 'Everything all right?'

'Got a delivery coming in soon. Two cases of malt whisky. I know a few landlords who'll pay through the nose for it. Been busy whilst I was away?'

'Yes, done quite a bit of trade. That blonde bird's been in again, bought another dress. And I sold her that black feather boa that's been hanging around, too. She brought her sister with her this time. I sold her a dress too.'

'Are they alike?' asked Sonny.

'No, couldn't be more different. The sister's a couple of years older, I would say. Quieter, more serious, not at all flighty.'

'I bet the parents are grateful for that!' Sonny wryly remarked.

Maisie had persuaded Kathy to go to a dance with her instead of wandering round the house like a lost soul.

'Jimmy wants you to enjoy yourself,' Maisie said. 'You told me so yourself, and frankly we are all sick of seeing your long face, so come on. Me, Milly and Hazel are going to the Guildhall on Wednesday evening.'

Kathy had been reluctant. 'I don't really want to,' she said. 'Besides, I've nothing decent to wear.'

'We can soon sort that out,' Maisie insisted, and had dragged her along to Sonny's shop. 'Come on, Kathy, you love to dance. It will take you out of yourself.'

And so Kathy went along with her, knowing she had to do something to take her mind off Jimmy being sent to the front line.

Wednesday evening at the Guildhall was never as packed as at the weekend. It was the night when the local girls who really liked to dance went along. The servicemen who were there didn't know that; they just went to have a good time whilst they had the opportunity.

The four girls, Maisie, Kathy, Hazel and Milly, went to the bar and bought a drink, then stood near the dance floor passing comment on the dancers and their ability, or lack of it.

'Look at that poor girl,' said Kathy, pointing out one couple. 'She's going to have sore feet. That chap she's with is spending more time treading on them than on the floor.'

'Well, we know to keep clear of him!' said

Maisie. She glanced at another couple. 'Now he's the man I want to dance with tonight. Watch him, he's terrific!'

'So's that one,' remarked Kathy. 'Actually, when you look around, there are quite a few good blokes here this evening.'

'There you are.' Maisie grinned. 'I knew you'd enjoy yourself if you came.'

The music stopped and the girls lingered near the edge of the floor and waited to be asked to dance. As the band started up again, all four had been claimed by various men and were enjoying the music as they moved around the floor.

The hours seemed to fly by. All the girls were having a good time. Kathy felt herself relaxing for the first time since she knew that Jimmy would be leaving, and she was enjoying herself. Hazel and Milly were a couple of bright sparks who kept a running score on the men with whom they danced, which was a source of great amusement, and when a ladies' choice was announced Maisie made a beeline for the man she'd picked out as the best dancer. As she swept past in the man's arms, she winked at Kathy and then closed her eyes as if she was in ecstasy.

Kathy started to laugh and her partner glanced at her with surprise. 'What's funny?' he asked.

Still chuckling, she said, 'Sorry, but I'm laughing at my sister who just danced by.'

His eyes twinkled. 'Well, I never find my brother amusing, so you're lucky!'

'Believe me,' said Kathy, 'there are times when I want to murder my sister as well, but that's family for you.'

At the end of the evening, Kathy had the last waltz with the same young man, who asked if he could walk her home.

'That's very kind of you,' she said, 'but I'll be going home with my sister and her friends. Besides,' she added, smiling softly, 'I'm engaged.' She held out her left hand to show her engagement ring.

'I saw that earlier,' he said, 'but I only wanted to see you safely to your door. But perhaps we'll meet here again. I always come on a Wednesday evening.'

He was tall, with wide brown eyes and clean-cut features, and dressed in a smart grey suit. Kathy wondered if he was in the services. To satisfy her curiosity she asked him.

'I'm in the police force,' he told her.

'I've never seen you on the beat.'

'Ah, well, I'm usually in plain clothes,' he explained.

'I'm a detective. Ian Harvey, at your service.' He held out his hand. 'You are?'

'Kathy Bates,' she said, 'so far without a criminal record.'

'Not if one day you do murder your sister,'

he teased. 'Come on, let's see if we can find her.'

Maisie was nowhere to be seen and Ian suggested that Kathy go to the cloakroom to see if she was there. She wasn't, but Kathy did find Milly and Hazel, who told her that a couple of soldiers were walking them home, and they had seen Maisie leaving with the man she'd danced with in the ladies' choice.

Kathy collected her coat and walked upstairs, where Ian was waiting.

'Any luck?' he, asked.

Somewhat annoyed, Kathy told him what she had learned from the others.

'Then I'd better walk you to your door,' he said. 'The pubs will be turning out and it's better that you have an escort.' She started to refuse, but he insisted. 'It's my public duty,' he told her with a smile. 'Come along, Kathy Bates. I promise you, you'll be quite safe.'

He was a pleasant companion. He didn't talk about his work, but asked her about her fiancé, and they talked about the war and how they hoped it would be over soon. Before long, they were outside Kathy's house.

'Well, here we are,' she said. 'Thank you for bringing me back. It was very kind of you.'

He shook her hand and said, 'It was my

pleasure. Thank you for your company. Don't forget I'm at the Guildhall most Wednesday evenings. I hope to see you there again ... and don't be too hard on your sister! I don't want to have to see you in an official capacity.'

Laughing, she said, 'Well, I'm not making any promises.' Then she put her key in the door and went inside.

'Is Maisie home yet, Mum?'

'No,' said Annie. 'Didn't she come back with you?'

'I couldn't find her,' Kathy told her. 'Her friends said she left before me.'

Shaking her head, Annie said, 'That girl, she takes too many chances. Did you have to walk home on your own?'

'No, a very nice, good-looking gentleman I met walked back with me, and before you say a word, Mum, he was all right. He was a policeman.'

'Oh, well then.' Annie seemed to think that was fine. 'I'm off to bed,' she said.

'Me too,' said Kathy. 'I'm on an early shift tomorrow.'

As she climbed into bed, she thought, You wait, our Maisie, until I see you. Leaving me without a word.

But Kathy was fast asleep when Maisie eventually crept into bed and so was unaware of her younger sister's distressed state.

# CHAPTER SEVEN

Kathy was the first to wake the following morning. She took the opportunity of using the bathroom before Maisie woke, or her sister would be continually knocking the door urging her to hurry.

When she'd finished she walked round the side of Maisie's bed and shook her. 'Wake up, you lazy devil, it's time to get up.'

Rubbing her eyes, Maisie asked, 'What time is it?'

'Seven o'clock. Are you all right?'

Looking somewhat startled, her sister threw back the sheets and swung her legs out of bed. 'Fine. Why do you ask?'

Sitting beside her, Kathy took hold of Maisie's arm. 'How did you get these bruises? Look, there are more on your other arm. What on earth has happened to you?'

Fighting back tears of anger, Maisie told her. 'It was that bloke who brought me home. He tried it on and when I told him to get lost, he got angry. We struggled and then I kneed him. He soon let go and I ran like hell.'

'Oh, my God! Why didn't you wait for me? I looked everywhere for you.'

'Well, I wasn't to know he was a bastard,

was I? He seemed a decent chap when we danced together.' She stood up and walked towards the door, then stopped. 'He wasn't too pleased, though, I can tell you.' She didn't tell Kathy of the threats he'd yelled after her. 'I hope he isn't at the Guildhall the next time I go.'

'Well, at least you'll know to keep out of his way. You don't think he'll cause any trouble, do you?'

'I don't know, to be honest; I suppose I'll find out if he turns up.'

Kathy didn't see the worried look on Maisie's face as she left the room, but she wasn't fooled for a minute. She'd heard the nervous uncertainty in her sister's voice; she'd seen the bruises and guessed the altercation had been more serious than she'd been told. She herself had been fortunate that Ian, the policeman, had been a decent sort, she thought. Looking at her watch, she fled downstairs to get some breakfast.

Annie was making some porridge when she entered the kitchen. 'Here,' she said, handing Kathy a dish, 'get this down you. I'll pour you a cup of tea. Is the duchess up yet?'

'Yes, she'll be down in a minute.'

'Right,' said Annie, putting on her green uniform jacket and matching hat, 'I'm off. We're going down to the docks today to meet a ship that's bringing back some of the wounded. Your father has already left, so I'll see you later.'

It was a harrowing morning for Annie Bates and her colleagues. When the ship docked, the walking wounded struggled down the gangways, while others were carried on stretchers to the waiting ambulances, but there were so many patients that many were laid down on the ground, in neat lines, to await transportation. The WVS women were told which patients were allowed a drink.

'Most of them just want a comforting word,' a nurse told them quietly. 'Many are badly injured, but try and not let it show in your face when you look at them.'

Annie knelt beside a young soldier and offered him a cup of tea, but his hands were shaking too much to hold it. 'Here you go,' she said, and, holding up his bandaged head to help him, she gently held the cup to his lips. 'Where are you from, son?'

'Brixham in Devon,' he told her in a soft West Country burr. 'You don't have a fag on you, lady, do you?'

Taking a packet from her pocket, she extracted a cigarette and put it between his lips lips before lighting it for him. He drew deeply on the nicotine and blew out the smoke. 'Thanks. I needed that.'

'You'll soon be home, lad, once they've made you better. Then you can have a proper rest.'

Tears filled the boy's eyes and he couldn't speak.

Pretending not to notice, Annie urged him to drink more tea, chatting away as she did so, giving him time to pull himself together. When he'd drunk it all, she gave him the packet of cigarettes and tucked the box of matches in the pocket of his tunic.

'Thanks,' he said and smiled at her.

'Thank you, my son,' she said and moved on to the next man.

The next few hours seemed to fly by as the WVS volunteers fed, watered and comforted hundreds of men. Annie's back ached from constantly bending down and her throat hurt from trying to keep back the tears that threatened to flow as she attended to more and more injured soldiers. She wondered just how many would survive. Many had lost limbs, some had been blinded by shrapnel and others knew that after their stay in hospital they would have to return to their regiment. It was heartbreaking.

At the end of her shift, Martha, who had been working with her, said, 'Come on, I need a stiff drink after that. We'll pop into the nearest pub before we go home.'

They walked up the road to the Duke of Wellington and entered the lounge bar where Martha ordered two gin and tonics. They each lit a cigarette and sat in silence for a minute.

At last, Martha leaned back in her seat and said, 'That was about the worst day of my life. Those poor devils. Never did I think I would have to see such dreadful things. Those poor boys.'

Annie felt the tears fill her eyes. 'I know. So many – and so young. There will be many a broken heart in many homes after this Normandy business, and this is only the beginning. Can you imagine if one of those boys was your son?'

'Mm,' said Martha. 'I'm thankful to have only girls.' She gazed around the bar. At the far end, a wall separated the lounge bar from the public one, but the counter swept round the room to accommodate both, so that you could see the customers standing near the bar itself.

'Oh, look,' she said. 'There's my neighbour, who's in the ARP. Her husband's away in the army but she's got a fancy man she works with, naughty girl!'

Annie was still looking at the woman when the man she was with turned to buy another drink. Annie caught her breath as she recognised her husband.

Kathy Bates, busy working at her machine, felt a tap on her shoulder. The foreman was standing there and signalled her to follow him. Shutting down her machine, she did so, wondering what on earth he wanted.

When they got to his office, he said, 'There's a phone call for you. Private calls are not allowed, as you know, but I'll make an exception this time – it's your fiancé.'

With great trepidation, Kathy picked up the receiver. 'Hello.'

'Kathy, darling, it's Jimmy. Just to let you know I'll be leaving in the morning and I wanted to say goodbye to my girl. The sergeant in the supply store is a mate and let me use the phone.'

'Oh, Jimmy,' she cried, 'you take good care of yourself, do you hear?'

'I love you, darling. I've got to go.'

'I'll wait near the dock gates and hope to see you. I'll be there early. Watch out for me, won't you? I'll stand by the cigarette kiosk in Latimer Street.'

'I'll look for you. I love you.' The phone went dead.

Kathy stood like a statue, the receiver still in her hand. The foreman took it from her and replaced it in its cradle.

'He's off then?'

The voice didn't quite penetrate her mind and Kathy looked at him and asked, 'Did you say something?'

'Your young man, he's off tomorrow then?'

She just nodded.

'Look, you'd better take a break,' the foreman said gruffly, concealing his overflowing sympathy beneath a veneer of brusqueness. 'Go to the canteen and get yourself a cup of coffee, pull yourself together. You need to be fully attentive at your machine. I don't want no accidents. Now go on!' He pushed her out of the door.

In a daze, Kathy made her way to the canteen, bought a mug of coffee and sat drinking it. Her Jimmy was going to war. She closed her eyes, trying to escape her thoughts, but all she could see in her mind was his smiling face. The tears trickled down her cheeks, unchecked. What would she do if he was killed? No! No, she must never ever consider such a thing. Never! Her man would come home, they would get married, have lots of children

Burying her head in her hands, she wept.

She broke the news to the rest of the family as they sat round the table eating their tea.

'I'm going down to the docks early to see him go,' she said.

'I'll come with you,' said Maisie immediately. 'Give you moral support.'

'Would you?' Kathy looked relieved. 'I would be so grateful.'

'What time are you thinking of leaving?'

'About seven o'clock,' she said. 'I have no idea what time he'll be going through to the docks. We may have a long wait.'

'I'll make you some sandwiches,' said

Annie. 'You'll need something to keep you going.'

'Thanks, Mum.'

Annie had other things on her mind. When Wilf had arrived home that evening, she had told him about her harrowing time with the wounded soldiers and casually asked about his day.

'Just work,' he said.

She stared at him, hating him for his lies. 'Martha and I were so shaken we went to the Duke of Wellington for a drink,' she said casually.

Wilf Bates hesitated for just a moment before replying, which didn't go unnoticed by his wife. She hurried on.

'Yes, we slipped into the lounge bar for a couple of G and Ts and a cigarette.'

Her husband relaxed visibly. 'I expect you needed it,' he said. 'Those poor lads, they must have been through hell.'

Not as much hell as I'm going to put you through if you don't soon come to your senses, she thought. 'Are you on duty tonight?' she asked. 'Only I thought we could go to the pictures after tea. We don't seem to spend any time together these days.' She saw the flush of guilt on his face.

Wilf was thinking quickly. He reflected how lucky he was that Annie hadn't seen him and Betty together in the pub. How foolish they had been to take such a chance.

He had planned to visit Betty that evening, as they were off duty. She had promised him a night of sex that he wouldn't forget ... but he thought it prudent to take his wife to the pictures instead. He wouldn't like to give her cause for concern. If she found out about his infidelity, the shit would really hit the fan and he didn't want to be faced with the fallout.

'What a lovely idea,' he said. 'Where do you want to go?'

'Let's go to the Empire. There's a George Raft film showing.' And that's one night you won't be spending with your bloody mistress, she thought.

The following morning, the girls left the house to take up their positions. Troops were already marching past and Kathy's dread was that they had missed Jimmy. Seeing a policeman nearby, she went up to him and asked, 'Do you know if the Hampshire Regiment has gone through yet?'

'No, love, not yet.'

'Are you sure?'

'Yes. My young brother is in it and I'm hoping to spot him.'

'I'm looking for my fiancé,' she told him.

He gave her a sympathetic smile. 'Not easy, love, is it?'

'No, not easy at all.'

The next few hours were surreal. English

troops marched by, followed by Americans on foot and in lorries, yelling and calling out to the crowd now gathered, throwing gum, money and candy. Maisie was in her element, waving, laughing and calling back to the troops.

Kathy waved too, but always she was looking beyond the passing soldiers, watching for Jimmy's regiment. Eventually she recognized the insignia of the next company of troops as they approached.

Grabbing Maisie's arm she said, 'Here they come! Keep your eyes peeled for my Jimmy!'

There seemed to be so many as line by line they passed by. Kathy felt the panic rise within her as despite scouring the face of every man who passed she couldn't see her fiancé. She ran up and down, frantically searching.

'There he is!' cried Maisie. 'There's Jimmy.'

He was fortunately on their side as they marched and Kathy ran alongside him, calling to him, 'You keep your head down, Jimmy Greene. I love you, darling!'

'I love you too,' he called back. He looked past her and saw Maisie. She was crying.

'I love you,' she mouthed at him. 'I really love you!'

By now the crowd was so dense that Kathy could no longer run beside her man. She blew a kiss at him, then watched as he disappeared into the distance. She pushed her way through the crowd and leaned against a wall. She was exhausted – and in despair.

Maisie, eyes red from crying, walked away, fighting her way through those in her path. No longer did she see or hear the troops who were still marching past. All she could think of was the expression on Jimmy's face as she told him of her love for him. He had just stared at her without turning away. She remembered how he'd kissed her, the passion that had momentarily been in his response. It still thrilled her to think of it. He couldn't love Kathy with all of his heart and kiss her like that! He couldn't!

Kathy just walked and walked until she found herself in the park where she and Jimmy had sat beneath the beech tree. She made her way to the same bench and sank down on it, feeling stunned. She closed her eyes, then let out a deep sigh. A moment later, she was aware that someone had sat beside her.

'Hello, Kathy. Are you all right?'

She looked up and saw Ian Harvey staring at her with some concern. 'Ian. This is a surprise.'

'I saw you sitting here, and you looked so unhappy I thought I had better see if you were all right.'

'You're very kind. I've just been watching my fiancé march off to war, so no, I'm not all right, to be honest.'

'Did he see you?'

'Yes. I ran alongside him for a bit, but now he's gone.'

'That's really tough. Come along,' he said, rising to his feet and catching hold of her arm. 'What you need is a stiff drink. A nice drop of brandy will help. Come on.'

He didn't make conversation as they walked to the nearest pub. It wasn't until they were seated and Kathy had taken a sip of brandy that he offered her a cigarette and said, 'That's better. Now you've got a bit of colour in your cheeks.'

'You always seem to come to my rescue when I'm in trouble,' she remarked with a wry smile.

He laughed. 'No white horse, I'm afraid.'

'The strong arm of the law, though?'

'No, just a friend, that's all. Feeling better?'

'Yes, thanks.'

He looked at his watch. 'Look, why don't we have a bite to eat? I don't suppose you had any breakfast, did you?'

'My mother made some sandwiches, but I've just realised we forgot to eat them.'

'We?' he queried.

'Maisie – my sister. She came with me but we lost each other in the crowd.'

'Right. We'll go to the Cowherds. I know the landlord, he should be able to find us a

decent steak. What do you say?'
'Steak! Are you joking?'
'No, I'm not. A bit of red meat inside you, you'll feel like a new woman. What do you think?'
'I don't know. I don't seem able to think at all at the moment.'
'We'll drink to the safe return of your fellow with a glass of wine, how about that?'
'That's a really kind thought, Ian. Thank you.'
'Good. I'll call a taxi.'
As she waited for him, Kathy thought how generous and kind the man was. It wouldn't do any harm to go. After all, he knew her situation and was just being a friend in need, and at this moment she didn't really want to be alone.

The landlord did indeed find them a decent steak, as Ian had promised. They both tucked into their meal, and didn't speak again until they had finished.
'Feel better?' Ian asked.
'As a matter of fact, I do. Thank you. I haven't eaten meat like that since the start of the war.'
Ian replenished their wine glasses, picked his up and said, 'To the safe return of your fellow. What's his name?'
'Jimmy Greene, and I'll drink to that.' She sipped her wine, then asked, 'Do you have

anyone special in your life, Ian?'

He shook his head. 'Not at the moment. There was a girl once, but it didn't work out.'

'I'm sorry to hear that,' Kathy said, wondering why.

'She couldn't face the long hours we have to work and the worry of the job, the dangers involved. You have to be special to be married to the force. It puts a great strain on relationships, I'm afraid.'

'What a pity. You'd make a lovely husband.'

'Well, thank you very much, Kathy, but you don't know me well enough to make such a sweeping judgement.'

'With some people you know immediately. Others you can know for years and they are still strangers.'

'You are quite a philosopher. I had no idea,' he teased. 'So, what are you going to do with yourself now that your young man is away?'

'To be honest I don't know. Jimmy said he wanted me to go out and about and not stay moping at home.'

'Wise man. Life is for living and it doesn't mean you think any the less of your commitments. Are you going to the Guildhall again next Wednesday?'

'I hadn't thought that far ahead.'

Ian called the waiter over and asked for

the bill, and whilst he waited he said, 'I'll look out for you. I go every week. Saturday evenings are too crowded to be able to dance properly.'

He took her home in another taxi, and as she got out of the car she turned to Ian and said, 'Thanks for the lunch. You turned up at just the right moment and I'll for ever be grateful for that.'

'Then come to the Guildhall on Wednesday.'

'Maybe. I'll see,' she said.

When Kathy entered the living room she found her sister sitting drinking a cup of tea, eyes swollen from crying.

'Where have you been?' Maisie asked.

'I lost you in the crowd and went to the park. I met the policeman who walked me home from the dance, and he took me to the Cowherds for some lunch.'

Maisie shot her an accusing look. 'Well, you don't waste any time, do you? Jimmy has just about set foot on a ship and you're off enjoying yourself. So much for being true to him!'

'It wasn't like that at all! I was in a state and Ian happened by. He took me for a meal to cheer me up.'

'It seems to me that I care more about Jimmy than you do. You swan off with another man the minute he's out of sight. If he was mine I would have come straight back here and started writing to him.'

'Well, he isn't yours, Maisie. He's mine!'

'But you don't love him as much as I do. I would die for him if I had to.'

'Now you're being childish and dramatic. You've had a crush on him for years, that's all. It's time you grew up!'

'Jimmy thinks I'm grown up enough to kiss me.'

'What are you talking about?'

With a smile of satisfaction, Maisie, gloating, said 'The last time he came here to call for you, I let him in. I was really upset that he was going away. I cried, Kathy. I cried for him! He took me in his arms and kissed me. And, let me tell you, he wasn't kissing me like you kiss a child. He enjoyed it ... and so did I! Write and ask him if you don't believe me. He can't deny it.'

'You bloody little liar! How dare you try and make trouble between us!'

'He knows I love him. I told him then and again this morning.'

Kathy's fury knew no bounds. 'You little cheat! You told me you were coming with me to see him off to give me moral support!'

'I couldn't let the man I love go away without being there to see him off. I had to go. I would have gone alone if I had to.'

'You rotten little bitch!' Kathy flew at her.

The two girls were struggling with each

other, exchanging blows, pulling hair, when Annie Bates walked in.

'What the bloody hell is going on?' she cried. 'Stop this at once!' She forcefully pulled the girls apart. 'I've never seen anything so appalling in my life. You're sisters, for God's sake.'

'She's a wicked little bitch!' Kathy cried. 'She's trying to make trouble between Jimmy and me and I'll never forgive her for that.'

'She doesn't love him!' Maisie was incandescent with rage. 'She went off and had lunch with another man after waving goodbye to her fiancé who could be killed fighting for his country. I hate her! I love Jimmy Greene more than she does and she doesn't like it.'

Annie was flabbergasted. 'You seem to forget, Maisie, that Jimmy and Kathy are engaged.'

'It's not me that's forgotten. I wouldn't be going out with another man the minute *my* fiancé was out of sight.' Grabbing her jacket from the back of the chair, she swept out of the house.

Fighting back tears, Kathy sat in a chair and looked at her mother. 'Maisie said he kissed her the last time he called here.'

'He was probably just saying goodbye. You know Maisie, she always dramatises everything. She should be on the stage. Go and wash your face, I'll put the kettle on.'

Alone in the kitchen Annie pondered over the incident. Wasn't it enough that she had to cope with the infidelity of her husband? Now Maisie was making trouble. Hopefully the situation between the girls would smooth over eventually, whereas she still had to bide her time, wondering what was going to happen next.

## CHAPTER EIGHT

Jimmy Greene stood in the landing craft, smoking a cigarette, wondering what awaited him and his mates on this side of the Channel. The sea was choppy after a stormy night and several men were hanging over the side throwing up. Others were just standing, lost in thought, tense as each moment brought them nearer to the beaches of Normandy.

'Get ready, lads!' called the company sergeant. 'Lose the fags and try to keep your rifles dry.'

The next moment they were jumping into the water. The sudden cold took Jimmy's breath away. 'Christ!' he exclaimed as he sank up to his armpits and struggled for the shore, holding his Enfield rifle over his head.

'Keep together when you get to the beach,'

came the cry from behind.

'If we get to the bloody beach!' The soldier beside Jimmy wasn't as tall as him; the water was up to his chin.

'Hang on to me,' Jimmy said. 'Grab hold of my kitbag – we're nearly there.'

'And I bet when we get there, they'll have run out of towels!' the other man quipped. 'Bugger this for a game of soldiers!'

After what seemed an eternity, Jimmy breathed a sigh of relief as the water became shallower. Hauling the other man along with him, he made it up the beach to where the rest of the company were gathered.

Looking around, his new companion said, 'Well, they can keep bloody France if this is what it's like!'

'Shut up, Shorty, for God's sake,' said Jimmy as they started to move off.

The battle of the beaches had been won by the earlier expeditionary forces and so the landing troops were not met by any enemy artillery, but as the men headed inland they knew it was only a matter of time before they would be fighting house by house, street by street.

Whilst Jimmy Greene was fighting his war, Annie Bates was fighting her own battle. She had long since suspected that Wilf was having an affair and the most obvious candidate was Betty Langdon, with whom he spent so much time, but she had been shocked to actually see them together in a public place. Even more shocking to her was the fact that Betty was so much younger than Wilf. Inside she raged. How dare he? What the hell did he think he was playing at? She supposed that he was flattered by the attention – but more to the point, what was she going to do about it? If she confronted him with it, how would he react? Even if he was contrite and promised to end the affair, their marriage would never be the same again, and of course she had to face the possibility that if she gave him an ultimatum, he might decide to leave and set up home with the woman. So many questions, and no answers!

She suddenly remembered that Martha had told her that Betty was married to a soldier who was serving abroad, so she too was playing with fire. Annie stood in front of the fireplace and looked in the mirror at her reflection. Since joining the WVS, she'd smartened herself up considerably and she wasn't bad-looking, she concluded, but she couldn't compete with Betty Langdon with her youth and blonde hair!

'You stupid bugger, Wilf,' she muttered. She supposed the woman fed his ego, making him feel young again. Well, he wasn't that exciting in bed. After so many years, sex was just a habit – and a pretty mechanical one, if she was honest. Now she came to think about it, it had been a lot less frequent over the past months, which was what had first led her to wonder if he was playing around. Was he more adventurous with his new woman, she wondered? That possibility angered her even more. Perhaps if she said nothing, it would all pass over and Wilf would get it out of his system. After all, Betty's husband had to come home at some time. Perhaps that was the best option for the time being.

The atmosphere between the two sisters could have frozen a rain-forest. They didn't speak to each other for days. Every time Kathy saw Maisie, she wanted to shake her. Make her understand just how far she had stepped over the mark.

Wilf had asked his wife what the hell was going on and she had told him.

'Maisie thinks she's in love with Jimmy Greene and told Kathy so. She also implied that he fancied her too.'

He was shocked. 'That's outrageous!' he said angrily. 'What on earth is she thinking of?'

'Well, that's just it: she's not thinking, is she? What she's doing and saying could have terrible repercussions.'

'What do you mean?'

'It could ruin Jimmy's and Kathy's relationship; make a family rift that can never be repaired. Illicit love is hardly ever worth it,' she said, taking the opportunity of making a point. 'Lives are ruined ... and for what?' She enjoyed watching her husband squirm.

'It's the war, love. Things happen in war-time that would never happen normally.'

'What a load of bloody rubbish!' she snapped. 'There are rules to be followed. Men who are abroad often have a fling, we all suspect that, although you never know for sure, but if they come home to discover their wives have been doing the same ... well, that's how murder can happen, and it's the same between the girls. If Maisie persists in declaring her love and tries to make more of it when Jimmy comes home, what then? It's the eternal triangle and it's dangerous.'

'The girls will get over their spat, you'll see. It'll all blow over in time.'

Maisie was fed up. Kathy wasn't talking to her, her parents were cool towards her and she was worried about Jimmy. Apart from this she was bored. Well, it was Wednesday, so she would go to the Guildhall this evening. Milly and Hazel were off to the cinema, but she didn't fancy it so she would go dancing

Kathy too had decided to go to the Guildhall. The atmosphere in the house was oppressive and she wanted a change. Ian had said he would be there, so at least she would know someone. He was a good companion and she felt the need of company.

She waited until her sister had left the house before she got ready, so she was a little late arriving. After leaving her coat in the cloakroom, she went upstairs to the dance hall and looked for Ian. She saw him on the dance floor and stood watching. He was a good dancer. He spotted her as he passed by, and when the music finished she saw him walking towards her.

'Kathy! I was hoping to see you. Let's dance.'

As they whirled around the floor to the quickstep, she saw Maisie dancing with an airman. Her sister was in animated conversation and didn't see her, and at the end of the dance when Ian took her to the bar for a drink, she lost sight of her.

'How are you?' Ian asked as they sat at a table.

'Fine, and you?'

'All right. Life goes on, you know how it is. Is your sister with you?'

'She's here, but not with me,' Kathy said.

He raised his eyebrows. 'Oh, dear. Have you two fallen out?'

'You could say so, but I don't want to talk about it.'

He began to laugh. 'Sibling rivalry is a nuisance, isn't it? My brother and I were always at odds with each other, but as we grew older, it changed … for the better, I mean.'

'I wish I could say the same.'

'Never mind, Kathy. Let's forget about her and enjoy the dancing.'

Which they did, until the end of the evening when Kathy saw Maisie arguing with the man who had taken her home the previous week. The man was gripping Maisie's arm and looking very angry.

'Oh, dear,' said Kathy.

'What's wrong?' Ian asked.

'I think Maisie is in a spot of bother. That man she's talking to walked her home last week and turned nasty.'

Ian looked over. 'This needs sorting out,' he said. Kathy followed him as he walked towards the couple.

The man's voice was raised in anger. 'You're just a little prick teaser,' he accused her. 'You led me on last week but you soon backed off when I took you home. I don't like being taken for a fool.'

Maisie struggled to release the hold he had on her. 'Let me go!' she cried.

By then a small crowd had gathered. Ian pushed his way through, followed by Kathy. 'What's going on here?' he demanded.

'Mind your own bloody business,' the man growled at him. 'You interfere and you'll be sorry.'

'This is my business,' said Ian firmly. 'You are making a public nuisance of yourself and I think you should leave.'

'And who the hell are you to tell me what to do?'

Ian produced his warrant card and showed it to him. 'I'm the law, mate, and I'm telling you to sling your hook before I arrest you!'

Scowling, the man reluctantly let go of Maisie and walked away, helped by one of the hall's security men.

Rubbing her arm, Maisie said, 'Thanks, that was turning very nasty. You must be Kathy's policeman.'

'Well, I am a policeman, but I'm not Kathy's – she's already spoken for. You look shaken; you'd better have a drink to steady your nerves.' He turned to Kathy. 'If that's all right with you?'

'It's fine,' she said. 'I'm a bit shaken myself. That was a nasty five minutes.'

Ian left the girls together whilst he went to the bar. 'That was very decent of your friend,' Maisie ventured. 'I'm not sure what would have happened if he hadn't come along.'

'You were right,' Kathy said. 'That man was a very nasty piece of work and after seeing him tonight, I think you had a lucky escape last time. You need to be more careful.'

'Don't lecture me, please. I don't need that right now!'

Fortunately, Ian returned at that moment and stopped any further argument and at the end of the evening he insisted on walking them both home, just in case the belligerent man was hanging around.

When they arrived home, Maisie had the decency to leave them alone. 'Thank you once again,' she said, and walked into the house.

'I can't thank you enough for tonight, Ian,' Kathy said. 'Maisie would have been in real trouble but for you.'

'I rather think that trouble is your sister's middle name.'

She laughed. 'You have no idea just how true that is.'

'Well, perhaps tonight will have broken the ice between you two. Life's too short, Kathy.' He leaned forward and kissed her forehead. 'Take care.'

When she walked into the living room, she found that Maisie had made them both a cup of cocoa. 'Will this do as a peace offering?' she asked, offering a cup to her sister.

'I suppose so,' said Kathy. They sat together drinking it before going to bed, but neither of them touched on the subject of Jimmy, who had been the cause of their animosity.

# CHAPTER NINE

The notice on the door of Sonny Nolan's shop read *Closed*, which was unusual at ten o'clock in the morning. Passers-by might think that Sonny was absent for an hour and that Gerry, his sidekick, was busy elsewhere, but the truth of the matter could be found in the room behind the shop. Sonny had his hands round the throat of a man whom he'd pushed up against a wall.

'You must be stupid to think you can pull a flanker over me!' he was yelling. 'Let's face it, you've hardly got the brains of a newt!'

There was a look of abject terror in the man's eyes. 'I'm sorry, Sonny. I won't do it again, honest.'

'You won't bloody well get the chance.'

'What do you mean?' asked the man in a quaking voice. 'You ain't gonna do for me, are you?'

Sonny released his hold and pushed the man flying across the room. 'You are certainly not worth the risk of the gallows, but if I hear you've been loose-tongued I'll send Gerry after you and you know what *that* means.'

'I won't say nothing to no one, you have

my word.'

'A lot of bloody good that is. Now bugger off and don't come anywhere near me again.'

The man ran out of the shop, leaving the door open behind him.

Sonny walked through and flipped the sign over. Now he would have to find someone else to deliver his clothing and petrol coupons to his customers. What he needed was someone who would be above suspicion from the police. Someone who wouldn't try to fleece him of the odd pound, like the miscreant he'd sent packing. But who? Who would fit the picture? The door bell tinkled as a customer entered. Sonny turned and saw Maisie coming in.

'You taking an early lunch today?' he asked.

Flicking through the dresses on the stand near the door she said, 'Yes. I swapped with another girl, so I thought I'd pop in and see if you had any new clothes.'

'I've got a couple just down from London,' he told her, 'hang on a minute,' and he disappeared into the inner recess of his shop, returning with two beautiful garments.

Maisie almost snatched them out of his hands, so taken with them was she. 'Oh, they are exquisite,' she said as she held up the cocktail dresses. 'But they look very expensive.'

'I'm afraid they are, my dear, but then of course they are couture gowns, a little out of your league, financially.' He could see the avarice in her eyes as she held them in front of her, twisting and turning in front of the long mirror.

'How much is this one?' she asked eagerly.

'Twenty pounds.' He watched the disappointment on her face.

'Could I pay you so much a week?'

'No, I don't do business like that. Cash on the nail is my rule, then I know I'll get all my money.'

'I wouldn't let you down,' she pleaded. 'I would die to wear this to the Guildhall.'

He looked thoughtful for a moment, making her wait. 'There is a way round your predicament,' he said.

'Tell me.'

'Once a week I need someone to deliver papers to various people, no questions asked. There would be a fee paid for your services, which would help you pay for your goods.'

'But not twenty pounds,' said Maisie.

'No, don't be ridiculous, but I would let you have that dress at fifteen pounds. I'll keep it until you can pay me.'

'And what will you pay me for these deliveries?' she demanded. 'If I'm not allowed to ask any questions, it sounds as if it might be dodgy, so it should be made worth my while.'

Sonny Nolan burst out laughing at her astute mind. 'You are certainly something, young lady. There are no flies on you, are there?'

'If you thought I was stupid you wouldn't have asked me, would you?'

'Definitely not. I can't tell you what you'll be paid; it depends on how many papers you have to deliver. But it will be a fair deal, you can take my word for that.'

'Like a gentlemen's agreement, you mean.'

'I'm no gentleman, girlie, but I do keep my word, and I expect those who work for me to do the same, no mucking about.'

Maisie considered this for a moment. She looked at the man, then at the dress. 'All right, but I would like you to give me first refusal of any decent clothes you get in the shop. Is it a deal?'

With grudging admiration for her, he agreed. 'All right, but you have to say you want the garment or not at the time I show it to you. I can't afford to keep things hanging about, understand?'

'I understand. When do I start?'

'Come in after work in three days' time; by then I'll have some papers ready for delivery. Needless to say, this is a strictly confidential business deal. You don't tell anyone about it, and I mean not a word to a soul. Understand?'

She gave him a sly smile. 'Of course.' Fishing for her wallet, she took out four pound notes. 'Take this as my first payment on the dress.'

'No, girlie, you save fifteen pounds and then it's yours. I told you that's the way I do business. Don't worry, I promised to save it for you.'

Putting the money away, she said, 'Fine. I'll see you in three days' time, after work.'

Sonny was pleased with himself. The greedy young woman was the perfect carrier for him. He had the things she craved which would keep her eager – and who better to do his work for him?

Maisie was equally pleased. The dress she had been promised was very classy and she couldn't wait to wear it. What's more, she would have the pick of the gowns in the future. For a young woman for whom appearance was everything, this was a perfect situation. The extra money would be really useful. It would help pay for her clothes and she would be the envy of all her friends. She thought it was fortunate that she had walked into Sonny's shop and discovered his wares, but she would have been very surprised to see her mother enter the same shop soon after her daughter had left.

Annie had decided to venture into the dragon's den and look at the clothes on display. She figured she had to fight fire with fire and try to win back her husband. She had spent some clothing coupons on a new nightdress and a daring pair of camiknickers.

Sex was the obvious answer to her husband's infidelity, she had decided, and so she was hell-bent on enthralling him in their marital bed. But now she was looking for something special to wear for him when he came home from work.

Sonny Nolan looked with interest at the woman as she walked in. She was a stranger to him but she had a certain air about her, a look of determination as she sorted the garments on the dress rail.

'Can I help you?' he asked.

'I'm just looking,' she said in reply. As she sorted the dresses in front of her she remarked, 'You have some very stylish things here.'

'I bring them down from London. Some come from rejected stock.'

'Rejected stock, in wartime?' She gazed at him suspiciously.

He didn't answer.

As Annie looked at the seams and the hem allowance she realised there was nothing utility about those dresses and wondered if they were stolen goods, but as she chose one she really liked and held it in front of her, looking at her reflection in the mirror, she thought, So what? Everyone had some kind of fiddle in these difficult times, and she smiled to herself as she mused that after all, in a funny way, this was to help her own war effort!

'If I find this doesn't fit, can I bring it back?'

'If you do so by tomorrow,' Sonny said. 'I say that because I don't want anyone to wear something for a couple of days and then return it. There are a lot of unscrupulous people about, you know.'

Annie thought this highly amusing coming from a man known in the town as a racketeer.

She paid her money and took the dress home, stopping on the way to have her hair shampooed and set. To her delight the dress fitted perfectly. She had finished her shift for the WVS, so, covering her new hairstyle with a scarf, she undressed, filled the bath with the permitted five inches of water, poured in some bath crystals, and sat soaking, planning the evening ahead. Wilf would wonder what had hit him!

Jimmy Greene and the rest of his company were taking a rest by a roadside scattered with burned-out vehicles belonging to the German army and the British, relics of the battle that had been fought before they arrived. There had been pockets of resistance during their journey, small villages not cleared of the enemy. House-to-house fighting, snipers who found their targets before being shot themselves, and now the tired men were trying to recharge their batteries before moving on.

Shorty was, as usual, moaning about everything. 'Bloody field rations,' he said. 'Nowhere near enough to fill a man's stomach! How the hell do they expect us to fight when we're hungry?'

'Wait till we make camp tonight,' said Jimmy, taking off his tin hat and lighting a cigarette. 'I could murder a nice stew ... with dumplings,' he added longingly.

'Oh, mate,' pleaded Shorty, 'don't do this to me. You start talking about food and I think I'll die right here on the roadside.'

'Just be thankful you're still here and able to complain, not like those poor buggers we passed a way back.'

For once Shorty was silent. The company had marched past several dead bodies scattered about earlier that day, which had brought home to the men how perilous war was and how lucky they were to still be breathing the air around them.

Jimmy pulled out the photograph that Kathy had given him and gazed at it, taking in every detail as he did whenever there was a quiet moment. Taking a notebook and pencil from his uniform pocket he started adding to the letter he had started days ago.

*Well, darling, we are sitting having a quiet five minutes by the roadside before moving on. I would like one day to come back to France when we are at peace because it seems a nice country. Friendly people, the French, very pleased to see us as we march through the towns that have been liberated. They give us wine to drink which is really nice, and cigarettes that smell and taste absolutely foul!*

*There has been some fighting, of course, but we are all fine. I miss you like hell and can't wait until I can hold you in my arms again. Then we can get married and put all this behind us. We'll be moving on soon so I'll finish for now.*

He closed the pad and put it in his pocket. It helped him to write to Kathy whenever he had time. He didn't tell her too much about the fighting, certainly not about the dead bodies he'd seen or the man who'd been shot right in front of him, or the one who was blown to pieces after walking into a booby-trapped house. These were not the things he wanted to share with her. Tomorrow, all being well, they might receive mail from home and be able to send some back; that would certainly lift the spirits of the men. But now they were being moved on. Ahead of them would be more fighting. A company of German troops needed to be cleared from a town before other British troops could proceed. A strategic position, they had been told. More bloodshed, he thought, and prayed it wouldn't be any of his.

# CHAPTER TEN

Wilf Bates put the key in his front door with a sigh of relief. He felt weary after a busy day in the factory and was looking forward to a quiet evening. He had a night off from fire-watching and had made no arrangement to see Betty, so he planned to have his meal, enjoy a nice bath and sit reading the paper before having an early night.

'Hello, love,' he said to his wife over his shoulder as he hung up his coat.

'Hello, Wilf. Supper won't be long. I've made your favourite, shepherd's pie, so have a quick wash and it'll be ready to dish up.'

It wasn't until he sat at the table that Wilf looked directly at his wife. She looked different, he thought, and as she placed his plate of food before him a waft of perfume drifted past him. Annie never used anything but lavender water! He looked again. She smiled at him.

'Now then, dear, you tuck in. A man needs a good meal after a day's work.'

He suddenly felt nervous. What was going on? You never knew with women. Had he forgotten a birthday? No, of course he hadn't. Annie's birthday was in November. It was then he realised she'd had her hair done in a new style – and she was wearing a new frock.

'You planning to go out this evening?' he asked hopefully, thinking of his quiet night.

'No, why do you ask?'

'Well, you're all dolled up. I thought you were off to a WVS meeting or something.'

She looked pleased and touched her hair. 'Do you like it?' she asked.

'Yes, very becoming. It suits you. Is that a new frock too?'

'Yes, I bought it today. I thought the least I could do was look nice for my husband.'

He cast a suspicious look in her direction. Was she going to ask for some extra housekeeping money, he wondered? He didn't say anything, just grunted and continued to eat.

'There's some nice apple crumble for afters,' she told him as she tucked into her food.

Where was this going, he asked himself? His two favourite dishes, a new frock...

When the meal was over, Annie cleared the table, putting the plates in hot water to soak, and came to sit by him on the old but comfortable settee. Wilf was just about to stretch out and read his paper, but Annie pushed his legs down and moved closer.

'Isn't this nice?' she said. 'Being on our own like this. Kathy has gone to the pictures with a friend and Maisie is off out somewhere, so we have the evening to ourselves.' She snuggled closer and, putting an arm round his shoulder, stroked the back of his neck.

'What are you doing?' Wilf asked in alarm.

Gazing at him she said softly, 'I'm making a fuss of my husband. Is that so bad?'

'It's not like you,' he said. 'Usually you don't have time for such things.'

'I know, and I'm trying to put that right. Oh dear, Wilf, I've been thinking that I've been neglecting you and I'm sorry, but you know how it is. What with the raids, you out all night and me busy with the WVS, romance has disappeared from our lives. Good gracious, we aren't too old for a kiss and a cuddle, are we?'

He was utterly confused now. 'No, of course not, but after so many years...'

'That's what's wrong with marriage,' she said. 'We start to take each other for granted and forget why we first married. Remember when we were courting? How we used to sit up after my parents went to bed and kiss and cuddle?'

'Of course I do. I'm not senile, I do remember.'

'Then kiss me, like you used to.'

He leaned forward and gave her a perfunctory kiss.

Smiling at him, Annie said, 'Come along, you can do better than that!' She put her arms round him and kissed him with a passion that had been missing for some time

... and what's more he enjoyed the kiss and returned it with equal enthusiasm, thinking, Why not, whilst the mood lasts?

Eventually Annie surprised him even more. 'Let's have an early night, shall we, love?'

They made their way to the bedroom where he undressed and got into bed whilst Annie was in the bathroom. When she returned, he watched her remove her new frock, and hang it up, and admired her new underwear, thinking it made her look very sexy, a thought that hadn't entered his mind about his wife for some time. The idea had only been associated with Betty these past months. He mused that she wouldn't be too happy if she could see him now, about to make passionate love to his wife. He had assured her that he and Annie just shared a bed and nothing more.

Perhaps it was a feeling of guilt that came between him and his performance, but to his great shame he was unable to have an erection, no matter how hard he concentrated.

'I'm sorry, love,' he said. 'I'm more tired than I thought.'

She was very understanding about it. 'Never mind,' she said, 'just hold me in your arms and maybe it will be all right.' But even her gentle touch failed to stiffen his flaccid manhood.

Eventually, Annie, sick with disappointment that her carefully laid plans had failed, turned away. Inside she was seething. Wilf, she was sure, had no trouble satisfying Betty Langdon! Well, the bloody woman could have him lock, stock and barrel ... smelly socks and all. Why should she wash his clothes, iron them and feed him when he couldn't be a real husband? And when Wilf tried to put an arm over her, she pushed him away.

He lay there, traumatised.

Two days later, when he lay with Betty, he was decidedly nervous. Usually their love-making was energetic and passionate; she was insatiable in her needs, always had been. She was astride him now, her full breasts waiting for his kisses and caresses. He obliged as he normally did, but there was no stirring in his loins. God! What was wrong with him?

Betty, suddenly aware that things were not right, looked puzzled. 'Come on, darling, I'm ready for you. Hurry up, I want to feel you inside me.'

There was no way that Wilf could oblige her.

Betty rolled off him. 'What the hell's wrong with you, Wilf? You can't get me going and not finish the job!' She was scathing.

'Sorry, love, but I can't seem to get it up.'

She was incensed. 'What are you saying,

that I am no longer desirable?'

'No, of course not. I want you as much as ever, but...' He was lost for words.

'Are you ill?' she demanded.

'No, I'm as fit as a fiddle,' he protested.

'I don't think so! You can get a tune out of a fiddle!' She got off the bed and reached for her dressing gown. 'I'll put the kettle on. It's the only thing that will be perking tonight, it would seem!'

Wilf wanted to curl up and die. What sort of man was he? He couldn't make love to either his wife or his mistress. What a bloody predicament.

Wilf Bates's predicament was nothing compared with that of Jimmy Greene and his company, fighting to clear the small town of German soldiers, bent on maintaining control of this important sector. It was a bloody battle as street by street was fought over, with casualties on both sides. The citizens of the town had mostly fled to the surrounding countryside, but a few remained, hidden in cellars or barns, trembling with fright as guns blazed around them. Grenades were thrown to clear enemy troops out of buildings; machine guns blazed as soldiers fled trying to escape the constant barrage of bullets.

And so it continued until there was just one building left. It looked like the town hall to the British troops, two floors to be cleared with German troops at every window, trying to hold their position.

Shorty and Jimmy were using an upturned car as cover, but they had to duck constantly as the whine of bullets passed over them. There were several pings as bullets hit the body of the vehicle.

'The owner of this car isn't going to be best pleased,' Shorty remarked as he took aim at a sniper in an upper window. 'Got you, you bastard!' he yelled as the man pitched forward and landed on the road, killed by the shot.

The sergeant ran over and threw himself beside them. 'We need to get inside,' he said. 'Have you boys any grenades left?'

They both nodded.

'Right then, when you hear my whistle, you make a dash for the front door. We'll give you covering fire.' And he ran back to his position.

'Fuck me!' said Shorty. 'Just our bloody luck to be first up.'

'Stop your bloody griping, will you, and listen for the signal,' Jimmy snapped.

The whistle blew and the two men ran as fast as they could as their comrades blasted away with covering fire. They made it to the door, shoved it open, threw in a grenade each and stood flat against the wall to avoid the blast, then ran inside, guns blazing, soon to be joined by the sergeant and the other men. It was a hectic fifteen minutes before the building was theirs. Each room was searched, each dead German checked to make sure he wasn't feigning death. Eventually the troops were told to take a break.

Shorty sat beside Jimmy on the floor, pushed back his tin helmet, took out a cigarette and lit it. 'Next time on earth,' he said, 'I'm definitely coming back as a woman. Sod this for a life!'

'What about the pain of childbirth?' asked Jimmy with a grin.

'Compared to this ... dead easy,' snorted his friend. 'When I've had enough children I'll cut my old man's cock off!'

'Then he won't be able to pee.'

'Or anything else,' laughed Shorty.

A while later, more British troops entered the town and tanks rolled in. The officers used what was left of the town hall to set up headquarters, and much to the men's delight camp kitchens were erected with a promise of a hot meal that night. And more important, mail was given out.

Jimmy found himself a quiet corner where he opened the first of three letters. It was the first he had received from Kathy. He devoured every word; it was like manna from heaven.

*Darling Jimmy,*

*I do hope you are well and keeping safe. I read the news every day in the papers to see how our troops are doing, but of course they can't tell us in much detail because, as the posters say, careless talk costs lives.*

*I think about you constantly and long to hear from you. I miss you so much, my darling, and can't wait until you come home. What a great day that will be!*

*There's not much news from here. Life goes on. Mum is still with the WVS running kitchens for the troops and taking her turn in the shop, and Dad is still fire-watching in the evenings so we don't see much of him. Maisie is still out gallivanting every night, so she's happy having a good time.*

*We've had some more raids by these flying bombs, but it's nothing like the Blitz, thank goodness. Apart from that life carries on the same.*

*Take care of yourself, remember that I love you and always will.*

*Kathy xxxx*

He read it twice before opening one from his mother. All was well at home, he was pleased to read. His parents were well and his father's allotment was helping with the food shortages; in fact he was making a few shillings selling surplus vegetables. He didn't recognise the writing on the envelope of the third and wondered who it was from. He was very surprised to see it was from Maisie.

*Hello, you gorgeous man,* it began. Jimmy grinned. How very like Maisie. He started to chuckle as he read on.

*Of course everyone here thinks you are off fighting the nasty Germans but I know what you are really doing is sitting back on a soft comfortable sofa in some French château, smoking cigars, drinking wine and bedding those sexy Frenchwomen, you naughty man. Just be careful that by the time you leave you haven't increased the population of France. It wouldn't be seemly to see lots of little Jimmy Greenes running around speaking French, would it?*

*I of course have had numerous invitations to increase the population of Southampton from the many men who fall at my feet, but I have refused them all. As you know, I am saving myself for you because you are the love of my life. So keep safe and alive.*

*Lots of love for ever,*
*Maisie xx*

As Jimmy folded the letter and put it away, he was still smiling to himself about the contents. What a character that girl was! She was quite outrageous, but she had made him laugh and that was a bonus during such tough days.

'Good news, then?' asked Shorty. 'It must have been, because I heard you laughing.

What did your girl have to say that was so funny?'

'Oh, my girl is fine. That was a letter from her sister, who is a case. She makes me laugh.'

'Cor! Strikes me you're the case, mate – two women writing to you and sisters at that. You want to be careful, or it'll cause trouble.'

'Don't be daft,' said Jimmy, 'there's nothing like that about it.' But as he spoke he knew that Shorty was right. He really would have to be careful in his handling of Maisie and her obsession with him. But as he bedded down for the night, it was Maisie's letter he remembered.

## CHAPTER ELEVEN

Maisie finished work for the day and walked down to the Ditches and Sonny Nolan's shop. It was time for her first delivery of his papers and she wondered where she would be sent. She felt a sense of excitement. It was like being a secret agent, carrying secret documents, dodging the enemy, saving lives. She opened the door of the shop and walked in.

Sonny was standing behind the counter,

reading the local paper. 'Ah, there you are,' he said. 'Here are the deliveries I want made. Let's go over the addresses to make sure you know where you're going.' He handed over several large envelopes. 'Be sure to hand them to the person whose name is on the envelope and no one else, understand?'

Maisie nodded. She was intrigued. There was one that was for a local butcher, another for a pub landlord, one to a private address in the Polygon area and one to a social club in Oriental Place. This final one worried her a bit. Oriental Place was not a salubrious part of town at all; it was part of the red light district. Not an area for a lone woman to visit after dark. She decided she would go there first whilst it was still light.

'Now, I want these all delivered by to-night,' Sonny told her.

'Fine. When do I get paid?'

'When I know my clients have received the papers,' he told her. 'You do this right and there'll be more work for you. And remember, you keep your mouth shut.'

'I'll remember,' she told him and walked out of the shop.

It took Maisie some time to get to Oriental Place and the Solent Social Club. She looked at the shabby door with its peeling paint work, and pushed it open. There was a large room inside with a long bar at one side. The lighting was subdued and it took her eyes a moment to adjust to the change. Behind the bar a man was wiping glasses. At several tables men sat drinking, some with flashily dressed women, others alone. There was an air of menace in the place and Maisie felt the short hairs on her neck rise. Walking over to the bar she asked to speak to Mr Hampton, the name on the envelope.

'He's busy.'

'Is he here in the club?' she asked.

'Yeah, he's here. Who wants to know?'

'Just tell him I have some papers to deliver to him personally.'

'Who from?' asked the barman.

Maisie glared at him. 'Just tell him!' She sat on a bar stool. 'I'll wait for him here.'

The man came from behind the bar and disappeared towards the door at the back of the room. Feeling somewhat nervous, Maisie took a cigarette from her bag and searched for her lighter.

'Here, try this,' a voice behind her said and a hand was thrust before her holding a lighter with the flame already lit. She lowered her head, lit the cigarette, then looked at the person standing beside her. He was a big man, wearing a pilot's leather jacket. His dark hair was short, but the thing that struck Maisie was the coldness of his piercing blue eyes.

'Thank you. Are you a pilot?' she asked.

He laughed loudly. 'No, dearie. I bought it

off a Yank who owed me money. What's a girl like you doing here?'

'I'm just delivering a letter to Mr Hampton. I've never been here before.'

'I can believe that. Can I buy you a drink while you wait? I happen to know that Mr Hampton will be some time.'

'And who might you be?' she asked.

'You can call me Leo,' he said. 'I'm a pal of Mr Hampton and he wouldn't want a young lady like you sitting here alone in case the punters misunderstood your intentions.'

'What do you mean?'

'Prostitutes come here looking for business.'

Her eyes flashed angrily. 'Well, I can assure you I am certainly not that!'

'I can see that, so what can I get you to drink?'

'A gin and tonic, please.'

At that moment the barman returned. 'Mr Hampton won't be long, miss,' he told her, then he poured the two drinks that Leo ordered.

Another man approached. He was reasonably decently dressed in a somewhat crumpled suit. He staggered slightly, having imbibed too much alcohol, and placed an arm round Maisie's shoulder.

'Hello, sweetie. Can I get you a drink?'

Almost inebriated herself by the alcohol fumes being breathed over her, Maisie shrugged off the hold and said, 'No, thank you. Please go away.'

'Well now, that's not very friendly, is it, darling?' He swayed in front of her.

'It wasn't meant to be. Now go and sling your hook!'

But the man was insistent. 'You are a hoity-toity little bitch, aren't you?'

Leo turned round then. 'You heard what she said. Now sod off or I'll deal with you myself.'

Through bleary eyes, the man suddenly seemed to recognise Leo and immediately backed off, full of apologies, to make his way unsteadily back to his table.

'Thank you,' said Maisie. 'He was becoming a nuisance.'

'You shouldn't be in here at all. Whoever sent you should have known better,' said Leo. 'Never mind, here comes the man you're waiting for, so I'll take my leave.' And he left her at the bar.

Terry Hampton was not a nice man, Maisie decided. He was tubby, and round-shouldered, with a loose mouth and bulbous eyes. 'You want to see me?' he said, and sat on the stool beside her.

'I have an envelope for you from Mr Nolan,' she told him.

He took it from her and said, 'Thanks. Tell him I'll be in touch.' He signalled to the barman, who poured him a glass of brandy.

Then he eyed her up and down and said with a leer, 'Well, I must say you are a lot more attractive than the weasel who usually calls here. What's your name?'

'Maisie.' Getting off the stool, she added, 'Now I've delivered the goods I'll be going.'

Hampton leaned over and grabbed hold of her hand. 'What's your hurry? Stay and have a drink with me. I'd like to get to know you better.'

Snatching her hand away she said, 'No, thanks. I have more deliveries to make for Mr Nolan. This is strictly a business call and that's all!'

'What a lucky chap he is,' said Hampton. 'He always manages to pick good-looking girls.'

'I work for him. We aren't friends,' she snapped, and moved away from the odious man.

Hampton got off the stool as if he would prevent her exit, but Leo came over and took her arm. 'I'll walk you to the end of the street.'

'No need,' she told him. 'I'll be fine.'

'But I'll feel better and with me you won't be hassled,' he told her, and led her outside.

It was the strangest experience walking with this big man, Maisie thought, because if they passed anyone on the pavement the others seemed to step aside to let him through, a bit like the parting of the Red

Sea. Some, she noted, even crossed the road to be out of his way. She wondered why.

At the end of the road, Leo said, 'On your way now, and if you have any sense you won't come back.' He left her before she could reply.

As she made her way to the next address in the Polygon she hoped that Sonny wouldn't send her to the club again. It hadn't been an enjoyable experience. The owner made her flesh creep and his grasp was sweaty and warm. As she thought about it, she wiped the hand he'd held down her coat as if to remove all traces of his touch.

Leo Banks walked back to the club. Terry Hampton was still sitting at the bar. Glaring at Leo, he said, 'There was no need for you to step in so quickly with that girl! What do you think you're playing at?'

'The trouble with you, Terry, is that you never can tell when to keep your place. She wasn't some cheap whore, but then how were you to know? That's the only female company you keep.'

Hampton's bulbous eyes nearly popped out of his head with rage. 'You watch your mouth!'

'Or what?' Leo looked at him with disdain. There was a sudden silence in the room.

Hampton got off his stool. 'One day you'll go too far,' he said and walked towards the back of the room and his office.

Leo Banks roared with laughter and told the barman to pour him another drink. The air of tension in the club passed and the customers started chatting once more.

'With respect, you upset the boss again, Mr Banks,' remarked the barman as he poured the drink.

Leo grinned broadly. 'I did, didn't I? But to be honest I get a lot of pleasure from rattling his cage. He's getting too big for his boots and it does him good to be put in his place from time to time.' He downed his drink and left the bar.

The barman breathed a sigh of relief. Leo Banks was not a man to be crossed. He had served time for grievous bodily harm and had been lucky to escape with a reasonably light sentence for such a serious crime, due to a very smart brief. His gang was feared by the local villains, who treated him with respect and made sure to keep on the right side of such a dangerous man.

Maisie, unaware of the type of company she'd been in, finished her task and made her way home. When she arrived it was to find her sister poring over a letter from Jimmy.

'What does he say?' demanded Maisie.

Looking up from the handwritten pages Kathy said, 'It's private, most of it, but he's fine. They have been in a bit of fighting, of course, but he's fine.' She continued to read.

'Was there any mail for me?' Maisie asked hopefully, wondering if Jimmy had received her letter and answered it.

'No. Were you expecting any?'

'Not really.' But she was bitterly disappointed.

Kathy sat quietly, rereading the letter for the umpteenth time. Jimmy was fine and he loved her. He couldn't wait to come home to her. She took out a pad and pen to write back.

The sight of this was more than Maisie could bear and she went off to her room.

Whilst Kathy was penning her letter, Jimmy Greene was in the thick of a battle, on the outskirts of a small town they had cleared, trying with his company to keep the Germans from reoccupying it. Bombardment from heavy artillery, hidden in the trees across open ground, was giving the British forces a lot of trouble and they were having to fall back.

Shorty as usual had a lot to say about the situation. As more shells burst near them, the men ducked, trying to shelter from the flying shrapnel.

'Bastards!' yelled Shorty. 'What we need is some bloody air cover to take out those guns.'

'Well there isn't any,' snapped Jimmy, 'and we would have to cross open ground to use grenades.'

'Christ! I hope you're not suggesting we have a go, are you?'

'Don't be stupid. We'd get cut down as soon as we started out. If only we had some tanks with us, but we haven't. As far as I can see we're fucked!'

'Fall back, men!' the officer in charge called out and the men slid and ran, keeping their heads down, stopping at some outbuildings some yards behind them. Machine guns were set up to fire on the enemy as they approached and at the windows soldiers took up their positions. Others hid behind low brick walls ... and waited.

The next twenty minutes were horrendous. German troops headed towards them en masse. The heavy guns aided them as they covered the ground towards the British soldiers. The noise from all the artillery filled the air. The sergeant yelled his orders above the racket. As the enemy drew nearer, machine guns were fired and grenades were thrown from both sides. Screams of pain filled the air as bullets and falling masonry found their targets.

The Germans had the upper hand, covering the open ground, advancing on the outbuildings, but suddenly in the background there was a rumbling sound, almost masked by gunfire.

'Listen!' yelled Shorty. 'I can hear tanks.'

'You're bloody dreaming, mate,' said Jimmy as he took aim. But the sudden whine of a shell which passed over their heads and burst amidst the enemy proved that Shorty was right. There were cheers from the British troops as more shells exploded, sending the German troops fleeing back to the trees as the tanks swept in.

A little later, with the enemy temporarily subdued, Jimmy and Shorty sat smoking cigarettes.

'I thought we'd had it that time,' Jimmy said. Patting his pocket, he added, 'I thought I would never get to see my Kathy again.'

'Yeah,' agreed his friend, 'me too. It scared the shit out of me. I'm not ready to die just yet. Believe me, I'd have had a lot to say at the pearly gates!'

With a laugh, Jimmy said, 'What makes you think you'd go to heaven and not hell?'

'Well, we've all got to hope, me old mate.'

They both knew how lucky they were to have survived the skirmish, but to have dealt with it in any other way than by joking about it was unthinkable. Every day, the men faced death and they knew it, but to linger on such thoughts was too frightening, so they took one day at a time and thanked God every time they pulled through.

'I need to go for a leak,' said Jimmy, getting to his feet.

'I'll come with you,' said Shorty.

The two men walked outside and round the back of the building. As they propped up their rifles and stood against the wall, Shorty glanced over his shoulder.

'Look out!' he yelled and pushed Jimmy as hard as he could.

As Jimmy staggered sideways, there was the sound of a shot, followed by another. Jimmy Greene cried out in pain and fell to the ground, clutching his leg. He looked up to see Shorty with his rifle in his hand.

'What the hell happened?' Jimmy asked as other troops came running to see what was going on.

Shorty pointed to a dead German on the ground nearby. 'That bugger wasn't dead. He had a revolver and took a shot at you. He's brown bread now, though.'

Jimmy looked down at his leg. It was bleeding heavily, and a medic was called for.

'You're bloody lucky, mate,' he said as he examined the wound. 'The bullet just nicked you. I'll put a dressing on for you until you see the doctor, but you'll be all right.'

Later the doctor agreed with the medic's assessment. 'I'll give you some antibiotics to take. You'll be a bit sore for a while, but it looks as if we will be here for a while so I'll keep an eye on it.' He handed Jimmy a crutch, saying, 'Use this to keep your weight off the leg for as long as possible. It will help stem the bleeding.'

Shorty came in and asked, 'Well, what's the verdict?'

'Thanks to you, it's nothing serious. I owe you one, Shorty.'

His comrade grinned broadly. 'Bloody right you do, and don't think I'll ever let you forget it.'

## CHAPTER TWELVE

Sonny Nolan was in the back room of his premises when he heard the doorbell tinkle. When he walked into the shop he was more than surprised to see Leo Banks standing there looking round.

'Morning, Leo. What brings you here?'

The big man sauntered over to the counter, and leaning forward he glared at Sonny. 'What the bloody hell do you think you're doing sending that girl over to see Terry Hampton?'

Nolan was completely taken aback by the man's interest. 'What's it to you?'

'She's not equipped to deal with Terry or any of his customers, unlike the others you've used as delivery boys. The Solent Club can be a dangerous place, as well you know.'

'Liked what you saw, did you?' asked Sonny with a sly grin.

Leo frowned. 'What game are you into now ... pimping? Is that it?'

Nolan's eyes flashed angrily. 'You know better than that!'

Leo Banks looked threatening. 'Don't send her again, that's all.'

Sonny eyed the man with interest. 'It isn't like you to take an interest in a young woman you don't know. Perhaps you can explain to me the reasoning behind your sudden change of heart.'

'I don't have to explain anything to you or anybody,' he snapped. 'If I see her there again I'll be back, and believe me that would not be in your best interest!' He walked out of the shop without another word.

Sonny Nolan puzzled over the incident for a long time. It didn't make any sense to him. Leo Banks was as hard as they came. He certainly wasn't known to be any kind of humanitarian, in fact quite the opposite, being particularly ruthless in his dealings with people. He wasn't known as a womaniser either. He had been married years ago, but he had lived alone for a long time. Sonny assumed that if he wanted a woman he had no trouble finding one; after all, every man needed sexual relief. Shaking his head, he returned to his back room.

Leo Banks walked into the Horse and Groom and bought a large whisky. Taking it over to a table, he sat down, lit a cigarette and sipped his drink. When that girl had walked into the club the other day, his stomach had turned. With her blonde hair and blue eyes, she reminded him so much of his daughter. Her colouring, her manner when she put the barman in his place. Sparky! Sharp – and although he sensed her nervousness, she put on a show of confidence. He admired her for that. Had his daughter lived, she would have been around her age. He closed his eyes for a moment to try to shut out the pain he felt. His beautiful girl had been murdered one evening in a bar room brawl. The man she was with had got into an argument with one of the local hoods. A fight had started and his daughter had tried to intervene and had been knifed. She had no right to be in the pub in the first place as she was under age. He had warned her about that more than once, when he heard she'd been drinking, but as usual his headstrong girl had defied him and had paid the ultimate price.

The man who had stabbed her had been arrested and sent to prison, which was just as well because had he not been incarcerated, he, Leo would have taken his life with his own hands. As it was, his estranged wife had always blamed him for the death of their daughter. He didn't hold this against her because he blamed himself and had to live with the feeling of guilt for the rest of his life. So no way was he going to see that girl in the bar put into any kind of danger when he could do something about it. That was why he had been furious to see Sonny's messenger out of her depth and had stepped in.

When, a couple of days later, Maisie called in at the shop in the Ditches, she blazed at Sonny Nolan. 'Don't you ever ask me to go to that crummy club in Oriental Place again, because I won't go!'

'Why? What happened?' he asked, filled with curiosity.

'Mr Hampton was busy and I had to wait at the bar. Some drunk came over and made a nuisance of himself, and if it hadn't been for some kind man I might have had trouble getting rid of him. And then your sleazy Mr Hampton tried to make a pass at me, pawing me! It made me feel sick!'

'But you got out unscathed.'

'Yes, thanks to this bloke who walked me out and along the road. You sent me to the red light district, for God's sake.'

'And who was this knight in shining armour?' he asked, already knowing the answer.

'I don't know, some bloke called Leo.'

Taking out his wallet, Sonny gave her a five-pound note. 'Here, this is for your trouble. I won't be sending you there again.'

Taking the money, Maisie said, 'You shouldn't have sent me there in the first place!'

'Don't get lippy with me, girlie. Do you still want the job or not?'

'As long as it isn't Oriental Place, yes. Your other customers were all right.'

'Fine. Come in again next week and I'll see if I have any more errands for you. I've still got your frock hung up in my back room.'

'I should hope so,' she snapped at him. 'That was part of the deal, remember?'

Glowering at her, he said, 'Don't get carried away, young lady. You treat me with a little more respect if you know what's good for you!'

Maisie recognised the threat and backed off. 'I'll see you next week,' she said, putting the money away in her bag.

'Go on, on your way or you'll be late back. Your lunch hour is nearly over.'

Maisie hurried back to Tyrell & Green's, pleased with the money she'd been given, hoping to add to it substantially the following week. At this rate she would soon have enough money to pay for the frock. After her visit to the Solent Social Club, the rest of her deliveries had been fine. Knowing she was probably breaking the law gave the whole thing a frisson of danger and excitement and she enjoyed that. And what's more it was lucrative. What more could she want? Kathy's policeman would have a fit if he knew and that pleased her even more.

Kathy, unaware of Jimmy's injury, was walking around in a haze of happiness having heard from him. As she signed on for work that morning, her friend Joyce joined her.

'You look like the cat that got the cream,' she remarked.

'I've had a letter from Jimmy and he's fine.'

'That's great news! You are so lucky. With Bob being at sea, there's no opportunity to post letters.'

Kathy was immediately sympathetic. 'I am sorry, Joyce, I never gave it a thought. Here am I crowing about it to you of all people.'

'Don't be daft,' said her friend, 'I'm delighted for you. I think we should celebrate and go for coffee and a sandwich when we finish here. What do you say?'

'That'll be lovely, and I'll pay!'

Later that day they sat in a small café, talking about the war.

'God knows how much longer it's going on for,' Joyce remarked. 'I'm so sick of the shortages, queuing for food, making do and mending. I'm saving my clothing coupons to buy something sexy for when Bob eventually comes home.'

'I'm lucky,' said Kathy. 'Mum does all the food buying. She can make a meal out of nothing, it seems. She's even started growing vegetables in the garden – what's left of it after the Anderson shelter was built – and of course she's doing her bit with the WVS.'

'And what about Maisie?'

'Oh, well, she's doing her bit for the war effort keeping the troops happy!'

'I can imagine,' said Joyce with wry grin. 'But she needs to be careful, these boys are a bit wild, knowing they're off to the war. They want to spread their wings before they go to fight, and who can blame them? At least with Jimmy away, you won't have any trouble with her flirting with him as she did.'

'No doubt she'll be up to her old tricks when he does come home, but I won't stand for any more nonsense. We actually came to blows one day, you know. Mum had to separate us.'

Joyce started laughing. 'Oh dear, I can't imagine you resorting to fisticuffs.'

'She pushed me too far and I completely lost it. How dreadful is that? Me a grown woman, after all!'

'With the right provocation, I've always

said, every one of us is capable of murder!'

It was Kathy who laughed now. 'I wasn't going as far as murder,' she said.

As they sat chatting, a man walked in, ordered a coffee and came to sit nearby to read his paper. Kathy recognised him as the person who had caused the scene with Maisie at the dance, when Ian had intervened. He looked up and met her glance. Recognition dawned and his jaw tightened in annoyance. He glared at her and Kathy quickly looked away.

The man finished his coffee and walked over to where Kathy and Joyce were sitting.

'I remember you,' he snapped. 'You were with that poncy policeman who had me thrown out of the dance hall. Well don't you think you'll get away with treating me that way because one day I'll get even with you both!'

'It was your own fault!' Kathy told him bravely. 'If you hadn't caused such a fuss, it wouldn't have happened.'

'It was that bloody little tart's fault. She led me on. I hate women like her. They cause trouble wherever they go, and then you had to interfere. Well, girlie, one day you'll be sorry!'

Kathy breathed a sigh of relief as he strode out of the café.

'What the hell was that all about?' asked Joyce, and Kathy explained. 'I told you, your

Maisie will push her luck too far one day.'

'I do worry about her,' Kathy confided. 'She is my little sister, after all.'

'Little sister my arse! Your trouble, Kathy, is that you still think of her as a child. She's a grown woman and don't you ever underestimate her or you'll end up being the injured party.'

Had Kathy seen the contents of the letter that Maisie had written to Jimmy Greene the previous night, she would have realised how true Joyce's prediction was.

*My darling Jimmy,*

*My heart is broken! Today Kathy received a letter from you, but where was mine? After all, I did write to you, wanting to cheer you up, doing my bit for the war effort. I'm told that letters from home are life's blood to those away fighting.*

*I miss you so much, more than Kathy that's for sure. She's been filling her lonely hours with a local policeman, not like me, curled up in a corner sometimes, pining for my hero. Life is pretty dull round here right now. Yes, there are thousands of men looking for excitement before they are sent over the Channel and I have in all honesty been trying to keep them happy – but I want you to know I'm saving myself for you, darling Jimmy, so keep your head down. If you get yourself killed, I'll murder you!*

*Lots of love for ever,*

*Maisie xxx*

# CHAPTER THIRTEEN

Kathy was more than a little surprised when she answered the knock on the front door in the early evening and saw Ian Harvey standing there.

'Hello, Kathy. I do hope you don't think this presumptuous of me, but Saturday evening is the annual police ball and I wondered if you'd like to come with me?'

'You'd better come in,' she said, and stepped aside. Once in the living room she introduced him to Wilf and Annie, who looked at him with puzzled interest.

'Ian has invited me to the police ball this Saturday,' Kathy explained.

The detective saw Annie frown and said, 'It's just that I'm expected to show up and I hate going to these events alone and I wondered if Kathy would come to my rescue? I know she's engaged but she would be doing me a great favour.'

Looking at the handsome stranger, Annie asked, 'Are you the bloke who walked Kathy home from the dance?'

'Yes, that's right.'

Annie looked at her daughter and said, 'I don't see why you can't help him out.'

Hiding a smile, Kathy said, 'Well, if you think it's all right.' She turned to Ian. 'Thank you, I'd love to go.'

'I'll pick you up at seven thirty then,' he said. He nodded to Kathy's parents. 'It was nice to meet you.'

As they walked to the door, Kathy chuckled. 'Mother gave me permission, can you believe that?'

He grinned broadly and said, 'I'm glad I passed muster. Have you heard from Jimmy lately?'

'Yes, the other day. He's fine.'

'That's good news. I'll see you on Saturday, and thanks, Kathy.'

A little later Maisie arrived home. 'I saw someone along the road and from the back it looked like your policeman,' she announced.

'He's not my policeman, he's just a friend, and yes, it was him. He's taking me to the police ball on Saturday.'

Maisie looked accusingly at her. 'Really?' she said with great sarcasm. 'You seem to have forgotten you're engaged to a soldier fighting for his country!'

'Don't start! I know that and so does Ian. I'm just doing him a favour, that's all.'

'Of course you are,' her sister said and walked into the kitchen.

'Ignore her,' said Annie. 'You know what she's like.'

Kathy didn't answer but went to her bedroom bristling with anger. Why did Maisie always have to make her feel guilty when there was nothing to feel guilty about? She'd be so pleased when she and Jimmy were married and living in their own home. Then she would be free of her sister and her snide remarks.

Kathy wasn't bothered by Maisie again that evening as Maisie was off to do another delivery for Sonny Nolan. She walked to the Ditches, wondering where she would have to go this time.

'Only one call tonight,' Sonny told her, handing her a package.

She looked at the address and frowned. It was a road in the Chapel area. Again a shady place, she thought, but at least it was a private house.

'Ask for Bert Smart,' she was told, 'and don't give this to anyone else, understand?'

'What if he isn't there?'

'He will be, but if not, bring it back to me. I'll be here until late.'

When she arrived at Standford Street, she searched for the number of the house. The area had been devastated by the bombing and although much of it had been cleared, the remaining buildings wore an air of depression. Snotty-nosed children in torn clothes played among the ruins, although they seemed happy enough, swinging on a thick rope with a knot in the end for sitting on, the other end thrown over a bare rafter and tied.

Maisie eventually arrived at the house she wanted. She noted the ripped, dirty net curtains hanging at the window. Outside, a rusting bicycle stood beside an old pram. Looking at the name written on the parcel, Maisie knocked at the door.

A scruffy unshaven youth answered. 'What do you want?' he snapped.

'I have a parcel for Mr Smart.'

The youth held out his hand. 'I'll take it.'

'Sorry, but I have to deliver it to Mr Smart in person,' she insisted.

'Please yourself.' He stood aside. 'Come in then.'

Maise followed him down a dingy corridor where paper was peeling off the wall. She tripped over a piece of torn carpet, and wondered just who lived in this hovel. She was led to the kitchen at the back of the house where several men sat round a table, drinking beer.

'Parcel for you, Bert,' said the youth.

A big man with his back towards Maisie turned and looked at her.

'Are you Mr Smart?' she asked.

'That's me. Who's asking?'

'Mr Nolan sent this for you.' She handed the parcel over.

He coldly eyed her up and down and said, 'Well, you're a sight better than the usual messenger. Thank him for me. Kenny will show you out.'

But as Maisie turned to walk out of the room her way was barred by a figure in the doorway.

'Well, this is the last place I thought I would ever see you!' It was the man who had caused the scene at the Guildhall.

Maisie froze.

He grabbed her by the arm and said, 'This little bitch kneed me in the nuts one night, then was the reason I got kicked out of the Guildhall. Now you are on my turf, dearie.'

'You let go of me,' she cried, trying to loosen his grip on her.

'Or what?'

'I'll tell Sonny Nolan about you, that's what!'

He laughed at her. 'You mixed up with Sonny? You are full of surprises, I must say. No, I think it's time I got what was due to me. You're coming upstairs.'

'Let her go, Jack!' Bert Smart demanded.

'Oh, come on, Bert, I won't hurt her. Well, not so it'll show.'

'You heard me. Let her go. Sonny has done me a favour, and he wouldn't be best pleased if you interfere ... and nor will I, so knock it off!' He nodded to the youth. 'Show the girl out.'

Maisie's legs were trembling as she had to pass by the man who had threatened her. He leaned towards her and whispered, 'You are unfinished business.'

Once outside in the street, Maisie ran until she couldn't breathe.

Leaning against a wall trying to recover, she held out her hands but couldn't still the shaking so she tucked them into her armpits and clamped her arms tightly to her sides. The threat from the stranger was not to be taken lightly, she realised. She would tell Sonny about him. If she was to be his messenger, then he would have to protect her.

In the kitchen of the house Maisie had just left, Bert Smart unwrapped the parcel and took out a revolver and a handful of bullets. He smiled with satisfaction. 'This will do very nicely,' he said.

At the morning meeting in the Southampton police station, detectives and uniformed police sat listening to their boss.

'There has been a spate of burglaries in the town,' he began. 'A warehouse has been broken into and stores for the NAAFI have been stolen, so someone is feathering their nest with black market goods. A supply of ration books was taken from an office in the Civic Centre together with a number of petrol coupons. The only fingerprints found belonged to the staff so obviously our perpetrators wore gloves. This is a professional job and has all the hallmarks of Bert Smart and his villains. So, gentlemen, we need to stop this now.'

The men listened to the plans laid before them, making notes before leaving to carry out their duties.

At lunchtime, Maisie made her way to the Ditches and Sonny Nolan's shop. Once there she told him what had happened to her when she made her delivery.

'That man scared me to death,' she told Sonny, 'and what's more he threatened me. You have to do something about it.'

'What can I do?' He looked at her coldly. 'He didn't harm you. If you work for me you've got to take the rough with the smooth.'

She looked appalled. 'You don't give a damn, do you? First you send me to the red light district, then to this thieves' kitchen. Well, I won't go there again.'

He laughed at her. 'My, you do like to get on your high horse, don't you? You won't go here, you won't go there! Fine, then let's call it quits.' He handed her five pounds. 'But I don't save any dresses for you; if you don't work for me then of course I'm not bound to help you. No more clothing coupons. You'll be treated just like any other customer.'

At that moment, the shop door opened and Ian Harvey entered. He eyed Maisie with surprise. 'Hello. What are you doing here?'

She sauntered over to the rail of dresses and said, 'Looking for a new dress to wear when I go dancing. Have you come to shop?' she asked cheekily.

'Not exactly.' He turned to look at Sonny. 'Can I have a word?'

'Just a moment while I see to my customer. Now, miss, found anything you like?'

'Not today, but I'll call again and perhaps you'll have new stock in.' She looked pointedly at him.

'Will I put your name down as a regular customer?' he asked, raising an eyebrow.

'I would think you could,' she said, and gazing across at Ian she smiled. 'I'm off back to work. Nice to see you again.'

The detective looked carefully at the contents of the shop and then asked, 'Mind if I look around inside?'

'Got a search warrant?' Sonny enquired.

'No, but I could get one. However, if you've nothing to hide, what's your worry?'

With a shrug Sonny stood aside. 'Help yourself. You won't find anything illegal on my premises.'

Probably not, thought Ian, otherwise the man would have denied him access, but sometimes villains get careless. It was always worth a look.

The room at the back of the shop was full of furniture, some decent stuff, some of little value like chairs, table lamps, crockery, cutlery, pots and pans, and clothes. The police were well aware that folk who had been bombed out shopped here for replacements on the cheap. Ian flicked his way through ladies' dresses on a rail. He realised that some were of fine quality but it wasn't illegal to sell used clothing, although many appeared to be new and he wondered where they had come from.

He opened drawers in an old desk, but saw nothing of any interest to him. Disappointed but not surprised, he was about to walk back into the shop when he spied something just beneath the desk. He knelt down and fished underneath with a handkerchief until he pulled the small object free. It was a bullet. He picked it up carefully in the handkerchief and put it in his pocket.

Walking back into the shop, he said, 'Everything seems fine.'

'What did you expect?' Sonny asked. 'I run an honest business.'

Ian Harvey gave the shopkeeper a hard stare. 'We both know you're up to your neck in the black market and one day it will give me the greatest pleasure to nick you, Nolan. Every villain makes a mistake and you're no different from the others, and I'm a very patient man.'

This was said with such confidence that as soon as the detective left the shop, Nolan hurried into the back room and searched it thoroughly. It was with some relief that he found nothing untoward. All the illegal stuff was hidden in the alcove behind the bookcase and he felt convinced that, even with a search party, it would never be discovered.

## CHAPTER FOURTEEN

Kathy stood in front of the long mirror and looked at her reflection. She was dressed in a long blue taffeta gown which she'd made long ago, before the days of clothing coupons. Fortunately it still fitted her. To brighten it she'd managed to find three navy rose-shaped decorations made of chiffon. They varied in size and she'd placed them on the skirt, the smallest near the waist, the others below at different heights. She felt they lifted the plainness of the dress. To fill the sweetheart neckline she wore a diamante necklace and matching earrings. Twirling, she thought it should be all right for the police ball. She knew the ball was a very prestigious affair and didn't want to let Ian down.

Walking downstairs she asked her mother, 'Do I look all right?'

'Oh, Kathy dear, you look lovely. Quite grand, in fact. Pity your dad is on duty and can't see you.'

'Never mind, you can tell him later how gorgeous I looked,' Kathy joked. She put on her coat, and looked at the clock just as there was a knock on the door.

'That must be Ian,' she said. 'I'll see you later.' She kissed her mother. 'I don't know what time I'll be home. Ian didn't tell me what time the ball finished.'

'Don't leave your glass slipper behind,' her mother teased.

The detective stood on the doorstep, resplendent in his dinner jacket. 'Hello, Kathy.' He smiled. 'You look lovely. Come on, I've a taxi waiting,' he said, and ushered her into the vehicle.

It wasn't a long ride, and they arrived at the Polygon Hotel at the same time as several other diners. Ian led her to the ladies' cloakroom and said, 'I'll wait in the bar for you.'

After depositing her coat and checking her hair and make-up, Kathy made her way to the bar and found Ian talking to a couple of men. She walked shyly up to him.

'Gentlemen, this is my good friend, Kathy Bates,' he said as he introduced her. 'These two reprobates are my colleagues, Tim Taylor and Bill Johnson. They are not to be trusted,' he added with a broad grin.

The two men laughed. 'Sadly, that is true, young lady,' said one, 'but neither is he, so beware.'

'What would you like to drink, Kathy?' asked Ian.

'Gin and tonic, please,' she said as she looked round the room. 'I must say everyone looks quite splendid.'

'And you look gorgeous,' he said. 'I'm delighted you agreed to come tonight.

'I'm sure you wouldn't have been without a female really, had I not been free.'

His eyes twinkled, and he chuckled. 'Oh, there were several ladies I could have asked, but there was no one but you I wanted to be with. Cheers,' he said as her drink arrived. 'We're going to have a great time. Gil Hume and his band are playing, so at least we'll have some decent music to dance to.'

Kathy didn't know when she'd enjoyed an evening more. Ian's two colleagues and their wives were at their table and were a lot of fun, teasing each other as men do, the wives friendly and charming. The food was good and the wine flowed freely, but what she enjoyed even more was the dancing. She and Ian danced well together and hardly missed an opportunity to take to the floor, much to the amusement of their fellow diners.

'Quite the Ginger Rogers and Fred Astaire you two are,' quipped Tim. 'I don't know where you get the energy. I'm absolutely knackered!'

'And you've two left feet,' complained his wife with a grin.

'Then allow me to help you out,' said Ian. 'May I have this dance, Mrs Taylor?'

'Willingly,' she said, and joined him.

Tim looked at Kathy. 'How brave are you?'

Laughing, she held out her hand and said, 'Come on, it can't be that bad, surely?'

''Fraid so,' he said, 'but at least it's a slow tune so you may come out of this relatively unscathed.'

As they danced, Tim praised Ian. 'He's one of the nicest blokes around and good at his job. He'll go far in the force, mark my words.'

Walking back to the table, he held Kathy's left hand and saw her engagement ring. 'Ian's?' he asked.

'No, I'm engaged to a soldier. Ian and I are just friends.'

'Pity,' he said. 'I'd like to see him settled with a nice wife.'

At the close of the evening, the lights dimmed as the opening bars of the last waltz began and everyone took to the floor with their partners. Ian held her close and put his head against hers. 'Thanks for coming with me,' he said as they swayed in time to the music. 'It's been so much fun. I hope you've enjoyed it as much as I have.'

Gazing up at him she said, 'I don't know when I last enjoyed myself so much. Thank you for asking me.'

He held her gaze and thought to himself, Oh, Kathy, if only you were not promised to another, things could be so different.

It had just gone midnight, and after bidding goodnight to their dining companions Ian and Kathy climbed into a taxi. As they drove home, they slowed down to let another taxi pass in a narrow space. Kathy glanced at the row of houses to her left and to her great surprise she saw her father walk out of one of the doors, pausing to kiss a woman who was wearing a dressing gown. She thought she'd been mistaken, but just as the taxi moved off the man turned and walked down the path to the gate – and she knew for certain that it was Wilf.

Kathy tried to hide her confusion from Ian as they arrived at her house. He helped her out of the car, kissed her cheek and said, 'I'll be in touch.'

The living room was empty, to Kathy's great relief. She assumed her mother and sister were in bed. She slumped down in a chair and tried to make sense of what she'd seen. Her father with another woman! She'd not seen her face, only her long blonde hair. What the devil did he think he was playing at? And what was she going to do about it?

One thing was certain, her mother must never know – it would break her heart. She felt the anger grow within her. How could he?

The following morning, Kathy was on the early shift so was up at the same time as her father. As they sat eating porridge and drinking tea, she gazed across the table at him and wondered how he could sit there so calmly, making conversation with her and Annie as if he didn't have a care in the world!

'I'll walk with you,' she told Wilf as they left the house.

'Did you have a good time at the police ball?' he asked.

'Yes, thanks. It didn't finish until midnight and Ian brought me home in a taxi.'

'Quite right too, but then he seems a real gent.'

'We drove along Threefield Lane,' she told him, 'just about the time you left that woman's house.'

Wilf looked shocked. His face paled under the hard scrutiny of his daughter.

'Don't try and deny it, Dad, because I saw you clearly. She was standing on the steps in a dressing gown ... and you kissed her.'

'Oh, my God!' he said, and fumbled in his pocket for a cigarette.

'What's going on, Dad?' she demanded. 'If

Mum finds out there'll be hell to pay.'

'You're not to tell her!'

'Who is this woman, this blonde?'

Wilf wiped his sweating forehead with the back of his hand. 'Betty ... Betty Langdon. She's in the ARP with me. We share fire watch duties.'

'That's not all you damn well share after what I saw last night. What are you thinking of, Dad? Don't you love Mum any more?'

He stopped walking. 'Of course I do. How could you think differently?'

Kathy just raised her eyebrows at him.

'Well, yes, that was a stupid question. I don't know how it all happened really. It was after a really bad raid – Betty was frightened and started to cry, and then she told me she was in love with me.' He looked at Kathy, silently begging her to believe him. 'That was a shock, coming from a young woman ... and it started then.'

'But the Blitz was ages ago!'

'I meant to stop it, really I did. I told her it wouldn't change a thing, and anyway nothing could come of it as we are both married – her husband's abroad with the army. We agreed on that. Nobody gets hurt.'

'Well, I'm bloody well hurt, Dad! How do you think I felt when I saw you? Answer me that!' Wilf tried to take her arm but she threw him off. 'How could you be so stupid and so selfish – all for a bit of sex?'

'Kathy! That's no way to speak to your father!' He was appalled.

She was infuriated. 'I don't have a father, just a sex-crazed old man who lives with my mother and will break her heart – and for that I'll never forgive you! You put an end to it, you hear – and soon, before Mum finds out.' She ran off, leaving Wilf standing alone.

Badly shaken, Wilf watched Kathy running away from him. He could still see the hurt in his daughter's eyes, hear her anger. My God, what a fool he was. He'd put his marriage in jeopardy and if Annie ever found out he didn't know what she'd do. Kathy wouldn't tell her, he was certain of that; she would protect her mother. He would have to tell Betty tonight that it was over.

But as he walked slowly to work, he remembered how it felt to be with his young mistress. How she made him feel a real man, had praised his prowess as a lover, how he enjoyed the sexual freedom she gave him, encouraged him even. With her he'd been able to live out his fantasies with a woman who had no inhibitions. He would miss it so much. Then he remembered how for a time his guilt had made him impotent. That had scared the living daylights out of him, but fortunately it had passed, at least with Betty. After the first time it had happened with his wife, he'd been too scared to approach her again. Indeed, it had caused a rift between them at bedtime. Annie now slept way over her side of the bed, almost as if she didn't want him to touch her. He really had treated her badly and, bless her, she didn't deserve it.

When he took Betty Langdon home that evening after their shift, she stepped back to let him into the house, but he hesitated. 'I won't come in tonight,' he said.

She looked surprised, then smiled at him. 'Not too tired, are you, darling?'

'We need to talk,' he said. 'Let's go for a drink – we've got time.'

They walked in silence to the nearest pub and settled away from the other drinkers.

'Kathy, my daughter, saw me leaving your house last night,' he told her.

The smile left Betty's face. 'What exactly did she see?'

'You in your dressing gown and me kissing you goodnight.' He scratched his head. 'I'm sorry, love, but it has to stop now. I can't put my marriage at risk any more.'

She looked furious. 'That hasn't stopped you all these months. You've been more than happy to share my bed!'

He put his hand over hers. 'I know, and you made me a happy man, but just think if it was somebody you knew who had seen us and maybe might tell your husband about us, how would you feel?'

Pursing her lips, she said, 'Yes, I know, but I'm in love with you, Wilf, and when my old man comes home, I don't know if I'll want to stay married to him.'

Wilf panicked. 'Now you're being silly! In the beginning we both agreed our affair wouldn't interfere with our marriages.'

She became petulant. 'That's all very well, but I can't say I like the way you are able to dump me, just like that, not after all we've been to each other!'

'Keep your voice down,' he pleaded, looking round to see if they had been overheard.

'Well, it's not very flattering,' she persisted.

'It wasn't meant like that, you silly girl. I'll really miss you. Surely you must know that.'

'What if we were very careful and your daughter thought we'd ended our relationship?'

'I can't take that chance; knowing Kathy, she'll watch me like a hawk. If she thinks I'm still seeing you I don't know what she might do. I think it best if we change our duties so we are on different shifts.'

She moved closer. 'What's the matter, Wilf? Scared you won't be able to keep your hands off me?'

'Now stop it! We've got to be sensible now. Being apart is the best way.'

Glaring at him, she said, 'You've just used

me, Wilf Bates, to get what you couldn't get at home with your wife!'

'Leave Annie out of this!' he snapped.

Betty rose to her feet. 'I'm going home and bugger you, go back to her if that's what you want, she won't please you the way I did. You'll miss me more than you'll ever know. I made a man of you, Wilf.'

Some of the customers in the bar had started to listen to her tirade and Wilf reddened with embarrassment. 'Please,' he began.

'Save it!' she retorted and stalked out of the bar.

Wilf could feel the beads of sweat on his forehead. That had not gone well, he thought. He only hoped that Betty didn't take it into her head to do anything foolish. Downing the last of his drink, he departed, a worried man. As he walked home, he knew that he didn't really want to finish with his lover. With her he was different. She made him feel young, vibrant – a real man. He wouldn't change their shifts, he decided. Perhaps if they just didn't meet other than for work for a while, Kathy would think he'd ended their affair and be satisfied. Once the coast was clear, he could continue sharing Betty's bed, but be more careful.

The following morning, he walked with Kathy as they left the house for work. 'I've finished with Betty Langdon,' he told her.

Kathy glared at him. 'I should damn well hope so! Perhaps now you'll pay more attention to your wife. You hurt her, Dad, and I'll *never* forgive you.'

## CHAPTER FIFTEEN

Kathy heard the mail drop on to the doormat and rushed to see if there was anything for her. She picked up an envelope, recognising Jimmy's handwriting, and tore it open as she walked back into the living room.

'Anything for me?' asked her mother.

Passing over two envelopes, Kathy said, 'Only these, but I've got a letter from Jimmy.' She took out the letter and started to read. 'Oh, my God!' she exclaimed as Maisie walked downstairs.

'What's the matter?' asked her sister.

'Jimmy's been injured!'

Maisie felt the blood drain from her face. 'Is he badly hurt?'

Quickly scanning the letter Kathy said, 'Thank God, no. Some German soldier they thought was dead wasn't and he took a pot shot at Jimmy.' She read on. 'The bullet just nicked him.' She slumped down into a chair. Putting her hand to her chest she said, 'My heart's racing, I had such a fright.'

'What else does he say?' asked Maisie impatiently.

'For goodness' sake,' Annie interrupted, 'the letter's private.'

'I only want to know if he's coming home.'

'No, he isn't,' Kathy told her. 'He's got a dressing on his wound, but he'll be fine. He said it was a narrow escape.'

'That's all right then.' Maisie grabbed a piece of toast and put on her coat. 'I'll be off to work now. I'm going out tonight, Mum. Don't wait up for me.'

'Where's she going?' asked Wilf as he sipped his tea.

'I've stopped asking,' Annie said. 'She never tells me the truth anyway.'

'Well, she's old enough to take care of herself,' her father said.

'I doubt that very much,' said Kathy, 'but whatever any of us say, she'll go her own way.'

Which was precisely what Maisie planned to do that evening. She was off to a pub with Milly and Hazel, to meet three servicemen there. The pub had a pianist and was supposed to be a good place for entertainment, and after the fright she'd got this morning about Jimmy it was just what Maisie needed.

The Grapes was a lively pub near the docks. The clientele were a mixed bunch. Several servicemen used it, knowing the landlord always had a few bottles of spirits under the counter, to be sold at inflated prices, but with the shortages no one minded paying black market prices. It was a favourite with merchant seamen too – and a meeting place for several local villains.

Maisie and her friends were unaware of this, as they had never visited the place before. But as the girls entered with their soldier escorts, they were struck by the buzzing atmosphere. A pianist was playing the latest tunes and an older man, with a good voice, was singing.

'This is a great place,' Maisie remarked as they found a table and sat around it. Already her feet were tapping to the music.

They all sang along with the songs made famous by the Andrews Sisters. 'Apple Blossom Time' was followed by 'Boogie Woogie Bugle Boy' and 'Don't Sit Under the Apple Tree'. Then they sang a selection of songs that Bing Crosby had made his own.

They were all having a great time until the bar door opened and Maisie saw Bert Smart walk in with two men, followed by the young lad who had opened the door to her when she made a delivery to Bert for Sonny Nolan. To her horror, Jack, the troublesome man from the past, also entered. She shrank back in her seat, hoping he wouldn't see her.

Milly noticed her behaviour, and knowing

Maisie so well asked, 'What's wrong?'

Maisie nodded over to where the men were standing and Milly recognised Jack from seeing him at the Guildhall. 'Oh, bugger!' she exclaimed.

'I need to get out of here,' muttered Maisie. Turning to Peter, her escort, she asked, 'Can we go somewhere else now?'

He was having such a good time he was very reluctant to do so. 'Whatever for? This is a great place. Relax; I'll get you another drink.'

'I don't want another drink! I want to leave, now.'

But it was too late. Jack had seen her.

He sauntered over. 'Well, hello,' he said with a sneer. 'We do keep meeting in the strangest places. It's almost like fate, don't you think?'

'Leave me alone!' she snapped.

He looked at the soldier sitting next to Maisie and said, 'Don't expect anything from this little bitch. She'll lead you up the garden path then shut the gate in your face.'

Peter stood up. 'That's no way to speak about this young lady.' His two mates, sensing trouble, rose from their seats.

'What's going on?' one asked.

'This bloke is being insulting about Maisie and I don't like it.'

Maisie tugged at his jacket. 'Please, Peter, don't make trouble, let's just go.'

'Why should we?' Glaring at Jack, he said, 'On your way, mate. Me and my friends aren't looking for trouble, but if you are, we will be only too happy to accommodate you.'

Bert Smart strolled over. He nodded in Maisie's direction then took Jack's arm.

'Enough!' he said. 'We came here for a chat with friends. You join us or you leave – for good!' There was a menace in his voice which they all recognised. It sent a chill down Maisie's back and she felt goose pimples rise on her arms.

Jack glared at Maisie and said softly, 'My time will come, girlie, make no mistake.' He turned and walked away.

Maisie tried to pick up her glass but her hands were trembling so much she couldn't hold it. Peter noticed.

'Who the devil is that man? You're as white as a sheet.'

'He took me home from a dance and turned very nasty,' she told him, 'and I keep running into him.'

'Well listen, love, he looks a bad egg to me, so you be careful. Come on, drink up. He's spoilt this place for us. We'll go elsewhere.'

As they all left the bar, Jack smirked to himself, but Bert saw the look and said, 'You stupid sod! You drew attention to yourself, which is the last thing we want. Will you never learn?'

'I owe that bitch one!' Jack snapped.

'Now you listen to me,' said Smart. 'You put us in jeopardy and I'll have your guts. I've already got a few doubts about you being right for the job, so don't push your luck.'

Jack's attitude changed. 'Sorry, guv. I'll catch up with her one day. Now what did you want to say?'

'Nothing here with too many ears flapping our way, thanks to you. We'll meet at my place tomorrow evening and go over the plans ... in the meantime, you,' he pointed at Jack, 'you keep yourself to yourself if you know what's good for you! Got it?'

'Got it,' Jack said and drank his beer. But inside he was fuming. He had a score to settle with that girl and he wouldn't be satisfied until he'd got even.

For Maisie, the evening had been ruined. Jack frightened her and she knew that if ever he caught her alone she would be in great danger. The way he looked at her terrified her and she wished she could turn back the clock. He had completely fooled her into thinking he was a charmer and she realised how fortunate she had been to get away from him before.

Betty Langdon felt she too had a score to settle when she turned up to fire-watch and found Wilf Bates already there, peering through binoculars, checking on nearby buildings.

'What the hell are you doing here? I thought you were changing watches.'

'I'm really sorry, love. When my Kathy found out about us, I panicked.'

'I'll say you panicked. You took off quicker than any greyhound I've ever seen! You shared my bed for months and then you dumped me. It made me feel no better than a whore!'

'I've never ever thought of you that way. I'm really sorry if I upset you – it wasn't my intention.'

'No, your intention was to save your neck! So what the hell are you doing here, I want to know?'

He tried to cajole her. 'I wanted to apologise and to make it up to you.'

'Really! If you think you can worm your way back into my affections, you'd better think again.'

'As if I would!' he lied. 'Want a cup of tea? I've got the kettle on.' He would have to tread very carefully to mend Betty's damaged pride if he was to resume his extramarital relations with her. It wasn't going to be easy, he felt.

As the days passed, Maisie realised just how much the encounter in the pub had unnerved her. Whenever she left the house to go to work, she found herself looking over her shoulder to see if she was being followed. It didn't stop her from making deliveries for Sonny Nolan, but she made sure she did it during daylight hours. The money she was making was too good to miss and she was getting together an impressive collection of expensive gowns – which didn't escape the notice of her sister, who shared the wardrobe space with her.

One evening, when the two girls were getting ready to go to the pictures together, Kathy aired her curiosity as she flicked through the new garments on Maisie's side.

'Another new frock! Good heavens, where do you get the money to afford to buy them?'

Maisie stiffened. 'I save up for them.'

'Don't take me for a fool. You never earn enough for these. There must be at least three new ones here ... and they're expensive models. These are not the ten-bob ones you see on Sonny Nolan's rails.'

Maisie was quick to defend herself. 'I buy a lot of his ordinary frocks, and because I'm such a good customer he saves me special ones until I can afford them.'

Kathy wasn't convinced but she couldn't argue with the excuse without any proof of its being a lie. Maisie was up to something, but what? Sonny Nolan had to be behind all this and that was a worry.

Later, they joined the queue at the Odeon

cinema to see Bing Crosby in *Going My Way,* settling quickly in the back of the circle before the lights went down for the evening performance. Maisie looked all around her.

'Whatever is the matter?' Kathy asked. 'You're like a scalded cat.'

Maisie was so on edge she felt the need to share her concerns. 'I met that awful bloke from the Guildhall in a pub a few weeks ago,' she admitted, 'and he threatened me.'

Kathy was shocked. 'Whatever happened?' When Maisie explained, Kathy became very concerned. 'You should go to the police and report him. He's a nasty piece of work.'

The last thing Maisie wanted was the police nosing about in her business, not whilst she was working for Sonny, delivering black market stuff. Then she would really be in hot water!

'No, I don't want to do that,' she exclaimed hurriedly. Anyway, what could they do? 'He hasn't laid a finger on me – well, apart from the time he took me home, and that was just a fumble in the dark. I'd look a fool.'

The lights dimmed, stopping any further conversation, but the more Kathy thought about it, the more concerned she became. She thought she would get in touch with Ian and have a quiet word with him.

## CHAPTER SIXTEEN

The following day was Kathy's day off. She walked to the nearest telephone box and rang the local police station. When Ian came on the line, she asked if she could see him.

'I have a meeting this morning, but I'm free around eleven o'clock,' he told her, and they arranged to meet at a nearby café. Kathy found it impossible to settle to anything else in the meantime, and she was already drinking her coffee when he arrived. She smiled across the room at him as he entered and walked towards her.

'This is a nice surprise,' he said as he sat down. 'Is this purely social or is there some other reason?'

'I'm always pleased to see you, Ian, but I must confess I do have an ulterior motive.'

Raising his eyebrows, he said, 'That sounds intriguing. Carry on.'

'Do you remember the man who caused the scene with Maisie that night at the Guildhall?'

'I do. A nasty piece of work.'

Kathy went on to tell him what Maisie had told her about the man. 'She's really scared, and I'm worried about him. Do you think she has reason to be so frightened?'

Ian stared at Kathy for a moment, deciding just how much he could tell her. Eventually he said, 'This man, Jack Winters, is a criminal. He works for a man called Bert Smart, an ex-con who runs a gang we are watching as we suspect it has been involved in various robberies. So yes, Kathy, I would say she does have reason to be scared. Jack is a man to hold a grudge.'

'Oh, my God!' Kathy's eyes widened with fright. 'What can we do?'

'At this stage, nothing, unless she comes to the station and makes an official complaint about him. Even then, we could only give him a warning.'

'She won't do that,' Kathy said. 'I've already suggested that to her and she refused.'

'Then my hands are tied.'

Kathy's eyes narrowed and she let out a deep sigh. 'My sister has no idea how much of a worry she is to me. I try to make her see sense but she'll never listen. What am I to do?'

'Unless she frequents the same places that he does, chances are they may not meet in the normal way, but she must make sure that if she does see him around, she is never alone. By that I mean if she sees him at a distance, she should make sure there are people about. If he bothers her again with his threats, let me know, and I'll have a word in his ear.'

'Won't that make it worse?'

'I'll put it to him in such a way that it won't involve her specifically. It's all I can do, Kathy, I'm afraid.'

'Well, thank you, Ian. I'm sorry to bother you with this, but I didn't know who else to turn to.'

'Don't give it another thought. How are you, anyway? Have you heard from your fiancé?'

'Yes. I had a letter to say he'd been shot in the leg, but fortunately for him it wasn't serious. The bullet just nicked him. Apart from that he seems fine.'

'That's good news.' He looked at his watch and said, 'I'm sorry, but I've got to fly. Fancy coming to see a film one evening?'

'Yes, I'd like that.'

'I'll pop round and see you and we'll make an arrangement for sometime next week. I'll have to check the duty roster first. Try not to worry too much about Maisie. As far as I could tell, she seems pretty well able to take care of herself, but a warning not to be alone if she sees Winter might not be a bad idea.'

'Thanks, Ian. I'll do that.'

He paid the bill as they left the café and kissed her on the forehead as they parted.

But as he walked back to the police station, Ian pondered on the problem of Maisie. He was more concerned than he dared tell Kathy. Winters was a sadistic bastard who had already served a sentence for grievous bodily harm when he was a teenager. His incarceration had not mended his ways. He was always in trouble around the local pubs and had been fined for disturbing the peace on more than one occasion.

Back at the station, Ian pulled out the file on Jack Winters. As he read it his brow furrowed. Maisie had made a bad mistake getting involved with such a man. Ian only hoped she wouldn't bump into him again.

Kathy too was thinking about her sister. She would have to admit she had spoken to Ian about her problem, otherwise how would she know Jack Winters was a criminal? Maisie would not be pleased at her interference, but she must warn her nevertheless.

Jack Winters had other things on his mind. Bert Smart was holding a meeting with his men, planning their next job. It was to be a big one.

The National Provincial Bank was an imposing building situated on the corner opposite Holy Rood church, or what remained of it after the Blitz, and Smart was planning to rob it. When he put his plans into words, his men looked understandably worried.

'Blimey, Bert, are you sure about this?' asked one. 'It's a pretty exposed situation.

How are we going to get away with it?'
'I've been watching the place for weeks,' he told them, 'and I'm convinced it can be done. But timing is crucial.' He smirked. 'Let's face it, surprise will be our biggest weapon and just in case things go belly up, I have this for insurance.' He produced the revolver that he'd bought from Sonny Nolan.
Jack Winters looked at Smart and said, 'You use that and you'll swing for it if you kill anyone.'
Smart glowered at him. 'I don't intend to fire the bloody thing, you fool. But one look at this and there'll be no trouble. Now listen up, this is what we do.'

Kathy had decided that if she was to pass on the information that Ian had given her to her sibling, it would be best to do so outside the house, as she didn't want to give her parents reason to worry. So after they had eaten that evening, she suggested to Maisie they might go for a walk.
'Whatever for? There's a cold wind blowing, or hadn't you noticed?'
Kathy was insistent. 'Oh, come along. It'll blow the cobwebs away. We'll pop into the local for a drink if it's too bad.'
'Are you paying?' asked Maisie, who was saving for yet another frock she'd seen at Sonny's shop.

'Yes, all right,' Kathy sighed. 'Just get your coat and stop arguing!'

The late autumn wind was indeed cold and the girls headed for the nearby pub after a very short while. There Kathy felt she would have her sister's attention. Once they were settled with their drinks, she took a deep breath and spoke.

'I don't want you to be mad with me when I tell you something.'

Maisie looked watchful. 'I hope you aren't going to give me another lecture about the way I live my life?'

'No, but I was worried about that bloke you told me about, and I had a word with Ian about him.'

'You what?' Maisie was furious. 'You had no right to interfere. I'll never confide in you ever again!'

'Just listen! Ian told me the man is a criminal.'

That was enough to silence her sister.

'Ian said he works for a man called Smart who they're watching at the moment.'

Maisie froze. Had the police been watching when she delivered a parcel there? She thought quickly. If they had, Ian would surely have been round to question her. 'What else did he say?'

'He said, if ever you were to see Jack again, you should make sure there were people around and not be alone with him.' She paused. 'He sounds like a really bad lot.'

'That doesn't surprise me one bit,' muttered Maisie. 'I wish I'd never met him.'

'You weren't to know. Just be careful in future, that's all. As they say, forewarned is forearmed.'

Maisie didn't want to dwell on the subject and asked, 'How is Ian?'

'Fine. He's taking me to the pictures one evening next week.'

'Don't you think that's unwise?'

Kathy laughed as she said, 'Don't be silly. We're only friends, nothing more. I'm sure Ian would say the same thing if you asked him.'

'I wonder what Jimmy would have to say about it?' snapped Maisie. 'I'm sure he wouldn't like it.'

'There's nothing between us that Jimmy would have to worry about. After all, he did tell me he wanted me to enjoy myself and to go out and about,' Kathy said defensively.

'But that doesn't include seeing another bloke, I'm sure. I don't think you are playing fair, that's all.'

Now Kathy was angry. 'You of all people have no right to judge me! You flit from one man to another.'

Maisie glared at her. 'But I'm free to do so. You aren't.'

'We didn't come here to talk about me,' Kathy retorted, 'we came to try and keep you out of trouble!'

'Which seems to be your mission in life. Not that I'm not grateful for the information, but I do wish you would realise I'm not a child any longer. I don't need you looking over my shoulder all the time.'

Kathy was livid. 'If I thought you were capable of behaving like a reasonable adult, I wouldn't have to bother ... and believe me, I could do without the worry of you. I have other things on my mind. More important things, let me tell you.'

'Like what?' asked Maisie disdainfully.

'Like our father having an affair!'

Maisie's eyes widened with surprise. 'An affair? Dad? You're having me on.'

With an angry glare Kathy said, 'Do you really think I would joke about such a thing?'

'So who is he having an affair with?'

Kathy explained how she saw Wilf the night of the police ball and how she tackled him about it. 'He says it's over, but I'm not sure I believe him,' she admitted.

'I'm assuming that Mum doesn't know about this?'

'No, she doesn't, and you are never to tell her, Maisie. It would destroy her.'

'As if I would!' She was astonished. 'Who'd have thought it? What's this woman like?'

'Blonde – and a lot younger than he is.'

'Sly old bugger! What makes you doubt that it's finished?'

Kathy pondered for a moment. 'He said it was and maybe he did stop it out of fright, but if you had seen them together they seemed so comfortable with each other. For a man of his age it must do wonders for his ego. That's all.'

'How can we find out?'

'I thought I'd leave it for a while and then I'll go to where he's on duty and see if they are still together.' With a frown Kathy added, 'I can't have Mum upset.'

'I should think not!'

'Now don't you go saying anything to him, will you?'

Maisie shrugged. 'What could I say that would make a difference? Either he's still mucking about or he isn't. We'll have to wait and see. Do you want me to come with you when you check up on him?'

'No, it's best if I go alone. I'll let you know what happens.'

'And if you find he's been lying to you, what then?'

Kathy flushed with anger. 'I'll certainly tell the woman a thing or two, that's for sure. And I'll threaten to tell Mum. That ought to be enough to put the cat among the pigeons as far as Dad is concerned.'

As they walked home, Maisie thought about her father's infidelity. He should be ashamed of himself. Imagine, betraying her mother that way, a woman who worked hard, who was a good and loyal wife. It wasn't right. She mused that her being in love with Jimmy Greene was an entirely different matter. He wasn't married – not yet anyway – and if he didn't truly love Kathy, she was saving them both from making a terrible mistake.

## CHAPTER SEVENTEEN

By the end of September, the Allies had control of most of France, but battles raged on beyond the Moselle along a line south of Alsace-Lorraine, notably around Metz. There had been further forays to the north, but there had been no breakthrough. The troops were tired and dispirited, and in early October Eisenhower warned of battle fatigue among the fighting men.

Jimmy Greene and his mate, Shorty, were certainly tired. Sitting in a foxhole, during a lull in the fighting, they smoked their cigarettes and cursed the war.

'Bloody Germans!' Shorty exclaimed. 'Don't they know when to give up? I'm pissed off and want to go home.'

'I suppose they think they can win. You know, the master race and all that bullshit,' Jimmy remarked.

'Do you think they are as tired as we are?'

Jimmy grinned at his friend. 'They're not any different from us, despite what they believe. I'm sure they all want to go home too.'

'Well, why on earth doesn't someone suggest we all pack it in?'

'Because there has to be a winner, that's why. Can you imagine Monty or that bastard Hitler settling for a draw?'

'No, suppose you're right,' Shorty conceded. He sat quietly, then said, 'You know, if we'd joined the Navy we would have led a quieter life than this. We made a big mistake signing on for the army.'

Remembering the crossing of the Channel, Jimmy said, 'I wouldn't be any good in the Navy. I would probably be seasick.'

'And I can't swim, so perhaps we didn't really have a choice.'

At that moment the order came along the line to prepare to move forward.

'Here we go again,' Shorty moaned. 'Right now I'd settle for a good meal and a good woman.'

Laughing, Jimmy said, 'A *good* woman's the last thing you need. I'd settle for a thoroughly bad one!'

'Now that's no way for a man who's engaged to talk, or have you forgotten you're spoken for?'

'Of course not, but a man can dream,

can't he?'

'That's about all we bloody well can do, me old mate,' Shorty said as they climbed out of the foxhole and once again faced the enemy.

During her stint at the factory, Kathy was bemoaning the fact that she hadn't heard from Jimmy for several weeks.

'I haven't heard from my old man either,' her friend Joyce said. 'Until his ship docks somewhere he won't get a chance to post any letters.'

'Fancy going to the pictures this evening?' Kathy suggested. '*Since You Went Away* is showing. I'd like to see that. Claudette Colbert's in it and I like her.'

'I saw it advertised. Jennifer Jones and Joseph Cotten are in it, too. It's a good cast.'

'Right. I'll meet you outside the cinema at seven o'clock in time for the last showing ... and I'll buy the ice creams!'

With a broad grin, Joyce said, 'With such an offer, how can I refuse?'

When the film was over, the girls parted to go their separate ways. 'I really enjoyed that,' said Joyce. 'See you tomorrow.'

Kathy had just missed a tram and the wind was cold so she decided to take a short cut through the park. Turning up the collar of her coat, she put her hands in her pockets to keep warm and set off. She cursed the fact that she'd left her pocket torch at home, but she knew her way, having walked through the park all her life. As she walked, she went over the plot of the film she'd just seen in her mind, thankful that such an evening gave you something to think about other than everyday worries.

She was suddenly aware of the sound of singing. Male voices; more than one, she decided. The sound got nearer as she walked, but she didn't pay much mind to it until she came across two drunken soldiers who blundered across her path, bumping into her.

'Sorry, darling,' said one. Shining his torch into her face, which blinded her, he said, 'Well, well. What have we here?'

Somewhat nervously, she said, 'Let me pass, please.'

'How polite the lady is. And where are you going, my little darling?'

'I'm going home. Please get out of my way!' The stale smell of beer filled her nostrils.

Another voice chipped in. 'That doesn't sound very nice. We're only trying to be friendly, that's all.'

In the darkness Kathy felt a strong grip on her arm. 'Let go of me!' she cried.

'Come on, darling, give us a kiss.'

Her head was gripped by the hair and a wet mouth covered hers; a tongue thrust down her throat made her feel sick. 'Come along, dearie,' said the drunk, 'let's you and me have a bit of fun.'

'And me!' said the other. 'I'm damned if you're going to have it all on your own. I want a bit too.'

She started to struggle, kicking out, using her nails to gouge their faces, but the two men were too strong for her. Between them they threw her down on to the grass.

'Hold her down, Bill,' said one as he opened her coat and tore at her clothes.

Kathy screamed but a hand across her mouth silenced her. 'Shut up!' she was told.

Her blouse was ripped open and a mouth covered a breast whilst hands tore away her undergarments and forced her legs apart. She felt one of the men on top of her and cried out in pain as he thrust himself inside her.

His companion was getting impatient. 'Hurry up, for God's sake, don't take all bloody night. I can hardly wait.'

The first soldier eventually rolled off his victim and was replaced by his friend, who uttered obscenities as he too raped Kathy.

When he had finished ravishing her, the two of them walked away, laughing.

Kathy lay stunned, bruised and battered. She slowly sat up, crying out in pain and calling for help, but there was no one to hear her. Eventually she managed to get to her feet and crawl home.

Once she reached her house, clinging to the wall for support, she frantically banged on the door until with great relief she heard her mother call, 'All right! I'm coming!'

Annie opened the door and Kathy fell in.

'Oh, my God!' Annie exclaimed when she saw the state her daughter was in. She knelt beside her and cradled her in her arms as Kathy sobbed.

Eventually Annie managed to get her into the living room and put her on the settee. She went to a cupboard and took out a half-bottle of brandy which she kept for emergencies. Pouring just a little into a glass she handed it to Kathy and said, 'Sip this slowly while I go and phone the doctor. I won't be a minute.'

She ran to the nearest phone box, made her call, then ran back home. Kneeling beside Kathy she asked quietly, 'Who did this to you?'

'Two drunken soldiers.'

'Did you see their faces?'

Kathy shook her head. 'It was dark. They...' But she couldn't continue.

Her daughter's sobs broke Annie's heart. She was consumed with anger to think that two men could have been so cruel and callous.

The doctor soon arrived and gently examined Kathy. Between them he and Annie removed Kathy's clothes and bathed her bruises before putting her nightdress on.

'She needs to go to hospital,' he told Annie. 'She may be injured internally.'

Annie covered her mouth to smother her cry of despair.

The doctor sat beside Kathy and told her he was going to send an ambulance for her. But she was too shocked to care and just nodded. Annie sat on her other side and cradled her in her arms whilst they waited.

'I'll have to report this to the police,' the doctor said. 'Rape is a criminal offence, after all.'

'I understand,' said Annie. 'The bastards shouldn't get away with it.'

The doctor placed a comforting hand on Annie's shoulder. 'I agree, but since Kathy says she's unable to identify either of the men, I'm afraid they will. All she knows is that it was two drunken soldiers.'

'When you do report this to the police, could you ask them to tell Detective Inspector Ian Harvey about it, only he's a good friend of Kathy's. It might be easier for her to be questioned by someone she knows rather than a stranger.'

'I'll certainly do that. Now I'll be off and get an ambulance to come round for her. Best pack her a few things in case they keep her in.'

'I will. Thank you for coming so promptly.'

Kathy, deeply shocked, lay in the ambulance only vaguely aware of what was happening to her. She gazed at her mother, who was travelling with her, holding her hand, but unable to speak for worry and distress. On arrival at the hospital, Kathy was taken to an emergency ward where she was examined by the duty doctor and a nursing sister.

Eventually the doctor sat on the side of the bed and spoke to her.

'Miss Bates, I'm going to have to take you to the theatre, I'm afraid. You have been badly torn and we will have to stitch you. I am sorry, after all you've been through, but we have to do it, do you understand?'

She nodded. She was in so much pain she didn't really care what they did.

Annie asked anxiously, 'Is she going to be all right?'

'I can repair the damage to her body,' the doctor said quietly, 'but the trauma your daughter has been through may take longer to heal.'

'Can I wait whilst she's in the theatre?'

'Of course you can. I'll get the nurse to take you to the waiting room. We'll let you know when she's back on the ward, then you can sit with her.'

'Thank you, doctor.'

'Pop into the cubicle and have a word with your daughter. I'm sure she'll be relieved to know you'll be here when she comes round from the anaesthetic.'

Pushing aside the curtain, Annie walked over to the bed. She said, 'I'll be waiting here for you, love.' She kissed Kathy's forehead and squeezed her hand.

As Kathy was wheeled away, a nurse took Annie to a nearby waiting room. 'I'll bring you a cup of tea,' she said.

Annie sat quietly weeping until she heard the sound of footsteps approaching and looking up saw Ian Harvey. He hurried to her and sat beside her. Putting a comforting arm round her, he said, 'Tell me what happened.'

She told him everything that had been said, from the moment she had opened the door to Kathy.

'She didn't see their faces?'

Annie shook her head. 'It was dark, but she said they were drunk.' She looked at him with red-rimmed eyes. 'They both raped her!' she cried. 'Oh, Ian, my poor Kathy!'

His expression grim, he said, 'I am so sorry, Mrs Bates. Unfortunately, if she can't identify them, I can't do anything about bringing these men to justice and that infuriates me.'

'Will you wait with me?'

'Of course I will. Here's the nurse with a cup of tea. Drink it up, it will do you good.'

Ian had forced himself to remain calm as he listened to Annie's sad tale. But inside his heart was racing, his anger difficult to control. Poor, darling Kathy! He was worried as to how badly she'd been hurt and how she would cope mentally after such an ordeal.

They both sat in silence, gaining comfort from each other's presence, until the doctor came to tell them that Kathy was back in the ward.

'You go to her, Mrs Bates. I need to have a word with the doctor.'

When they were alone, the doctor told Ian the grim details of Kathy's injuries. 'It was a particularly vicious attack,' he said. 'The poor girl was torn inside and she's going to be in a certain amount of pain when she comes round, but we'll make her as comfortable as possible. It's the mental anguish that worries me. She was in deep shock, as you can imagine.'

'Thank you, doctor. I'll need a report from you, of course.'

'I'll do it tonight. By the way, the young lady put up quite a fight. There was skin beneath her fingernails, so whoever did this to her will be badly scratched.'

'Thank you. That might just help me to trace the men.' Ian walked away towards the ward to see Kathy for himself, and the nurse on duty showed him the way.

Taking a deep breath, Ian quietly opened the curtain and, drawing up another chair, sat beside Annie. When he saw the pale face on the pillow, bruised about the cheeks and neck, he felt the anger grow inside him. Somehow he had to find the men who were responsible.

He and Annie sat in silence until Kathy came round from the anaesthetic. Quietly Annie said, 'Hello, love. Here I am,' and took her daughter by the hand, patting it as she would a child's.

As Kathy opened her eyes, Ian stood up and looked down at her. He wanted to hold her, to comfort her.

It took a while for the patient to take in her surroundings. She recognised her mother and gave a wan smile; then she looked up. 'Ian,' she said. Then she closed her eyes and slept.

'I need to let Wilf know what happened,' Annie said. 'He was on duty when Kathy came home.'

'Don't worry, Mrs Bates, I'll see to it,' Ian told her. 'I'll leave you here now and call on your husband.'

# CHAPTER EIGHTEEN

Once Ian Harvey saw that Kathy was sleeping naturally, he left Annie at the hospital and went to her house.

A worried Wilf came to the door. Maisie had returned home, found an empty house, seen bloodstained clothing and phoned the ARP station in a panic. He paled when he saw Ian on the doorstep.

'What's happened?' he asked, as Maisie came and stood by him.

'Can I come in?' asked Ian.

'Of course,' said Wilf, stepping aside.

Ian explained what had happened to Kathy and assured them that she was now sleeping peacefully with Annie watching over her.

Wilf's hands balled into fists as he listened. 'The bastards! If I get my hands on them I'll kill the buggers.'

'No, Mr Bates, you will leave it to the law, that's our job. Unfortunately, Kathy is unable to identify the men. It was dark and she couldn't see their faces, but I'll do my best to find them.'

Maisie, who had been silent, asked, 'How on earth will you do that?'

'The doctor said she put up quite a fight

and one if not both of them will be badly scratched. It's a start anyway.' He told them which ward Kathy was in and suggested they get some sleep and go to visit her tomorrow.

Maisie showed him out. 'I hope you can find the men who did this,' she said, remembering only too well how frightened she had been when Jack had turned on her. But for the grace of God, that could have been her in hospital.

The following morning, Ian visited the various army camps in the area and called on the officers in charge of the military police. He explained his quest to all of them in turn. They all agreed the chance of finding the perpetrators was very faint, but promised their cooperation.

As one angrily declared, 'This is a slur on our service. We will do all we can to assist you. We will have the company sergeant major review the troops on parade. If any bear any scratches, we'll call them in for questioning.'

'If you do find anyone, I'd like to be there when they are questioned.'

'Of course. We'll let you know.'

There was nothing more the detective could do but wait.

Kathy woke early. She moved and moaned

with pain.

Annie, who had spent the night in the chair beside the bed, caught hold of her daughter's hand and said softly, 'Kathy, I'm here.'

Kathy glanced at her with glazed eyes, then looked around at her surroundings, and finally realisation dawned. Tears filled her eyes.

'Mum, oh, Mum,' she murmured, and started to weep. 'Those men, they were like animals. I fought as hard as I could...'

'I know, I know,' Annie whispered, fighting back her own tears.

'I couldn't stop them... I'm sorry.'

'Oh, my dear girl, why are you apologising? It wasn't your fault!'

'I feel so ashamed.'

Annie's anger grew. 'Ashamed! You have nothing to be ashamed about. Those two buggers are the ones who should be ashamed, not you. How could you think such a thing?'

'They made me feel dirty. The things they said to me.'

Annie could barely force herself to listen, but she knew she had to. Sitting on the bed, she held her daughter in her arms.

'Will Jimmy still want me now?'

'What do you mean?'

'I'm damaged goods, aren't I?'

'You certainly are not! Jimmy loves you. He will be devastated at what happened to you, but that's all. Why would it make a difference?'

Clutching hold of her mother, Kathy pleaded with her. 'Please don't let anyone write and tell him. He'll only worry, and what can he do about it? I'll tell him when he gets home.' She gave a deep sigh. 'Am I going to be all right, Mum?' she asked pitifully.

'Yes, love,' Annie hastened to reassure her. 'It will take a bit of time to recover from your injuries, but you'll be fine, you'll see.' She stroked her daughter's brow, knowing she had to be strong for her.

Kathy lay back against her pillows, and then said, 'I must have been dreaming, but I thought that Ian was here.'

'He was. He came last night. He stayed with me whilst you were in surgery.'

With a wan smile, Kathy said, 'That's just like him. He's a very kind man.'

A nurse came over and took Kathy's pulse. Before putting a thermometer into her mouth she asked, 'How are you feeling this morning?'

'Awful. I feel as if I've been run over by a steamroller. I hurt all over.'

'Open up,' the nurse said and whilst she was waiting added, 'I'm sure you do, but each day you'll feel better, I promise.' Turning to Annie she said, 'Why don't you go home and get some rest, Mrs Bates? You've been here all night; we'll take good care of your daughter.'

Annie began to refuse but Kathy, seeing how drawn her mother looked, intervened.

'Go home and rest, Mum. I'll be fine. Come back later. After all, I'm not going anywhere, am I?'

'Are you sure you don't mind being left, love?'

Kathy nodded. 'Honestly, you look so tired. Go on, please.' Relieved as she was to wake and see her mother beside her, Kathy wanted to be alone. She had to come to terms with what had happened, and she needed to be on her own to do that.

As Annie left, somewhat reluctantly, the nurse said, 'The doctor will be round to see you later. Do you think you could face up to a little breakfast now?'

Eating was the last thing Kathy wanted to do but as she shook her head the nurse gently persuaded her. 'Look, Kathy, you need to keep up your strength. How about a nice cup of tea and just a little scrambled egg? Try it, just to please me.'

'I could really do with some tea, and I'll try to eat a little,' she conceded.

The nurse gently bathed her face and washed her hands, gave her a toothbrush with paste on it and said, 'You'll feel fresher now.'

When at last she was alone, Kathy, impervious to the bustle of her surroundings, went over the previous evening's events. She closed her eyes to shut out the vision of the two men raping her, but she relived every violent moment and tears trickled down her cheeks. She opened her eyes as a voice broke into her thoughts.

'Hello, Kathy.'

She looked up to see Ian Harvey standing by her bed. She couldn't speak, but started to sob.

Ian sat on the bed and gently enfolded her in his arms. He remained silent as she let out the anguish she felt deep inside, until eventually the racking sobs subsided. He handed her a clean handkerchief and watched her wipe her eyes.

'Feel better?' he asked quietly.

'As a matter of fact I think I do,' she said with some surprise.

'A doctor I met said that tears were the best safety valve he knew.'

The nurse came with two cups of tea and left them alone.

Ian sat beside the bed and said gently, 'Kathy dear, I have to wear my policeman's hat and ask you some questions. Are you up to it?'

'Yes.'

'I know this isn't going to be easy,' he said as he closed the cubicle curtains around them to give them privacy, 'but I need you to tell me exactly what happened.'

With some difficulty Kathy began to relate the facts.

The detective took notes, his face grim as he listened. He made no comment until she had finished. Then, with pursed lips, he said, 'The doctor said you put up quite a fight as there was skin under your nails. Do you remember scratching your attackers?'

'Yes, I do.'

'Was this just the first man or did you manage to scratch the second one too?'

She closed her eyes, trying to remember. 'I think I did, but by then...'

'Did either of the men address the other by name?' he asked hopefully.

Shaking her head she said, 'No. The second man was foul-mouthed, though. All he did was utter absolute filth as he raped me, but I will *never* forget his voice. It was deep and harsh ... with a northern accent, I think.'

'Excellent! That's another clue. It may be a vital one at that.'

'I should never have walked through the park alone,' she said in a pitiful voice. 'It was asking for trouble.'

'Don't blame yourself. Hundreds of people do so every night during the black-out and nothing bad happens to them. You were just very unlucky.'

Her chin quivered but she fought to control her emotions. 'How could men do such a thing? They used me as if I was nothing. They had no pity – no conscience.'

Ian was trying to be professional, but it was difficult because a terrible anger raged within him as he looked at the girl in the bed.

'Drink is a destructive force, Kathy, but even so, no decent man even in a drunken state would treat a woman so.' He took hold of her hand. 'I'll do my level best to find them, I promise.'

The nurse arrived with the scrambled egg and looked pointedly at the detective.

'I'll leave you now,' he said and bent over to kiss her forehead. 'Try to eat a little.'

'Will you come back?'

'Of course I will. Can I bring you anything?'

She shook her head.

'I'll see you later then.'

As he walked out of the ward, Ian Harvey was fuming. If he could have got hold of the two men who had attacked Kathy, at that moment, he knew he would have lost control. During his years on the force, he had seen many dreadful things, but it was the first time that anyone he knew had been involved – and that made a difference. Especially with such a despicable crime, and against such a lovely girl. He knew now, without a doubt, that he was in love with

Kathy Bates ... and, if he was honest, had been from the first time they met. To see her in such a dreadful state tore him apart and he would do his damnedest to find the two men who had done this to her.

Maisie went straight to the hospital when she finished work, stopping only to buy some flowers and grapes to take with her. It was with some trepidation that she walked down the ward, glancing at all the patients, looking for Kathy. When she finally found her and approached the bed, she drew a sharp breath when she saw the state of her sister.

'Hello, Kathy.' She pulled up a chair. 'How are you?'

'I feel rotten, to tell you the truth,' Kathy replied. 'Take a good look at me, Maisie, and learn by it. I would hate the same to happen to you.'

'What do you mean?'

'You take so many chances. If you only knew how terrifying an ordeal this was, how those men treated me... I couldn't bear the thought of it ever happening to you.'

Maisie was unusually quiet. 'Are you going to be all right?'

'The doctor says my injuries will heal – but I'll never be the same again. How can I ever forget what happened? Those men took away my pride, my dignity – and left me with nothing!'

'Oh, Kathy!' Hearing the utter sadness in her sister's voice touched Maisie. She caught hold of her hand. 'I am so sorry. You didn't deserve this.'

'Ian came to see me. He questioned me about it all. I was so thankful it was him and not a stranger. He's promised he'll do his utmost to try to find them.'

'Well, let's hope he does. No one should be allowed to get away with this!'

Kathy gazed at her sister with a worried frown and said, 'Maisie, I wish you weren't mixed up with Sonny Nolan. His associates are a dangerous bunch.'

'I don't see any of them,' Maisie lied hurriedly. 'Believe me, I'm in no danger.'

At that moment, Wilf walked down the ward with an armful of flowers. He kissed Kathy's cheek and flushed with anger as he studied her.

'If I get my hands on the men who did this to you, I'll kill them!'

Kathy put out her hand and pleaded with him. 'Dad, please leave this to Ian. Don't give me anything else to worry about. I don't think I can cope with it.'

He was immediately contrite. 'Sorry, love, of course I won't do anything, but I'm your father. How do you think I feel when I see you lying there?'

'I really don't want to talk about it,' Kathy

said, 'but thanks for the flowers, they're lovely. When you go home, tell Mum not to come back tonight. She looked worn out and to be honest I'm feeling so tired, I just want to sleep.'

'I'll tell her. You have a good rest, and get well so you can come home soon,' he said, his voice choked with emotion. Seeing how weary she looked, he said, 'Maisie and I'll leave you to rest.' He kissed her cheek, Maisie followed suit, and they left together.

Although Kathy was pleased to see her family, she really didn't want to talk about what had happened. The pain she was in was enough to remind her. The nurse gave her a mild sedative and she slept for a time. She was delighted when she saw Ian walking into the ward a few hours later.

Sitting down beside her bed, he said, 'You have a bit more colour in your cheeks.'

'I must look a wreck.'

With a slow smile he said, 'You could never look a wreck, Kathy Bates. You have an inner beauty, did you know that?'

'You are better than any tonic, Ian, did *you* know that?'

With a chuckle he said, 'I'll have to put that down on my notes for when I next need a reference.'

They chatted together easily. Ian made no mention of her predicament, thinking that if Kathy wanted to talk about it she would do so, so that by the time he left her spirits had been lifted considerably, and when the ward lights were put out she slept soundly without medication.

The following morning Ian received a phone call from one of the army camps. The officer in charge of the military police informed him that two men had been picked out on parade that morning. He quickly left and headed for the camp.

When he arrived at the gate he showed his warrant card to the sentry on duty and was let in. He entered the headquarters of the MPs and spoke to the officer in charge.

Captain Graves asked him to take a seat. 'There are two of the men whose faces are badly scratched,' he told Ian. 'Both are somewhat undesirable types, although decent soldiers. They are under guard in another room. I waited until you were here before I sent for them.'

'Thank you,' said Ian. 'I'm grateful to you.'

'Sergeant, bring the men in,' the captain ordered.

A few minutes later the men marched in and stood to attention before their officer, reciting their number and name.

Ian scrutinised their faces. One was badly scratched, the second one less so, but it was obvious that the two of them had been in some sort of altercation.

'At ease!' barked the officer. He spoke to the one who was marked more than the other. 'Now you, Baker, tell me how you came by those scratches on your face.'

'I was drunk and got into a fight, sir.'

'Where did this take place?'

'Outside a pub, sir.'

Turning to the other man he asked, 'Were you with him?'

'Yes, sir.'

The officer sat back in his chair and asked, 'What started the fight?'

The first man spoke. 'It was a couple of locals, sir, being disparaging about the army. Well, we couldn't have that, so it got a bit heated.'

'Blows were exchanged, I suppose?'

'That's right sir.'

'How strange then that you don't carry any bruises, no black eyes for instance. Scratches would seem to me to be a woman's way of fighting, wouldn't you say?'

Both men became watchful and Baker looked at his superior and said, 'There was no woman involved ... sir.'

Looking at the other man, the captain said, 'What have you to say, Matthews?'

As the other man put his side of the story, Ian sat upright. His voice was deep and harsh, with a marked northern accent.

# CHAPTER NINETEEN

Ian Harvey stared hard at the two men in front of him. He was certain they were responsible for the attack on Kathy, but he also knew that he had no definite proof. He watched the reactions of the men as they were questioned.

'What was the name of the pub in which you were drinking?' asked the officer.

'The Lord Roberts in Canal Walk,' replied Baker.

Ian made a mental note. The pub was only a stone's throw away from the park where Kathy was raped.

'Did anyone see the altercation outside?'

'Don't know, sir. We just got stuck in, then walked away when it was over.'

'Where did you go after that?' Ian interrupted.

Baker's eyes narrowed. 'We came back to camp.'

'Which way did you come? Back through the park?' Ian watched their reaction closely. The men shifted uncomfortably beneath his steady gaze. Then they both answered together.

'We got a taxi,' said Baker.

'We caught a tram,' said Matthews.

Ian raised his eyebrows and said with heavy sarcasm, 'Dear me, this is one part of your story you have not rehearsed. How very remiss of you.'

Matthews glared at him. 'We got on a tram,' he insisted. 'Baker was too far gone to remember.'

'That's right,' agreed his mate, 'we got on a tram.'

'You're both lying,' said Ian. 'You walked through the park in a drunken state, singing, until you met a young lady. You accosted her, there was a struggle, and then you both raped her. That's how you sustained those scratches. You know it and I know it!'

Baker paled and looked shifty, but Matthews, the harder of the two men, just stared at the detective. 'You'd have to prove that, sir.'

Ian returned his arrogant look. 'Oh, believe me, I fully intend to.'

'Do you have any further questions?' the captain asked.

'Not at the moment.'

The men were led away.

Captain Graves turned to Ian and said, 'I can keep them in the guardhouse temporarily, but unless you come up with some evidence I'll have to let them go free. I'll give you two days.'

'Is it possible for me to take a look at their records?'

'Certainly,' said the officer. 'I'll get my man to take you to the records office. I am as keen as you to get this all cleared up, one way or another.'

Ian rose to his feet, shook the officer by the hand and said, 'Thanks for your co-operation. I'm sure they are the men I'm looking for, but there is only one way I can prove it. I'll get back to you.' After leaving the camp, armed with the personal details of the two men in question, he telephoned the police station and sent two of his men to their home addresses to glean as much about them as they could. Then he made his way to the Lord Roberts with the photographs he had acquired from the military and showed them to the landlord of the pub.

'Do you recognise these two men?'

Nodding, the landlord said he did. 'They come in here regularly; I wish they'd go elsewhere, to be honest. Nasty pieces of work, both of them. Always looking for trouble. I've warned them about being argumentative a few times.'

'When were they last in?'

The landlord thought for a moment. 'About three nights ago. Thursday, it was.'

'Do you know if there was a punch-up outside when they left?'

'If there was I never heard about it. In fact

they seemed in a good mood that night. They were drunk, of course, but they were singing. I told them to shut up and they left before closing time.'

'Do you remember what time that was?'

'Just before I called last orders ... about ten fifteen.'

Ian thanked the man for his help and left. The timing was right. The film finished about ten fifteen, which would put Kathy and the two soldiers in the park at the same time. But it wasn't enough evidence to charge them with. There was only one option open to him.

Kathy's attack had taken its toll on the members of her family. Annie was so upset that her usual stoicism deserted her and she turned to her husband for comfort.

'Will she ever get over this?' she asked him. 'You saw the state of her.'

Putting a comforting arm round her he said, 'God alone knows. She must have gone through hell. There can be no greater crime against a woman than rape.'

'What if she's pregnant?'

Wilf was shocked. The thought had never occurred to him.

Seeing the look of horror on his face, Annie said, 'It is a possibility, after all, although I don't think for a moment it's dawned on Kathy.'

'And let's hope it doesn't! That poor girl

has enough to cope with.'

'But we must think of it. I hope to God it doesn't turn out that way, but imagine ... knowing you were carrying a child fathered by a rapist, that could turn a woman's mind.'

'I think in those circumstances a doctor could perform an abortion, couldn't he? Wasn't there a case a few years ago?'

'Oh, Wilf, how terrible that would be after what she's been through already.' Annie's eyes filled with tears.

Wilf held her close to him. 'Now then, Annie, love, don't get upset about something that may never happen. Come on now, wipe your tears and I'll make us a nice cup of tea.'

Maisie too had been shaken by the events. When she saw her sister in hospital, she was devastated. Kathy was so strong, so decisive, that to see her weak and vulnerable had been a shock. It had made Maisie more aware of the risks she had taken in the past. She had told Milly and Hazel about it and they had all decided they would walk home together in future.

As Maisie said, 'I was lucky to get away from that dreadful man at the Guildhall and I don't want us to end up like poor Kathy.'

But it didn't stop her from continuing to run errands for Sonny Nolan. There was no way she was going to pass up the opportunity to earn her dress money. After all, a girl had to keep up appearances.

Ian Harvey called to see Kathy in the evening. He was pleased to see her looking brighter.

'The doctor says I can go home tomorrow,' she told him.

'That's excellent news,' he said as he sat down beside the bed. After some hesitation he caught hold of her hand. 'Kathy, I'm going to have to ask you to do something you will find very difficult.'

She frowned. 'What's that?'

'There is a possibility that I have found the two men who attacked you.'

Her eyes widened and with a look of fear she said, 'Really? And what do you want me to do?'

'I have no definite proof against them, but you said you would recognise the voice of one of the men.'

'Yes?'

'I want you to come with me to the barracks. You won't have to see them,' he hastily told her, 'but I want you to listen in whilst I question them and see if you recognise that voice.'

'But even if I did, it would only be my word against theirs.'

'True, but if it is the man, I can question them with certainty. Baker, the other one, can be broken, I'm sure. If I can get him to confess, I've got them both. It's our only chance. At the moment they are in custody at the camp, but in a couple of days' time they'll be free if I don't nail them.'

Her pale cheeks flushed with anger. 'Free? Free to do this to some other poor girl when they're drunk again?' She gave a brave determined look and said, 'I'll come with you, Ian.'

He kissed her hand. 'Well done! I know this will be an ordeal for you, but they won't see you or you them, and I'll be around. I'll call the officer in charge. I'm afraid it will have to be tomorrow, which is asking a lot of you.'

'If you ask the doctor what time he'll discharge me, you could pick me up. Let's get it over with.'

He looked at her with admiration. 'Kathy Bates, you are an amazing woman.'

With a wry smile she said, 'I certainly don't feel that, but I am an angry one. I want those two bastards to get what's due to them!'

'I'll have a word with the doctor and we'll make the necessary arrangements. I have to ask you one other thing.'

'What's that?'

He handed her a writing pad and pen. 'I need you to write down the things the second man said when he raped you. You said it was filth, but it will show me something of his character that I may be able to use when I question him. I know it's asking a lot, but I need it. Will you do it for me?'

Kathy put her hand to her head and closed her eyes for a moment. Then she gazed at Ian with a look of anguish. 'He was foul,' she whispered.

'I wouldn't ask you, Kathy, if it wasn't absolutely necessary,' he urged quietly.

She made no further comment but held out her hand for the pad.

Ian left her to go and find the doctor.

After a moment, Kathy started to write with tears trickling down her cheeks. When she'd finished she called for the nurse and was violently sick.

When Ian returned he took the pad from her and put into his pocket without looking at it, to Kathy's great relief, but once outside, seated in his car, he started to read the words she had written and was outraged.

The following afternoon, Ian arrived at the hospital to collect Kathy and borrowed a wheelchair for her to use. He had made all the arrangements with the officer in charge of the military police post, and in due course he arrived there with a very white-faced young lady.

In the office he introduced Kathy to Captain Graves.

'I'm so sorry that we have to meet under

such circumstances, Miss Bates, but we'll make it as easy for you as possible,' the captain said. 'I've set up a link with the interview room so you will be able to hear what's going on,' he told her. 'I'll be sitting in with Detective Inspector Harvey, but one of my men will be here with you. I'll get him to bring you some tea. Please make yourself as comfortable as you can.' He made room for her at the desk. 'There is a pad and pen in case you want to make any relevant point. If you want to send a message into the interview room, my man will see to it.'

'Thank you,' Kathy said quietly.

Ian looked at her and said, 'This isn't going to be easy for you to listen to, Kathy, but it's imperative that you are here.'

'I know, I understand,' she said. 'I'll be fine; you go and do your job.'

The two men left her alone, and after a few moments an MP entered the room with a tray of tea, which he set on the table.

'Here you are, miss. A good strong cuppa is a great thing for nerves, I always say.'

'Thank you,' said Kathy. 'You're very kind.'

Over the intercom, Captain Graves and Ian could be heard chatting as they entered the interview room. 'I'll see Baker first,' Ian said.

Kathy poured a cup of tea with trembling fingers as she waited. Then she stiffened as she heard the door of the interview room open and assumed the man had entered as he was told to sit down.

Ian didn't waste words. 'I am Detective Inspector Harvey and you, Arthur Baker, are very lucky not to be sitting in front of me with a murder charge hanging over your head.'

'What? What the bloody hell are you talking about?'

'Come on, soldier, don't be coy with me, you know very well what I mean. You and your mate Matthews brutally raped a young lady in the park, known as Hoglands, last Thursday night after you left the Lord Roberts.'

'I already told you we got into a fist fight outside the pub. We never touched any woman.'

'You say you were in a fight, yet the landlord says differently. He says there never was a fight and that you and Matthews were in a good mood, singing loudly. In fact he asked you to stop.'

'He was busy,' argued Baker. 'He wouldn't necessarily know if there was a fight.'

Ian changed tack. 'You come from Brighton, don't you?'

With a shifty look, the man said, 'So what?'

'It seems you have a bit of a reputation for causing trouble, for preying on women. Is that because you have a problem finding one who'll go out with you?'

The man's face flushed with anger. 'I can pull any bird I like!'

'Now come along,' said Ian with a smile, 'we know that's not true. It's common knowledge you have no success with women. It's a bit of a joke among your mates, isn't it?' Isn't it true that the only women you have ever had have been prostitutes? You have had to pay for female favours, isn't that the truth?'

'You bastard! This is all a pack of lies.'

'So that night as you walked through the park with your mate and met a young lady making her way home, you took the opportunity to chat her up and when she wasn't interested, you attacked and raped her!'

He glared at Ian, 'That's not true and you can't prove any different!'

'Wrong, Baker! I intend to get the army dentist to take an impression of your teeth. I'm sure they will match the teeth marks on the lady's body.'

Kathy's cup clattered on to the saucer as she nearly dropped it. The blood drained from her face. She hadn't told anyone about that, she'd been too ashamed. The doctor must have passed the information on to Ian.

In the other room, Baker was equally shocked. 'I don't know what you're talking about,' he said, but the bravado had gone from his demeanour.

'Don't muck me about any longer, soldier.

I've got you and you know it. Let's get down to brass tacks, shall we, and start at the beginning? What happened when you and Matthews left the Lord Roberts?'

Kathy felt sick as she sat and listened to Baker make his confession. Seeing her distress, the MP standing in the room with her passed her a packet of cigarettes and a lighter without saying a word. She took one out of the packet and lit it.

Eventually, Baker was led away to write out a statement. Ian spoke over the intercom. 'I'm sorry, Kathy, I know that was hard for you to hear. I am now going to call in the other man. This will all be over soon, I promise, then I'll take you home.'

Mathews was heard to enter the room.

Ian spoke. 'I am Detective Inspector Harvey and I am arresting you for the rape of a young lady in Hoglands Park on Thursday night.'

'You are not arresting me for that unless you have proof.'

Kathy felt faint. She would have recognised that deep, coarse voice anywhere.

The MP, noticing the state of her, quickly stepped forward and told her to put her head between her knees, talking quietly to her until she felt well enough to sit up in the chair.

'Your friend Baker has just made a full confession,' she heard Ian say, 'and that's all the proof I need. You're nicked!'

The string of oaths uttered by Matthews filled the room. Ian looked coldly at the man. 'You have no respect for women, have you, Matthews? Is it because your own mother was on the game?'

The man glowered at the detective and his mouth tightened. 'All women are whores ... all of them!'

'Take him away,' ordered the officer.

Ian rushed back to the room where Kathy was sitting. He knelt beside her and held her close. 'You were very brave,' he said.

'That awful voice,' said Kathy, choked with emotion. 'It will haunt me for the rest of my life.'

The officer in charge came into the room carrying a tray with three glasses of brandy on it. 'Here,' he said, handing a glass each to Ian and Kathy. 'We can all do with this, but perhaps, Miss Bates, you need it the most.'

She was unable to speak, but smiled her thanks.

Shortly afterwards, the two men were taken away in a Black Maria, to face the court.

Kathy sat beside Ian as he drove her home. 'I'll never be able to thank you enough for what you've done,' she said.

'I've just done my job.'

'No, you did much more. You were unbelievably understanding and kind. I couldn't have got through this without you.'

'I wish with all my heart it hadn't happened,' he told her, 'but now we must try to get you back on your feet again.'

'Will you be there to help me?'

He turned to her and smiled. 'Try and stop me.'

## CHAPTER TWENTY

Bert Smart and his men were making preparations to carry out their bank robbery. Gathered in Bert's front room, they studied the crudely drawn plan on the table.

'The bank reserves arrive around ten o'clock, give or take,' Bert informed his men. 'We'll be parked in this side street beside the bank. You, Jack, can linger at the corner, read a paper or something, and when the van arrives, give us the wink. We'll drive down and stop in front of it, blocking its path.'

'What then?' Jack asked.

'The driver will keep the motor running whilst we get out of the back and force the guard to open up.'

'He won't do it just like that!' Jack argued.

Picking up the revolver he'd bought from Sonny, Bert said, 'When they see this, I don't think we'll have any problems.'

'Christ! You're not going to use it, are you?'

'Only if I really have to,' said Bert, his expression grim but determined.

'They'll recognise you,' Jack persisted.

Grabbing him by the jacket Bert said, 'You are really beginning to piss me off with your constant arguments! We'll be wearing balaclavas, of course.'

'I can hardly stand on the corner wearing one, can I?'

'Are you stupid or what? Of course you won't. You are just a bystander, and you'll wander off and get lost as soon as you see us drive the van round. No one will suspect you.'

Jack breathed a sigh of relief. 'Shall I meet you back at your place?'

'Don't be a bloody fool! We mustn't be seen together. We'll ditch the money and lie low for a bit. The police will be on the prowl and we will need to be careful. I'll be in touch when I think it's safe.'

'You got an alibi?' Jack asked.

Bert smirked. 'I've been staying with my sister in Chandlers Ford, haven't I? She'll back me up. I suggest you get as far away from the bank as possible. Go shopping, then to a pub, make sure you're remembered.'

'How much do you think we'll get?'

'Enough! Now shove off, Jack, and be outside the bank in the morning just after nine thirty and don't buy your paper at a shop near the bank. Get it before you go. The boys and I have to arrange a place to meet.'

He reluctantly made his way to the front door. Jack always felt he wasn't really an integral part of the gang. He knew that Bert kept things from him which he shared with the other men, but you didn't argue with Bert Smart. Being in the gang brought him a certain kudos among the local villains. Besides, if things went wrong, being the lookout man meant he had more of a chance of getting away.

The following morning, Jack was feeling sick with nerves as he dressed. He went to his local paper shop and bought a paper, then walked to Holy Rood. He waited outside the remains of the bombed church as he was early and didn't want to be seen lingering near the bank for too long. He watched as the good citizens of Southampton went about their business; the road sweeper, the customers for the various shops and the flower seller, seated, surrounded by buckets of flowers, right next to the bank. He hoped she wouldn't be a problem for Bert and his men. He expected that she would be so taken by surprise as to be rendered useless.

Eventually it was time. His heart was racing as he crossed the road, and stood on the corner by the bank. Leaning against a lamp post, he unfolded the paper.

Just round the corner, Bert Smart and his men waited for the signal as they watched Jack. Bert was on edge. He didn't altogether trust the man, but felt using him as the lookout was safe enough.

The time seemed to drag on and on and Jack started to read an article about a London gang being prosecuted for black market dealing. He became so involved that before he realised it the van carrying the money for the bank had arrived and the guard was already out of the passenger seat, making his way to the back of the vehicle. Jack hurriedly gave the signal.

Bert's gang drove speedily round the corner and blocked the delivery van in. His men clambered out of the back, their faces covered with balaclavas. Somewhere a woman screamed, which alerted the guard and he ran to get back into the passenger seat.

Smart called to the man to stop and when he didn't a shot rang out and the guard collapsed beside his vehicle. Pandemonium ensued. Jack panicked and started to run up the High Street away from the bank, knocking over a pedestrian in his flight. The would-be robbers clambered back into their van and made their escape at speed, tyres squealing, leaving the injured man on the pavement.

In a very short time, the police and an ambulance were called. Ian Harvey, too, was soon on the scene. He and his team started taking statements from passers-by who gave descriptions of the hooded men and the one seen running away. The flower seller, from her stationary position, was able to be very precise with her description of the failed robbery.

When, later, Ian visited the South Hants Hospital where the injured man had been taken, he was relieved to hear he'd only been nicked in the shoulder. He was now in the operating theatre, having the bullet removed.

'Tell the surgeon I want that bullet and not to lose it,' Ian told the nurse. 'It's vital evidence.'

In the meantime, Jack, breathless from running, had walked into a café. The pubs were not yet open and he needed to sit and gather his senses. He knew he'd screwed up and that Bert Smart would be out for his blood. What was he to do? If only he hadn't started to read that article. Well, it was too late for self-recriminations. He'd sit and get his breath back and think about his next move.

It wasn't long before Sonny Nolan heard about the failed bank robbery. One of the local prostitutes came into his shop later that day and told him about it. He listened with casual interest, but when she told him the guard was shot he questioned her closely.

'Is the man dead?'

'Apparently not, just injured. Lucky bugger. I don't know what the world's coming to. Don't we have enough aggro with the war without needing another one on our streets? The place was crawling with cops.'

'But you say the robbers got away?'

'Yeah, they took off like rockets.'

'Did they find the gun that was used?'

Shaking her head, she said, 'No, don't think so. Anyway, got to get on.'

Alone, Sonny went over the details in his head. There was no doubt in his mind that Bert Smart was the perpetrator and that he'd used the gun Sonny had sold to him. Thank goodness it wasn't left at the scene, although there was no way it could be traced back to him, he'd made sure of that. When Maisie delivered it to Smart she'd had no idea what was in the parcel, so there was no problem there, and Smart was canny enough to dump the weapon at the first opportunity. The one thing that puzzled him was what had gone wrong. Bert was a smooth operator who planned his work with precision, usually. He would not be happy that this job had fallen through.

Sonny was right. Bert Smart was livid. He and his men had dumped the van they had used, with its false number plates, and were sitting in a pub outside the town discussing what went wrong.

'It was that bloody fool Jack Winters. Why the hell didn't he give us the word earlier? It was obvious that time had elapsed otherwise the guard wouldn't have been out of the vehicle. Stupid bastard! I knew he was going to be a problem ... but not for much longer. I want him found.'

'What now, boss?' asked one of the men.

'Go home. I'll stay at my sister's for a couple of days, then I'll come back to my place. In the meantime, find that bastard. I want him!'

Kathy Bates had been home for a few days and was slowly getting over her ordeal, physically at least. But she suffered from terrible nightmares. She would wake screaming in the night, and both Annie and Maisie would rush to comfort her.

Ian called in to see her at some time each day, trying to help her through the aftermath, but he knew, as did Kathy, that it would take time.

'I need to keep busy,' she told him. 'I want to go back to work next week.'

'Are you sure you are well enough?' he asked.

'I don't honestly know,' she admitted, 'but I can't stay home all day with nothing to do. It gives me too much time to think. If I find it's too much, I'll ask to work part time.'

'Let me take you out to the New Forest on Sunday,' he suggested. 'We'll go for a walk, have a bite to eat and then see how you feel, all right?'

'That would be lovely,' she said.

But when she told Maisie of her plan it didn't meet with her approval at all.

'Aren't you seeing too much of the policeman?' she snapped. 'You seem to have forgotten about Jimmy.'

'How dare you say such a thing! Of course I haven't forgotten him. I love him and we are getting married when he comes home. Ian is just helping me get back on my feet, that's all. Surely you don't object to that?'

'No, of course not. I just think you should be careful you don't get too fond of him is all I'm saying.'

'I can assure you I know what I'm doing. Ian is just a friend; he knows my future plans. But I have to tell you, Maisie, without his help, I doubt I could have come this far. So please don't try and decry him to me – in any way!'

But even as she defended herself and her friendship with Ian Harvey, Kathy knew in her heart she wasn't telling the whole truth. She was fond of Ian. He had been such a brick, so kind and understanding, and they had grown very close. It was only natural after what they had been through together, of course, but even when Jimmy did come home she wouldn't want to lose touch with the man. After this weekend she would try to settle down and write to her fiancé. He would wonder why she hadn't done so this past two weeks, when he did eventually get his mail. But she was finding it difficult to know what to say without giving anything away. She couldn't possibly write about being raped. It wouldn't be fair to worry him when he couldn't do anything about it.

She was faced with an even greater dilemma after her trip to the New Forest, where she and Ian had walked and talked for hours. It was as if the rest of the world had disappeared. Now she knew, without a doubt, she was falling in love with him.

## CHAPTER TWENTY-ONE

Things were getting back to some kind of normality in the Bates household. Kathy had remained firm in her decision to return to work, in an attempt to put the past behind her. It wasn't easy at first as everyone knew of her ordeal, having read about it in the local paper. She had known that she would be a centre of attention when she did go back. Some had questioned her out of sympathy, others wanting to satisfy their morbid curiosity. Kathy, however, had no intention of satisfying them and had made that clear in very strong terms.

'What are you trying to do?' she asked one or two of them who had persisted with their questions. 'Rape me all over again?' They had walked away somewhat shamefaced, and as the days passed she was no longer subjected to their avid desire for detail.

Wilf had cut down his fire-watching duties for a while to be a comfort to his wife and it had done much to restore their relationship. He felt needed and Annie, for once, wanted a shoulder to lean on. But now she was once again caught up with the WVS and Wilf with his ARP duties.

Betty Langdon had been sympathetic when she'd heard about Kathy's ordeal and the rift between her and Wilf had been healed. She made it clear Wilf was welcome back into her bed, but so far he had declined, making the excuse that he had to be at home to look after his daughter.

Maisie was getting more and more involved with Sonny Nolan. She sometimes went with him when he made deliveries of black market goods, as his man, Gerry, had fallen one night in the dark and broken his wrist. Maisie was in seventh heaven, earning even more money, which she kept very quiet about, spending some and secretly stashing the rest away for when Jimmy Greene came home, when she planned to buy a new outfit and some fancy underwear to tempt him with. She was determined to reignite the fire she had discovered when she kissed him goodbye. The opportunity was to come sooner than she thought. Jimmy Greene was being sent home.

It was during a skirmish near Nancy that Jimmy took a bullet from a sniper during house-to-house fighting. It caught him in his thigh and he was to be flown home for surgery. His mate Shorty was angry when he went to visit him in a field hospital.

'What is it with you and your bleeding legs? The last time you was shot it was in the leg. Bloody fool that you are! What the hell am I supposed to do when you go home?'

Hiding a smile, Jimmy said, 'Make sure *you* don't get shot – and keep your head down.'

'If I keeps it down any further, I'll not be able to see where I'm going!'

The two men had been through harrowing times together and the bond between them was strong. They both knew they would miss each other in the days to come.

'When you do get back to Blighty,' said Jimmy, 'you make sure you come to see me. Don't you forget.'

'Forget? I expect to get a bloody invite to the wedding! I'll even go AWOL to get there if I have to,' Shorty joked. 'You'll be pleased to see your family again,' he added, 'and that good-looking girl of yours.'

'Perhaps if I'm able when they fix my leg, we'll make the time to get married.'

'You don't expect them to send you back here, do you?' Shorty looked alarmed.

'I hope by the time I'm fixed up, the bloody war will be over.'

With a sly wink Shorty said, 'Well, me old mate, you make sure you don't get better too quickly.' And with a grin, he tapped the side of his nose. 'If I was in your place, no way would they get me back to fight on, let me tell you!'

Jimmy Greene was unable to inform his family and Kathy of his move as he was sent home immediately on a transport plane and admitted to the Middlesex Hospital in London to undergo his surgery.

The following day the surgeon came to see him. 'You were a lucky chap, Greene – there was no bone damage, although the bullet tore a muscle badly. I've repaired and stitched it, but you'll be on crutches for some time. I need your bed, so I'm sending you to convalesce at Netley Hospital, which is near your home. At least your family will be able to visit you fairly easily.'

Jimmy eased himself up higher in the bed, wincing with the pain. 'Thank you, sir, that's great. How long do you think I'll be like this?'

With a grimace the surgeon said, 'I have no idea. We had to do quite a lot of work in there, so it will take some time. Anyway, you'll be out of the war zone and I'm sure that's a relief.'

'Yes, sir. It wasn't much fun, but I hate to leave my mates there.'

'We'll just have to hope we beat the Boche soon, then. We'll be moving you in a couple of days.'

Jimmy lay back against his pillows and pondered the situation. Of course he was pleased to be out of the fighting, but he felt a strong loyalty to the men in his company, and wondered how many of them would eventually come home. He asked a nurse for some writing paper and envelopes and began to write to Kathy and his family.

It was Maisie who picked up the mail from the mat. She immediately recognised Jimmy's handwriting but was puzzled by the English stamp and postmark and went rushing into the living room. Thrusting the letter at her sister, she said, 'It's from Jimmy, but it's got an English stamp! How could that be?'

'Perhaps he got someone to bring it home and mail it,' Annie suggested.

Hurriedly opening the letter, Kathy quickly scanned its contents. 'No, he's coming home,' she cried and then with a gasp said, 'He's been injured. Shot ... he's had an operation ... well, would you ever?'

'What? What does he say?' demanded Maisie.

'They are sending him to Netley Hospital to convalesce. He should arrive tomorrow!'

Her face pale with concern, Maisie asked, 'Is he badly wounded?'

Avidly reading the letter, Kathy said, 'The bullet tore a muscle in his thigh, but no bones were broken. However, he'll be on crutches for some time to come, apparently.'

Maisie sank down on the sofa. 'Well, that's a relief.'

Eyeing her younger daughter with some determination, Annie turned to Kathy. 'That's good news, love. You must be over the moon. When he recovers maybe you'll be able to plan your wedding?'

'We'll have to see just how badly he's been hurt, Mum, before we start thinking of wedding bells.'

'What's the matter, Kathy?' said Maisie tartly. 'Not so keen on the idea now?'

But Annie was prepared; she'd seen the

look in Maisie's eyes. 'Now you can stop right there, missy! We'll have none of your nonsense. Hasn't Kathy been through enough?'

'I wonder what Jimmy will have to say when you tell him you were raped.'

'Maisie!' Her mother was horrified at the girl's insensitivity.

Glaring at her sibling, Kathy said, 'Well, I certainly don't intend to march into the hospital ward and blurt it out just like that, for Christ's sake. We have to make sure that Jimmy gets well before we give him any more bad news.'

'You'll be able to see him tomorrow, anyway,' Annie ventured.

'Unfortunately I can't,' said Kathy. 'He's arriving in the afternoon and I'm on late turn. I'll have to go the day after.'

'Never mind, love, you can call the hospital and leave a message for him,' Annie suggested.

'Yes, I'll do that on my way to work.' She looked at her watch. 'Oh, blimey, I'm late already! I must rush,' she said as she gulped what was left of her tea. 'See you tonight.'

But as she walked down the road her mind was in turmoil. It had all been so sudden, it was hard to comprehend. What was even harder to admit was the strange lack of enthusiasm she felt about seeing her fiancé so soon. Of course she was pleased that he was home and there were no life-threatening wounds to worry about. It was the talk of marriage that had startled her. In no way was she ready to contemplate that. And, she admitted to herself, the reason she wasn't was because of Ian Harvey.

Back at the house, Maisie was not beset with any such problems. She knew exactly what she was going to do. During her lunch hour, she would shop for a new outfit, and tomorrow evening – when her sister was working – she would go to Netley and visit the patient. She could hardly wait.

Just after lunch the following day, Jimmy arrived at Netley Hospital and was put in a ward with other soldiers all from different companies. There were several Americans there as well as British lads who had met their nemesis in various parts of Europe. Many were in bad shape. Some had lost limbs, one was blinded by shrapnel and a few were merely there to convalesce and continue with their treatment, as he was. As he looked around, he realised just how lucky he was to have escaped serious injury.

A nurse came along and told him his fiancée had called and left a message. She was unable to come to see him until tomorrow due to her roster, but sent her love, and his parents would call later that afternoon in the hopes of seeing him.

'They can only stay a little while,' he was told. 'You'll be here for some time and we don't want you overtired today.'

Indeed, when his parents did call and spend time with him, he was relieved when the nurse curtailed their visit with a promise of a longer stay next time. Jimmy felt exhausted.

He ate a light supper and was dozing afterwards, when he felt a soft touch on his arm and opened his eyes.

'Hello, you gorgeous man,' Maisie said, as she leaned forward and kissed him softly on the mouth.

'Maisie! How lovely to see you.'

'Wild horses wouldn't keep me away!' she declared, grinning broadly. 'So how is my hero?'

He could see such a change in her. Suddenly she looked all grown up. She was wearing a smart costume in pale green with a white blouse which frilled down the front She had truly blossomed.

'I can assure you, heroic is the last thing I feel,' he said as he tried to sit up.

Maisie quickly called a nurse over to make him comfortable. 'There,' she said, when the nurse had gone. 'Is that better?'

'Yes, thanks. So how are you, Maisie? Keeping out of trouble?'

Chuckling, she said, 'I'm doing my bit for the war effort, keeping the troops happy, dancing them off their feet. Keeping them fit.'

'Thanks for the letters,' he said. 'I did enjoy them.'

'Then why didn't you answer any of them, you rotten devil?'

He shrugged. 'It wasn't that easy, Maisie. We were on the move most of the time, stuck in dugouts or trenches, or running for our lives.'

'Or fighting?'

'Oh, yes,' he said with a wry smile. 'We did rather a lot of that.'

She held his hand. 'Was it really bad, Jimmy?'

He met her steady gaze. 'Yes, it was really bad. War isn't kind or dignified. It's cruel beyond belief. Men shouldn't die like that, it wasn't meant to be.' He looked up and saw the tears brimming her eyes. 'I'm sorry, Maisie. I didn't mean to upset you.'

She squeezed his hand. 'It's all right. I'm just *so* happy that you're home, among people you love and who love you.'

He caressed her cheek and wiped a fallen tear away. 'You are a strange creature, Maisie Bates.'

'What on earth do you mean?'

'Beneath that stubborn, selfish streak, you have a great capacity to care and that's *very* unexpected.'

'I care about you. I always have, and you

know that.'

'I didn't, not until the night you said goodbye and when I marched to the docks to go to France.'

'You can't marry Kathy!'

'Now don't be silly, Maisie. I love Kathy and we are engaged. Of course I'm going to marry her one day.'

'She doesn't love you as much as I do. No one will ever be able to do that!'

A nurse came down the ward and stopped at the foot of the bed. 'Come along, miss. We don't want to wear the young man out the day he arrives. We have to get him better.'

Maisie rose from her seat. 'I'll come and see you again,' she said. 'We have a lot to talk about, you and me.' She leaned forward and kissed him, gently but thoroughly. 'Just to give you something to remember me by,' she said with a slow smile. 'Goodnight, Jimmy. Sleep well.'

He watched her retreating figure with some amusement. What a character that girl is, he thought, and he could well understand why men were drawn to her like a moth to a flame. She could be dangerous to know, he realised, but he was determined not to get burned.

The next afternoon, Jimmy watched the door of the ward as visiting time drew near.

He couldn't wait to see Kathy again. The picture he carried of her was propped up against a jug of water on the locker beside him. He glanced at it now, remembering the day it was taken when they went to the pier. It was this image of her that had kept him going through difficult times, and he was longing to see her.

The doors opened and the visitors hurried through. Jimmy craned his neck, trying to see if Kathy was among them. At last he saw her and raised his hand to catch her attention.

Armed with flowers, Kathy walked over to the bed.

'Hello, darling,' he said, his voice suddenly choked with emotion. 'You're a sight for sore eyes.' He held out his arms to her.

Kathy was enfolded in a grip that was like steel. 'Hello, Jimmy,' she said, and kissed him. His mouth claimed hers with a desperation that left her breathless.

'You have no idea just how long I've wanted to do that,' he declared.

'Oh, I think I have,' she said, feeling her tender lips.

'Sorry, love. It's just that I've missed you so much.' Holding her hand, he fingered her engagement ring and gazed lovingly at her. 'You look wonderful.'

Looking at his pale face, which was much thinner than she remembered, Kathy thought her man looked as if he'd been through hell and back. 'And you look as if you need care and attention. How are you feeling really?'

'Sore, but that's to be expected. I have to have some physiotherapy whilst I'm here. The doctor says there will be some muscle wastage, of course, but exercises will help. But looking around at some of these poor devils in here, I know I've been more than lucky.' He took her hand and kissed it. 'How are you, darling? Tell me what's been happening since I've been away.'

Oh, Jimmy, if you only knew, she thought, but she just smiled at him and said, 'Things go on as usual. Mum and Dad are fine, and Maisie. We spend most of our days working or queuing for food like always. But for goodness' sake, that's nothing to what you've been through.'

'I don't want to remember that now,' he said. 'Although I do worry about my mate Shorty.'

'Who's he?'

'We met when we landed in France,' he told her. 'Shorty almost drowned as the water was up to his neck, so he grabbed hold of my haversack as we waded in. We stuck together after that.' He chuckled. 'I promised to invite him to our wedding.'

'We have to get you fit and well before we even think about getting married,' she said, and changed the subject. 'Have you any idea how long you'll be here?'

Shaking his head, Jimmy said, 'No. It all depends how my leg heals, but at least we're close to each other.'

'Perhaps you'll be out by Christmas. That would be nice.'

They chatted away, remembering happier times, until it was time to leave. As the bell sounded, Kathy rose from her chair and kissed Jimmy goodbye. 'I have to work tomorrow during visiting hours, but I'll be in the next day. Is there anything you need?'

'No, all I need is you, sitting there, talking to me. What else could I need?'

As she walked away, he realised he hadn't told her of Maisie's visit.

## CHAPTER TWENTY-TWO

Ian Harvey had been very busy. The failed raid on the National Provincial Bank and the shooting of the guard had taken up much of his time. Despite the many statements made by the bystanders on the day, the fact that the would-be raiders had been wearing balaclavas had been a dead end as far as identification went. There was, however, a good description of the man who ran away and Ian was convinced that man was Jack Winters. Despite a concerted effort by the police, they had been unable to find him.

'The bastard's gone to ground,' remarked Ian. 'Pity. We might have been able to make him talk.' He also had another problem. Ballistics had confirmed that the bullet removed from the injured guard was the same make and calibre as the one he had found in the back room of Sonny Nolan's shop. Ian knew there was little point in getting the man in for questioning yet as Nolan could deny all knowledge of it. Ian needed to be able to show that Nolan had sold the gun and ammunition to Bert Smart before he could arrest him as a conspirator.

He had been so tied up with it all that he hadn't been able to see Kathy. This he would put right today, he decided. He rang the factory to find out what shift she was on so he could be there when she finished.

That evening, at the end of the shift, women came through the gates of the factory en masse and Ian watched carefully in the darkness until he saw Kathy walking with another woman and strolled over.

'Hello, Kathy.'

'Ian!'

She looked surprised and pleased to see him, but he thought she also looked a little pale. 'Could we have a word?' Her friend Joyce left them together and they walked away from the gates. 'I've got the car round the corner,' he told her. 'Let's go and sit in it.'

Kathy looked down at her dungarees and said, 'I'm not very clean, Ian. Will it be all right?'

Laughing, he caught hold of her hand. 'Of course. Don't be silly.'

Once settled in the vehicle he put his arm round her shoulders and apologised to her. 'I've been busy these last days and I've not been able to see you. I am sorry. How are you?'

'Not so bad. And you?'

'Fine, just busy. I wondered if you would like to come out for a meal tomorrow?'

'I can't, Ian. I'm sorry, but Jimmy's come home. He's in Netley Hospital and I'm going to visit him.'

Ian felt as if someone had punched him in the solar plexus. 'When did this happen? And what's wrong with him?'

'He was shot in the thigh and the bullet damaged a muscle. It was badly torn and they operated on him to repair the damage, and now he's convalescing at Netley. He was very lucky – it could have been so much worse. He's been there a couple of days.'

It felt as if suddenly there was a great divide between them. Now things would never be the same, Ian thought, and found the idea unbearable.

'You must be pleased to have him home.'

She hesitated for just a moment. 'Of course, but it was so sudden, I haven't quite got used to the idea. It'll take some time before he's fit and well again. He's staying in hospital as he has to have treatment, but we don't know for how long.'

Ian gazed steadily at her. He wanted desperately to take her into his arms, but held back. 'I'm going to miss you very much, Kathy. You have become such an important part of my life.'

'And you mine,' she said quietly, holding his gaze.

He could see the anguish in her eyes, and, cupping her face in his hand, he leaned forward and kissed her. As soon as he felt her respond, he held her close and the longing they both felt was suddenly released as they clung together.

Eventually, Kathy moved away. 'This is ridiculous!' she exclaimed. 'I'm engaged and Jimmy is home.'

'Do you still love him?'

She looked confused. 'I don't know! I don't know anything any more. I'm in such a muddle I can't think straight.'

'And I'm only making matters worse,' he said. 'It's best we don't see each other. With me out of the way, you can start getting your life back together.'

'Oh, Ian, I don't think I can bear not to see you.'

'Listen, darling, you have to give Jimmy a chance. You've been apart and also you've been to hell and back. You have to try. It's only fair to both of you.'

'I suppose you're right,' she said, somewhat reluctantly. 'Everything seems to have happened all at once. I haven't really got over being attacked and then Jimmy comes home. It's almost too much, too soon.'

'He doesn't know about what happened to you yet?'

'No, I want to see him getting better first. He's been through a lot too, you know.'

'I'll take you home,' he said, and started the engine. They drove through the streets in silence. When he stopped the car at her door, Ian said, 'I'm at the other end of the telephone if you want me. I thought you looked a bit peaky as you walked out of the factory. Are you all right?'

'I have felt a bit off colour,' she admitted, 'but with one thing and another it isn't surprising, is it?'

'Perhaps you went back to work too soon?' he suggested.

'Maybe, but I'm better keeping busy.'

'Just you take care of yourself, you hear?'

Kathy opened the door of the passenger seat, then looked at him and said, 'I'm going to miss you so much.' Then she got out of the vehicle before he could reply.

As Ian drove away, he felt deeply dispirited. Kathy had a place in his life far beyond the professional interest arising from the attack she had endured. He had found and charged her attackers, and would need her cooperation when the case was brought against them, but now he was concerned for her mental wellbeing after such a trauma. Although she was putting on a brave face by returning to work, it didn't take a fool to realise that no one recovered that quickly and he wanted to be around to comfort her when she needed it, as he was sure she would. And now she had to pretend that all was well for the sake of her fiancé. He felt it was too much to ask of her. He was in love with her, yet he was going to have to step out of her life and give her a chance of happiness with the man she had promised to marry. Remembering how she had returned his kisses only made the matter worse, because it showed that she did have feelings for him which would only add to her dilemma. What a mess!

When Kathy walked into the living room, Annie was sitting by the fire reading. She put down the paper and asked, 'Want a cup of tea, love? You look as if you could do with one.'

Kathy sank into the chair on the other side

of the fire. 'Thanks, Mum. That would be lovely.'

Pouring the tea, Annie handed it over. 'You look tired. Are you finding work too much at the moment?'

Kathy sipped the hot drink and said, 'Perhaps, but I can't just sit at home. And now that Jimmy is back I have to get on with my life.'

'What about Ian?'

'What do you mean?' Kathy was startled by the question.

'The man is in love with you, surely you know that?' Annie watched her daughter, concern etched on her face. 'And if I'm not mistaken, you feel the same.'

'How can I be? I was in love with Jimmy. I promised to marry him, for heaven's sake!'

'Do you realise what you just said?'

'No, what?'

'You said I *was* in love with Jimmy. You used the past tense. A Freudian slip, they call it, I believe.'

'Oh, Mum, I'm so muddled; I don't know what to think.'

'You can't think of marrying Jimmy if you love Ian Harvey. It wouldn't be fair to the lad.'

Kathy put down her cup of tea and said, 'Ian ran me home tonight. He said we shouldn't see each other any more, he would only be in the way.'

'Then he must love you very much, because he's putting your happiness before his own. At least he's given you the space to make up your mind.'

'And if I decide that it's Ian I want, how can I tell Jimmy? He's been through hell by the look of him. I have to let him get fit and well before I make any decision.'

Annie rose from her chair, picked up the dirty cups and walked to the kitchen. 'Just make sure your decision is the right one. Marriage isn't easy, but if you choose the right man, you'll weather all the storms together.'

There was a storm brewing in Bert Smart's house when he returned from his sister's home in Chandlers Ford and discovered that his men had been unable to trace Jack Winters.

'What do you mean, you can't find him? Jack Winters has only half a bloody brain, how can he have hidden away so well he's invisible? Tell me that!'

'He's shit-scared, that's how, boss,' said one.

'He's got every reason to be scared. He screwed up that robbery. If he'd been on his toes we'd have had the money and been out of there in a flash.' He ran his fingers through his thinning hair in frustration. 'I wouldn't have had any reason to shoot the guard. Now, if I should ever be caught, I'll go down for a long stretch, all because of that stupid bleeder!'

'What did you do with the gun?' asked one of the men.

'I threw it out of the window into the water as we drove along the Esplanade. I want you men to keep searching for Winters. I don't want the filth to get to him first. He's got no balls. He'd talk eventually and then we'd all be in the shit.'

It was with a somewhat heavy heart that Kathy entered the ward of Netley Hospital the following afternoon. Jimmy was sitting in a chair beside his bed and when she saw the look of delight on his face, she was filled with guilt.

'Kathy, darling! Look at me. I'm up – I'm one of the walking wounded!'

She leaned forward and kissed him. 'That's great. How's your leg?'

He pulled a face. 'Well, I'm not up for a game of football yet, and it is uncomfortable, but I've taken a few steps this morning. I walked to the door and back.'

The nurse came along and made a suggestion. 'If I get a wheelchair for Jimmy, you could push him into the recreation room for a chat. It's so much better than sitting in here.'

'That would be lovely,' Kathy said. And

when the chair arrived, and the patient was settled, she pushed Jimmy out of the ward.

'This is better,' he said as they settled near a window overlooking the green of the lawns sweeping down to Southampton Water. 'I can't wait to get out of this place and be able to walk about. We'll go out for a slap-up meal and celebrate when I do.'

'Of course we will,' she said, 'but you must learn to be patient. Your recovery will take time.'

He looked at her with longing. 'I want to be able to take you in my arms and kiss you to death.' He grinned broadly. 'I've got a lot of time to make up for, after all.'

'We have lots of time ahead of us.' What else could she say? He was so happy.

'I forgot to tell you,' he said, 'Maisie came to see me the other afternoon. My goodness, she has grown up these past few months since I've been away.'

'She didn't say anything about seeing you,' said Kathy with some surprise. 'And what did she have to say for herself?'

'Oh, you know Maisie; she told me she was helping the war effort, dancing with the troops, keeping them fit. She was full of beans.'

'I bet she was.' Crafty little beggar, she thought, I wonder what else she had to say? Remembering the scrap they had had over Jimmy, Kathy was sure that her sister would have taken advantage of the visit to flirt with her fiancé. But knowing him she was sure he would have taken it in his stride as he usually did.

'Well, I'm sure she cheered you up,' she said.

'She made me laugh. I have to say she was good company.'

When Kathy arrived home, Maisie was sitting having a meal with her parents. She looked up and asked, 'How was Jimmy today?'

'A little better. He was up, sitting beside the bed. He was given a wheelchair so we were able to go into the recreation room.'

'Oh, that was nice. So much better than sitting in the ward surrounded by all those wounded men.'

'The way you were when you went to see him,' said Kathy pointedly.

Annie looked up. 'You never told me you'd been!' she accused her younger daughter.

'She didn't tell anyone!' Kathy said shortly. 'I find that very strange. I would have thought you could have told me, especially as you knew I was working and couldn't go. Why keep it a secret?'

Tossing her blonde hair, worn like Veronica Lake's, she said, 'It was no secret. I just thought I'd go and see him. After all, it isn't fun being in hospital ... is it, Kathy?'

Wilf looked at his two girls and said, 'Now that's enough! You, Maisie, watch your tongue and don't start making trouble.'

'I'm not making trouble. I'm not the one with a fiancé in hospital and another man on the side!'

'Ian is just a friend, as well you know!' snapped Kathy.

'For just a friend, he seems to be around rather a lot is all I'm saying.'

'Well, he won't be coming round in the future now that Jimmy's home.'

With raised eyebrows and a sardonic smile, Maisie said, 'So you've dumped him now, have you, now that Jimmy's home? That seems a bit unkind.'

Annie rose to her feet. 'I'll have no more of this! Maisie, if you can't keep a civil tongue in your head, you'd best go to your room.'

'I'm no longer a child, Mum, you can't just send me to my room. I'm entitled to an opinion like anyone else. Besides, I'm going out.' She got up, grabbed a coat from behind the door and swept out of the house.

'That girl!' exclaimed Annie. 'She'll be the death of me.' Then, looking at Kathy, she asked, 'How was your meeting with Jimmy?'

'He's so excited about being up, and it was good for him to get out of the ward.'

Annie waited, but Kathy made no further comment. 'Time can heal many wounds,' she said and walked into the kitchen.

## CHAPTER TWENTY-THREE

Jack Winters walked into one of the bars in Southampton's dockland and ordered a pint of bitter and a sandwich. His coat collar was up to keep out the cold wind and his trilby pulled down to hide his face. This pub was not one frequented by anyone he knew, but even so, he kept looking around, scared of being recognised.

Ever since the botched bank raid, he had been in hiding, knowing for certain that Bert Smart's men would be looking for him and terrified of the consequences. Smart was not a forgiving man and Winters feared for his life. He hadn't the money to leave town and escape detection that way, so he had been sleeping rough, frightened to return to his shabby flat in case he was discovered. That had been hairy with the doodlebugs falling every night: the V1 flying bombs that sputtered overhead, then suddenly cut out – later, an explosion. Terrifying. He was now desperate and all but penniless. He would have to get some money from somewhere. If only he could get enough to catch a train to London, no one would find him there. But how? He couldn't approach anyone he knew because he would give himself away. He sat sullenly in a corner and begged a cigarette from another customer.

Thank God it was warm in here, he thought. Sleeping rough in the winter was no picnic; the cold seeped through his bones. He'd used the public lavatories to wash every morning but without a razor he'd been unable to shave and he knew he looked disreputable.

He ate his sandwich and lingered over his pint, enjoying the warmth of the place, until the landlord came over to him.

He picked up Jack's pint glass, which now held just the dregs of his beer. 'You ready for another?'

'Not yet.'

'I thought not,' growled the man. 'I'm not running a doss-house here. Order another pint or bugger off!'

Muttering angrily to himself, Jack downed the remains of his beer and left the bar.

The cold air hit him as he emerged. Digging his hands into his pockets he thought the only way to keep warm was to walk. He stopped a man in the street and asked for money to buy food and to his relief he was handed half a crown. Jack decided to go to the afternoon showing of a film to get out of the cold and away from prying eyes. He would spend one and ninepence on the cheapest seat in the front stalls and the rest on fish and chips later.

It was dark when he emerged from the cinema, which made him feel a bit safer, but he needed to try to beg for more money, enough to buy him a room for the night at some dosshouse or other. He decided to go to East Street where the Horse and Groom was situated, as it was the haunt of lots of servicemen and they were often good for a few bob.

As he turned into East Street, he saw a young lady in front of him. The way she walked looked very familiar, so he strode along at a faster pace to get closer. Bloody hell, he was right, it was that bitch from the Guildhall, whom he'd last seen in the Grapes when he'd been there with Bert Smart. The street was fairly busy with pedestrians and so he was able to follow her without being obvious. When she turned into Canal Walk, he was close on her heels and surmised that she was going to see Sonny Nolan.

Canal Walk was quiet, it being too early for the brasses to turn out, and Jack decided to make his move. He grabbed Maisie by the arm and dragged her into the doorway of the pub, which was not yet open, covering her mouth with his hand to smother her cry of alarm. He saw the look of fear in her eyes as she recognised him.

'Keep quiet, you bitch, or I'll do for you, understand?' Maisie nodded, so he slowly removed his hand from her mouth. 'Give me any money you've got in your bag, and don't try to be clever or you'll regret it.'

Maisie opened her bag and with shaking hands took out her purse and handed it over.

Jack opened it and was delighted when he saw several notes inside. 'Bit flush, ain't you?' He pocketed his ill-gotten gains and grabbed her by the throat. 'I ain't got the time to waste on you now, 'cause I'm in a hurry, so you can count your blessings, girlie. You stay put for the next twenty minutes before you move ... right?'

'Yes,' she managed to croak through the grip that was squeezing her windpipe.

Pushing her roughly away, he made off into the gathering gloom.

Maisie's legs were shaking so much she couldn't stand, and she slid to the ground, gasping for breath as she did so. She was still terrified, wondering if Winters would return, and knowing she would be unable to move if he did. Eventually she felt strong enough to stand up, and carefully peered round the doorway. Seeing no one, she ran to Sonny Nolan's shop, threw open the door and almost fell inside.

Sonny and Gerry looked startled at her sudden entrance.

'What the bloody hell is going on?' demanded Sonny.

Maisie collapsed on a chair by the counter. 'I've been robbed!' she cried, rubbing her throat.

'Robbed? What do you mean, robbed? And what's wrong with your throat?' asked Sonny, seeing the fingermarks on her flesh.

'It was that bastard, Jack. The one who threatened me at Bert Smart's when I delivered that parcel for you.'

Sonny almost had a fit at the mention of the delivery. It was the last thing he wanted her to remember, knowing the police were making enquiries around the town after the furore at the bank.

She told the two men what had happened and, now feeling safe, was absolutely furious. 'He took all my money! It took me weeks to save enough to buy that dress you were keeping for me,' she told Sonny. 'He took all twelve pounds.'

With a grim expression Sonny told her, 'You can think yourself lucky that's all he did. Jack Winters is a mean bugger – and violent.' He paused, then added, 'Forget about that parcel too, if you know what's good for you.'

'Are you threatening me as well?'

'You were never there and you've never heard of Bert Smart, that's all. It's for your own good.'

Maisie was suddenly afraid. What had she got herself into? She wasn't a fool. Yes, she had found working for Sonny daring and exciting, but now for the first time she realised that there could be consequences of her actions and she was scared – but she hadn't lost her arrogance.

'In that case, I think you should still give me the dress anyway. Payment for my silence, so to speak.'

'Don't try and mess with *me*, girl. This isn't a game.'

She sat and stared back at him, daring him to refuse, but secretly quaking inside.

Sonny disappeared into the room behind the counter and returned with a bag. 'Here, take the bloody thing, but I don't want to see you in here again, not even to shop. Our business is finished and my shop is out of bounds to you. Understand?'

Taking the parcel, she glared at him. 'Perfectly!'

'Gerry will walk you out to East Street, make sure the coast is clear. Now off you go. And keep out of trouble!'

'I might say the same to you, Mr Nolan,' she said as Gerry opened the door for her.

Sonny had to smile. This girl had guts and he admired her for it.

When Gerry returned he looked at his boss and asked, 'Do you think she'll keep her mouth shut?'

'Of course she will. She knows that she's been dealing in dodgy stuff. Fortunately she doesn't know she delivered a gun in that parcel, and tonight Jack scared the shit out of her. She'll keep stumm all right. She's done well out of it with her new dresses.'

Maisie caught a tram to the bus station, where she climbed on one going to Netley and to Jimmy Greene. Fortunately she had enough change in her pocket to cover her fares after her purse had been taken. She'd slipped into the ladies' room and changed into her new dress first. She was going to be late, thanks to Jack Winters.

Jimmy was sitting in the chair by his bed when Maisie walked quickly down the ward towards him.

'Good heavens, Maisie, I didn't expect to see you this evening.' He looked at the ward clock. 'Visiting time is almost over.'

Taking off her coat, she perched on the bed. 'I know, I was delayed, but the ward sister said she would let me stay an extra ten minutes.'

He admired her new outfit. 'Lovely dress. The colour suits you. The mixture of blues complements the colour of your eyes.'

'Well, what a silver-tongued man you are, Jimmy. I never would have thought it of you,' she teased.

He leaned forward and looked at her neck. 'What are those marks?'

She automatically put her hands to her

throat. 'I was robbed in the street earlier tonight.'

'Oh, my God! What happened?'

'This man pushed me into a doorway and demanded that I give him my money.'

'Did you report it to the police?'

'No of course not. I didn't see his face clearly,' she lied. 'It was dark, so what was the point? Besides, then I wouldn't have been able to visit you. That's why I was late.'

Jimmy was stunned by her tale. 'You are an amazing girl. You get robbed, which must have been terrifying by the look of things, and still you come here. I don't know what to say.'

She took hold of his hand. 'You just don't understand how much I love you. Nothing, but nothing would keep me away!'

'Now then, enough of your nonsense, young lady. Not that I'm not touched by your words, but you know how things are.' To try to lighten the atmosphere he said, 'I am a lucky man today. Kathy was here this afternoon and now you. I'll be the envy of the ward.'

She looked around at the other patients and said, 'Well, they're not as good-looking as you. Two women fighting over you must be good for your ego. It certainly should help to make you better.'

He laughed at her cheek. 'Sadly it will take a little more than that.'

The smile left her lips. 'Is it possible that they'll send you back to France once you're well?'

'It all depends on what state I'm in when I recover, I suppose.'

She gazed lovingly at him. 'Oh, Jimmy, I couldn't bear it if they sent you back. My heart would break.'

He was about to tease her about being so dramatic, but when he saw her expression he knew she meant every word and the words died on his lips. 'Maisie, you have to stop thinking about me this way. I'm going to marry your sister.'

'I must mean something to you! I remember the way you kissed me before you went away. You wanted me then, I know. I felt it.'

'You took me by surprise and I was touched by your distress, the way you really cared what happened to me. It was a vulnerable time for us all.'

She sat up straight and asked, 'Are you sure that Kathy still wants to get married to you?'

'What a strange question. Why wouldn't she?'

'Well, you know, time passes, people change. Absence doesn't always make the heart grow fonder.'

'Are you trying to tell me something?'

With a toss of her hair she said, 'Just don't take too much for granted, that's all.'

The ward sister came along. 'The bell went ten minutes ago, young lady, and now you must leave. We have to get the patients settled for the night.'

Maisie slipped off the bed, put on her coat and leaned forward to kiss Jimmy goodbye. 'I'll be in again soon. Is there anything you need?'

He shook his head. He was still puzzling over her remarks, made with deliberation he was sure. But why? He watched her walk away. Was she just trying to cause trouble or was there something behind her words?

'Time passes people change,' Maisie had said. If only she knew how prophetic that was!

Kathy was faced with a huge problem. She had missed a period and was terrified that she was pregnant. At first she had pushed the idea to the back of her mind, unable to face the possibility that one of the terrible men who'd raped her had put her in this predicament. The very idea made her feel sick.

But if this turned out to be true, what was she to do? How could she tell Jimmy? What *would* his reaction be? She felt soiled.

Jack Winters had spent the night in a cheap dosshouse with the money he'd taken from Maisie. It had been wonderful to lie on a proper bed, even though the mattress was thin and lumpy. But after locking the door and putting the rickety chair under the handle, he had felt safe, and slept solidly. He'd started the day with a proper breakfast for a change, but he still had to be careful. Twelve pounds was a lot of money, but not enough to take him out of Southampton and sustain him for long. He needed more. He hadn't shaved, thinking it would help to disguise him from prying eyes.

He strolled through Hoglands Park, then on until he came to the rose garden near the Civic Centre, where he sat on a wooden bench. He saw an elderly lady walking towards him, carrying her shopping. As she came abreast of him, he tipped his hat.

'Can you spare a copper for a cup of tea, madam?'

She looked startled for a moment, then angry. Looking scathingly at him, she said, 'No I can't and you should be ashamed for asking. Why aren't you in the army, I'd like to know?' And she walked off.

Jack was humiliated. Wicked old bitch, he thought, how dare she speak to him like that? But it made him all the more desperate. He had to top up his money to keep him going.

The exchange had been witnessed by a policeman on the beat and he walked over to have a word with what he saw as a vagrant.

He approached from behind Winters so it wasn't until he stood facing the man that he recognised him, despite his altered appearance.

'Well, if it isn't Jack Winters! My boss will be pleased with me. There's a warrant out for your arrest.'

Winters paled. 'What do you want me for? I ain't done nothing!'

'I just saw you begging,' the constable declared. 'But anyway, you're wanted for questioning. Now don't argue. We're off to the station.' And before Jack could take flight, he was handcuffed and led away, much to the curiosity of a few bystanders who had heard the interchange.

Inside the police station, Ian Harvey was told of Winters' arrest. 'Read him his rights and put him in a cell to stew for a bit,' he ordered. He knew that Jack Winters would be no pushover; his fear of Bert Smart would stop him giving information. It would be Ian's job to make him more frightened of the law and that would take time. Making him wait in a cell would help to unnerve the man.

He read the latest report on the guard who'd been shot. The man was recovering after surgery. But Winters didn't know that. It might just be the lever to use to break him.

## CHAPTER TWENTY-FOUR

Jack Winters was eventually taken into an interview room where Ian Harvey and another detective were waiting, and told to sit down. He sat opposite the two men but remained silent.

'Looking a bit rough, aren't you, Jack?' Ian stared hard at the man opposite him.

'What's it to you?'

'Usually you take a pride in your appearance, that's all. Been living rough, have you?'

Jack stared back arrogantly. 'No, I just decided to grow a beard, but I'm flattered by your interest.'

'Where were you last Monday morning at around ten o'clock?'

Jack could feel his heart pounding, but he paused, thought for a moment and said, 'To be honest I can't remember precisely. I got up late, did a bit of shopping and went for a coffee in the morning sometime.'

'What did you buy?'

'Nothing in the end, apart from some fags and a paper.'

'Was that before or after you ran away from the National Provincial Bank?'

'I was nowhere near Holy Rood,' he protested. 'I caught a tram from Bernard Street up to Tyrell & Green's.'

'You're lying!'

'About what exactly?'

'You were hanging about outside the bank waiting for Bert Smart to knock over the delivery of money, except it all went pear-shaped and you ran off in a panic, sending some poor pedestrian flying in the process.'

'I had nothing to do with that! I was up the town.'

'Shall I tell you what I think happened?' asked Ian with a confidential air. 'You were the lookout and you screwed up somehow. Smart was late and the guard was warned when he heard a woman scream as she saw the would-be raiders. Then you took to your heels after the guard was shot.'

'You're talking a load of rubbish!'

Ian lit a cigarette slowly and deliberately. 'Funny, I never took you for a fool, Winters.'

'What do you mean?' He wiped the sweat from his brow.

'Well, I never thought I'd see you in the dock charged as an accessory to murder.'

'Murder?' The colour drained from his face. 'What do you mean, murder? I read in the paper the injured guard was recovering.'

'Sadly the man took a turn for the worse last night,' Ian lied. 'We're waiting to hear the latest news about him. If he dies, well...'

'I had nothing to do with it! I wasn't there, I tell you.'

'Bert Smart must be furious. He's known for meticulous planning in everything he does. Word on the street is he's looking for you. I wouldn't like to be in your shoes when he finds you – he doesn't have a forgiving nature, does he?'

Winters remained silent.

Ian Harvey picked up his cigarettes, rose to his feet and said, 'I'll send a barber in to shave you.'

'No thanks, it doesn't matter. I'm used to this.' He rubbed the growth on his chin.

'Actually, it does matter, Winters. You were clean-shaven on the day of the raid, and this evening you will take your place in a line-up. We have several witnesses coming in to take a look. Your days are numbered, Jack.' Turning to the constable at the door, he said, 'Take him back to the cells and get him shaved.'

Ian and his sidekick walked back to their office.

'How do you think it went, guv?' asked the young detective.

'He's worried to death. If anyone fingers him in the identification parade, we've got him, if not we'll push a bit harder. Now he's got time to think about it. An accessory to murder is a frightening thing to be charged with. It means years locked up inside.'

Meanwhile, under the watchful eye of a police officer, Jack Winters sat handcuffed to the chair as the barber began to shave him. He eyed the open razor with suspicion.

'I hope your hand is steady,' he snapped. 'I don't want my bloody throat cut!'

'I haven't cut anyone's throat in twenty years,' was the reply. 'Mind you, there's always a first time, and if you don't keep still, it could be today!'

This was enough to keep the prisoner quiet until the job was done and he was returned to his cell. Once there he weighed up his options. No way was he going down with Bert Smart; he would keep protesting his innocence, but would he get away with it? So far there was no concrete evidence; it would all depend on the identification parade. If no one picked him out, he was home free. He would wait.

Early that evening, the flower seller and two other people who had been outside the bank on the fateful morning arrived at the police station. Ian Harvey spoke to them.

'In that room are several men, lined up. You will walk, one by one, with my officer, down the line and look closely at each person, and if you recognise the man you saw on the day of the raid, you will point him out. Understand?'

They all nodded their agreement. One

asked somewhat nervously, 'Will we be safe if we pick one out?'

'Of course,' Ian assured the woman. 'One of my officers will be with you and two others are standing by inside the room. It will only take a couple of minutes, then you'll be free to leave.'

The flower seller was the first one in. She walked slowly down the line and stopped in front of the last but one.

'This is the man I saw!' she declared. She was taken outside.

'Are you sure?' the detective asked.

'No doubt about it. I first noticed him standing on the corner reading a newspaper. Then after the shooting he took off.'

'Are you prepared to go into court and say that?'

'I am. The poor bloke who was shot was only doing his job. It isn't right!'

The other two bystanders also picked out the same man – and Jack Winters knew he was in serious trouble.

When Kathy next went to visit Jimmy Greene, he had some good news for her.

'I can come home at the weekend!' he said gleefully.

'That's wonderful news!'

'I have to go to the South Hants Hospital for some physio treatment, but at last I'll be sleeping in my own bed and we'll be able to spend more time together.'

'I am so pleased for you,' she told him.

'There was a time,' he admitted, 'when I wondered if I would ever get home in one piece.'

'Oh, Jimmy, don't say such things.'

'It's true, darling. It was pretty rough out there, you know.' He gazed lovingly at her. 'I can't tell you how I longed to see you, take you in my arms, feel you close to me.' He gave a wry smile. 'They say absence makes the heart grow fonder. It certainly worked for me.'

He waited for her answer, but Kathy just squeezed his hand.

'Of course,' he said slowly, 'that's not always the case. Sometimes it's out of sight, out of mind.'

Laughing, she said, 'For goodness' sake, stop talking in clichés and tell me how you're getting home. Will they help you with transport?'

'Yes, the WVS will send someone for me and drop me at the door. We'll go out, you and I, and have a romantic dinner together to celebrate. How about it?'

'That'll be lovely. But you mustn't do too much too soon.'

'I won't, but they want me to exercise and keep my muscles moving or I'll seize up. At least I'll be home for Christmas. Once I know how long I'm going to be around, maybe we can think about getting married. What do you say?'

'I say you're jumping the gun, Jimmy Greene. Let's get you well first. One thing at a time.'

'You do still want to marry me, don't you?'

Kathy wanted an end to this conversation. She didn't want to be pushed into making any such decisions, and now she felt trapped. 'Of course,' she said. What else could she say under the circumstances? It wouldn't be fair to complicate Jimmy's life even further. It was going to be difficult enough, because she had yet to tell him about being raped ... and now its possible consequence. She prayed her period was just late, for the horror of the alternative was almost more than she could cope with. The last thing she wanted to discuss was marriage.

Jimmy struggled to his feet. 'Come on, let's take a walk outside.'

'It's a bit cold. Will you be all right?'

'I'll be fine. I'll put my greatcoat on and there's a partially covered place where we can walk.'

Once outside and away from everyone, Jimmy paused. Putting his crutches aside and leaning against the wall for support, he said, 'Come here,' and took her into his arms.

His kisses were full of urgency and need, but Kathy, with her own worries, was unable to match his mood.

'What's wrong?' Jimmy asked. 'Before I went away, you were far more enthusiastic than that, as I recall.'

'I'm sorry,' she said. 'I'm just tired, that's all. Come on, let's sit on this bench and have a cigarette and decide where we're going to have this celebration dinner.'

As Kathy waited for a bus to take her back to Southampton, she felt guilty that she'd been unable to fulfil Jimmy's expectations of her. What must he be thinking? But the very idea that she could be carrying the child of a rapist was all-encompassing. It brought back the whole trauma, which to a certain extent she'd managed to push to the back of her mind, since that was the only way she could go on from day to day. She felt she couldn't tell either Annie or Maisie of her fears. There was only one person she could confide in and that was Ian. Unable to carry the burden alone any longer, she went to a phone box as soon as she arrived in Southampton and rang him.

'Kathy! How lovely to hear from you. How are you?'

'Ian, I need to see you. Can we meet? I'm at the bus station.'

He sensed the urgency in her voice and said, 'Wait there, I'll come straight away. Sit in the waiting room out of the cold.'

Kathy's heart was pounding as she waited. Would she still feel the same about Ian when she saw him, and what would he say when she told him of her fears? Would he be able to help her solve her problem ... and would he still want to?

As soon as he walked in the door and saw the expression on her face, she knew the answer to her questions. As she stood up, he gathered her into his arms and held her tight.

'Kathy, whatever is the matter? You look worried to death.'

'Can we go somewhere more private?' she asked.

He took her by the arm. 'Come along.'

Outside, he called a taxi to take them to the Polygon Hotel. There Ian sat Kathy in the lounge, which was almost empty, and ordered a drink for them both.

'Now, what's the problem?' he asked.

In a voice that was all but a whisper she said, 'I think I may be pregnant.'

'Oh, my God!'

'I'm two weeks late, which is unusual.'

'Have you seen a doctor?'

'No, it's too soon – and I may be mistaken.'

The waiter delivered the drinks and left them alone.

'I have to ask you, Kathy. If you are pregnant, do you want this child?'

Her eyes widened in surprise. 'How could

you think I would want the child of a rapist? Those men were foul. It was bad enough that they raped me, but to have to give birth to an offspring of theirs ... I'd rather die!'

He took her hands in his. 'There will be absolutely no need for such drastic measures, Kathy. We'll get you to a doctor, and if your fears are right, then we'll make arrangements for you to have a termination. Under the circumstances there won't be a problem in getting it done.' He looked thoughtful and asked, 'Does Jimmy know yet what happened to you?'

She shook her head. 'No, I haven't told him yet. He's being sent home this weekend. I'll tell him once he's settled.'

'How is he?'

'Slowly recovering. Today he was talking about getting married.'

Ian's expression didn't change. 'How do you feel about that?'

'I can't even think about it now. First I have to know if I *am* pregnant; everything else will have to wait.' With a look of concern, she asked, 'Will this have to come out in court when the case comes up? I'd hate to have to read about it in the papers and have everyone know.'

'I'm sure the court will use its discretion. I'll see to that.'

'What about my family, do they need to know?'

He frowned as he said, 'They know what happened to you. I'm sure the possibility has occurred to your parents, at least.'

'I'll wait and see what happens at the doctor's before I decide what to tell them.'

He tried to reassure her. 'Please try not to worry too much, Kathy. We'll sort everything out, I promise.'

With a deep sigh she said, 'I don't know what I'd do without you, Ian. You always seem to be around when I'm in trouble.'

Trying to lighten her mood, he smiled. 'Perhaps I've been designated as your guardian angel!'

'Well, whatever it is, I'm so glad you're here.'

'Have you eaten, Kathy?'

'I had a sandwich earlier before I went to the hospital, that's all.'

'Why don't we stop here for a meal?' he suggested. 'Unless you have to hurry off somewhere.'

The last thing she wanted was to lose his company, so she agreed. 'Yes, that would be lovely.'

Kathy had never been in the Polygon dining room and was delighted by its opulence. The head waiter sat them at a table for two and left them to read the menu.

'Goodness me,' she said, 'considering there's a war on, this menu is very tempting.'

'Well, a clever chef can work wonders, you

know. Now, let's see what looks the most appetising.'

In the end they decided to have roast chicken. Although chicken was not rationed, it was seldom seen for sale in butchers' shops, so it was a real treat. Kathy couldn't help but think how her sister would view her dining with Ian, but she didn't care. It was a welcome break from all her worries and she intended to enjoy every moment.

During the meal, Ian told her a little of their progress with the failed raid on the bank. 'We're holding a suspect now and we're hoping he will lead us to the gang who organised it all.'

'Will the guard recover?' Kathy asked.

'Fortunately yes. He took the bullet in his shoulder, which may impair his movements a little in the future, but he'll be fine. I'm sure that Sonny Nolan's mixed up in this too.' He looked at Kathy and said, 'I saw Maisie in his shop one day, looking at the clothes.'

With a sinking heart, Kathy said, 'I believe she does sometimes buy dresses there. He has some good stuff, you know. I've bought one myself before now. I was wearing it the night we first met.' But although she made light of it, she was hoping that Maisie wasn't involved with Nolan in any way. She never seemed to be short of money these days and some of her new dresses looked very expensive. She quickly closed her mind to the possibility. She had enough to worry about at the moment without her wayward sister adding to her troubles!

## CHAPTER TWENTY-FIVE

Bert Smart was furious that his men still had not tracked down Jack Winters. None of them were aware that he was sitting in a cell in the local police station, waiting to be questioned further.

He was mulling over his options, knowing that he'd been identified on the line-up. If he was to cop a plea and give the police the information they required, how much time would be knocked off his sentence, he wondered? He knew for a fact he would be going down. If only Smart hadn't used the gun!

The cell door opened and Winters was taken once more into the interview room.

'Well, Jack,' said Ian triumphantly, 'you're really swimming in the brown stuff now. Three people have identified you as the man outside the bank. So what have you got to say for yourself?'

'Nothing until I know what's in it for me!'

'The judge will of course take into consideration your cooperation with the police when it comes to sentencing. I can't say more than that.' He pushed a packet of cigarettes across the table. 'Here, have one whilst you consider what might be a murder charge.'

'I didn't shoot the bloody guard! It was Bert Smart. He said he would only use the gun as a threat. It wasn't my fault the bastard panicked!'

'Let's start at the beginning, shall we?' Ian suggested.

Knowing he had little choice, Jack told them about the plan and how he had been so busy reading the paper he'd missed the van's arrival, and what happened afterwards.

'Where did Smart get the gun?'

'He bought it off Sonny Nolan.'

'Did you see him do that yourself, or were you only told about it?'

'I didn't see Sonny hand it over, if that's what you mean. Sonny sent his runner over with the parcel.' Winters suddenly realised the connection and grinned at Ian. 'You know the bird who delivered it! It was that bitch who made all the trouble at the Guildhall. She's the one what brought the gun to Bert's place. You've been mixing with a criminal, Mr Harvey!'

Ian was stunned but he kept his feelings hidden. 'I've been mixing with criminals since the day I joined the force. Tell me more about this girl.'

'She's Nolan's runner. She makes deliveries on his behalf. You know, petrol and clothing coupons for a start. Oh, she's quite a busy little spitfire, that one.'

'I'll need you to make a statement, Winters.'

'I know that. In any case, it will be a pleasure to get back at the girl, 'cause I owe her one.' And he started to laugh.

Ian left his colleague in the room and returned to his office. Maisie! What an idiot that girl was, getting tied up with the likes of Nolan. And for what, he wondered? Now that she was implicated, he would have no choice but to question her. If she told him the truth, then he could get Nolan on dealing in black market goods at least. But first he needed to get a search warrant for Bert Smart's house. He didn't for one minute expect to find the weapon there, but he had to look. The getaway van had been seen driving along the Esplanade before being abandoned in Woolston and Ian had men searching the route. He'd wait another day or two before bringing in Nolan and Maisie Bates.

Bert Smart was surprised when there was a battering on his door and several uniformed police marched in, followed by Detective

Inspector Harvey, who waved a search warrant under his nose and told him to sit down in the kitchen with a constable on watch, whilst his men took the place apart.

'What's this all about?' he demanded.

'Shut up and wait!' he was told.

Each room was searched thoroughly. Apart from one or two items, like nylon stockings and cartons of American cigarettes, nothing of an illegal nature was found and there was no sign of the weapon.

Smart sat smirking when the search was over. 'Satisfied?' he asked.

'Take him to the station for questioning,' Ian Harvey told the constable.

'Questioning about what?'

'You will be helping us with our inquiries,' Ian told him.

'What inquiries?'

'You'll learn soon enough. Now get into the car outside. I'll see you at the station.'

Maisie, unaware of the trouble she was in, was planning her weekend. Jimmy was being driven home on Saturday and she intended to see him, come what may. She knew he would be calling on Kathy on the Sunday and staying to tea, and she hoped at least to steal a moment alone with him. She could hardly contain herself at the prospect.

Kathy didn't share her sister's enthusiasm. She was delighted that her fiancé was leaving hospital and of course she wanted him to recover completely from his injuries, but her period hadn't started as she had hoped and with each passing day her dread of being pregnant grew. The fact that she would have to wait before going to the doctor's to find out was only adding to her concerns. And to see Maisie rushing around like a dog with two tails, talking incessantly about Jimmy coming home, didn't help.

'I thought you'd be over the moon that Jimmy was coming out of hospital,' Maisie accused her, 'but you don't seem at all excited. What's wrong? Don't you care about him at all?'

'Don't be ridiculous! Of course I care. I'm sure he's delighted to get out of Netley. It isn't much fun being surrounded by patients who have hideous injuries and I'm sure he'll improve more quickly being among his family.'

'And us, of course.'

'Us?' queried Kathy. 'What do you mean – *us?*'

'Well, I certainly intend to make a fuss of him if you don't!'

'Of that I have no doubt,' Kathy said with heavy sarcasm. 'Now for God's sake shut up, will you? I've got a headache.'

'Well you certainly don't have an aching heart, that's for sure,' Maisie snapped, and flounced out of the room.

Annie had been in the kitchen listening to the exchange between her daughters, and when Maisie left she went into the living room.

'What's up, love? Not feeling well?'

'I'm all right, Mum. Just a bit off colour, that's all.'

'Never mind. When Jimmy's home you'll be able to see more of him and that'll cheer you up a bit.'

Forcing a smile, Kathy said, 'Yes, of course it will. Meantime, let's put the radio on. *ITMA*'s on in ten minutes. That'll give us a laugh, at least.'

'Good,' said Annie. 'I'll make us a cup of tea.'

But as she returned to her kitchen, she had her own ideas as to why Kathy was feeling under the weather, although she prayed that she was wrong. If Kathy was with child, what would happen then? Would she want to carry a child fathered by a rapist, and what effect would it have on her relationship with her fiancé?

She took out her concerns on the dough she was kneading, pummelling it vigorously. Why was life so full of problems? She had no idea that she had another to add to them.

Wilf Bates, relieved to have mended his fences with his wife, was frustrated. He missed the exhilarating sex he'd enjoyed with

Betty Langdon. He'd not felt he could ask Annie to be more adventurous in their love-making and therefore he was not a happy man. The day came when he could resist it no longer, and once more he succumbed to the temptation of his associate after finishing a fire watch with her.

As he climbed into her bed and felt her bare flesh against his, he moaned as the ache in his loins longed for release. He buried his face in her voluptuous breasts.

'Oh my God, Betty, I'm not sure I can control this need I have for you.'

'You'd better bloody well try,' she snapped. 'I've waited long enough for you to come back and I don't want it over in five minutes!'

He tried as hard as he could, but he failed. Shuddering over her, he spent his passion as quickly as he'd feared – and far too quickly for Betty.

She was furious. 'A lot of bloody good that did me, Wilf Bates!'

'Sorry, love. I couldn't help myself.'

'Then you'd better try again, and this time think a bit more about my enjoyment.'

'Christ, Betty, I'm not superhuman.' But seeing the look on her face he said, 'Give me a bit of time and I'll see what I can do.'

When eventually he crept home and climbed into his own bed, he felt as if he'd aged ten years.

There was a buzz of excitement at the police station. Jack Winters had made his statement and now Bert Smart was in custody, being questioned about the raid on the bank.

At first, Smart denied everything. 'You're plucking at straws,' he told Ian Harvey. 'You have absolutely no proof that I was even there! If you want to know, I was staying with my sister at Chandlers Ford.'

'And she'll testify to that, will she?'

'Why ever not? It's the truth.'

'It's a pack of lies and you know it.'

'Prove it!' Bert Smart challenged.

Picking up two sheets of paper, Ian waved them in Smart's face. 'Here's the proof. I've got you tied up in knots.'

The villain's eyes narrowed and became watchful. 'What do you mean?'

'This is the statement of one Jack Winters. I've got it all here, from beginning to end.'

Bert Smart now realised why his men had been unable to find their erstwhile lookout. He tried to tough it out. 'You are going to trust the word of that man, with his criminal record?'

'Have you forgotten your own? Neither of you have an ounce of decency between you.' Turning to his colleague, Harvey said, 'Book him!'

The arrests made the headlines in that evening's edition of the *Southern Daily Echo.* When Sonny Nolan read them he was a worried man.

Maisie Bates read them too and was horrified when she realised that she had met Bert Smart, but relieved when she saw the name of the other man in custody. At least she could stop being scared of meeting Jack Winters again. Little did she realise how her connection with these men was going to influence her own future.

It was Sunday afternoon. The table in the Bateses' living room was laid for tea. Annie had been able to buy some ham and she opened a tin of salmon she'd been saving for a special occasion. She would serve it with potato salad, pickled onions, pickled red cabbage and a fresh lettuce, grown in the garden. The loaf of home-made bread was placed on the bread board, waiting to be cut. There were home-made scones and a fatless sponge, with jam.

Kathy eyed the spread and smiled at her mother. 'Gosh, Mum, you wouldn't think there was a war on. Thanks, it all looks lovely.'

'Well, this is a special occasion. I haven't seen Jimmy since he left for France.'

Maisie flounced into the room, wearing one of the dresses bought from Sonny Nolan. She'd put her hair up to make her look older and Kathy noticed she was wearing silk stockings.

'My goodness, where did you manage to get those?'

'I happen to know the right people, that's all.' She patted her hair in front of the mirror over the fireplace.

'You'll do,' said Annie. 'Now get another cup out of the cupboard. I've only got four on the table.' As Maisie was about to do as her mother asked, there was a knock on the door.

'I'll go!' she said, but Annie grabbed hold of her arm.

'No, Kathy will answer the door. Jimmy is *her* fiancé, remember?'

Glaring at her mother, Maisie went for the cup, as requested.

As Kathy opened the door to him, Jimmy Greene leaned forward and kissed her. 'I was going to bring you some flowers, but it would be a bit difficult to carry them with two crutches.'

'Don't be silly, that wasn't necessary. Anyway, how are you feeling?'

'It's great to be home. But come here and give me a hug. I need that more than anything else.'

Kathy held him close, realising as she did so that he'd lost a lot of weight.

'Come on in,' she said. 'Mum has got a feast on the table, especially for you. It feels as if you could do with some flesh on your bones.'

Wilf, who had been reading the paper, stood up to greet him. 'Good to see you, lad. Glad you're home in one piece. Here, come and sit down.'

Annie crossed over to him and kissed his cheek. 'I'll put the kettle on,' she said.

Maisie sauntered over to him and kissed his cheek too. 'You look better than the last time I saw you. You've more colour in your face.'

'Yes, I'm doing all right. Leg throbs a bit sometimes, but with a bit of physio I'll soon be on the mend.' Smiling at Kathy, he said, 'Before you know it, darling, we'll be dancing round the floor at the Guildhall.'

'I'll really look forward to that.' She laughed. 'But the jitterbug will have to wait a bit, I think.'

The tea was made and they all sat around the table to eat. Jimmy told them about his mate Shorty. 'He's only pint-sized but he's a brave little devil. He saved my life by pushing me out of the way when a Jerry I thought was dead took a pot shot at me a few months ago.'

'Ah well,' said Wilf, 'in a war, you look after each other.'

'That's right,' Jimmy agreed. 'But I have to say, it's wonderful to be able to sleep in a decent bed and have a bath when you want it, even if you are only allowed a few inches of water.'

'Did you get a taste for wine out there?' asked Wilf.

'Yes, we were given the odd bottle when we pushed the Germans out of various villages. I liked what I had but no way can I smoke their cigarettes, they're bloody awful! They taste and smell like a bonfire.'

Before anyone could comment on the qualities of French tobacco, there was a knock on the door.

'I'll go,' said Wilf.

'I'm not expecting anyone on a Sunday afternoon,' Annie remarked.

They were all taken by surprise when Wilf returned, followed by Ian Harvey.

## CHAPTER TWENTY-SIX

Annie Bates was the first one to recover. 'Ian, come in. This is Jimmy Greene, Kathy's fiancé. This is Detective Inspector Harvey,' she told the soldier.

The two men shook hands. 'Glad to see you're getting better,' said Ian.

'Let me get you a cup of tea,' Annie offered.

'Thank you, Mrs Bates, but this isn't a social call, I'm afraid.'

'What's wrong?' asked Jimmy.

'I need Miss Bates to come with me to the station and help me with my inquiries.'

Kathy rose from her seat. 'I'll get my coat.'

'No, Kathy, it's Maisie I want to talk to, not you.'

With a startled look Maisie asked, 'Me? What on earth do you want to talk to me about?'

'I'll explain at the station. There's a car outside with WPC waiting. If you will just get your coat, we'll be on our way.'

'Are you arresting my Maisie?' asked Annie in alarm.

'No, Mrs Bates, it's just routine, that's all.'

'I'll come with her,' Wilf said.

Maisie got to her feet. 'No, Dad, that won't be necessary. Ian will take care of me, won't you?'

Ian placed a reassuring hand on Annie's shoulder. 'Don't you worry; I'll get her home safely.' To Maisie he added, 'Ready?'

The occupants of the living room were silent as they watched Maisie leave with the detective.

'What's that daft daughter of mine got herself mixed up with now?' Wilf voiced all their thoughts.

Jimmy turned to Kathy with a puzzled expression. 'I don't understand why you thought it was you that bloke wanted. Why on earth would you think he would need to question you, of all people?'

Kathy cast a glance in her mother's direction. Annie just raised her eyebrows.

'I am a witness in a case he's in charge of. I assumed it was about that.'

'A case? What case?'

'I'll tell you about it later,' she said.

Tea was over, and Kathy had taken Jimmy into the front parlour. Sensing the tension in her, he was filled with trepidation. Wordlessly, he sat down in the chair she indicated, and waited to hear what she had to say.

Taking a deep breath, Kathy began. 'The case that I am involved in is to do with two soldiers who attacked me in Hoglands Park one night.'

'Oh my God, Kathy! Did they hurt you badly?'

Tears brimmed her eyes and her throat seemed to close. 'Yes, they did. They both raped me.'

Jimmy was so shocked he was lost for words.

Kathy continued valiantly. 'I tried to fight them off, Jimmy, honestly I did, but they were too strong for me. I managed to crawl home and Mum called an ambulance.'

'You were taken to hospital?'

'Yes, I was badly hurt. Of course the doctor had to report it to the police and Mum asked for Ian to be told, as I knew him. She thought it would be easier for me than to talk to a stranger.'

He sat shaking his head, unable to believe what he was hearing.

Kathy started to cry. 'It wasn't my fault!'

Her anguish reached his shocked brain and he caught hold of her and held her close.

'Of course it wasn't. It must have been terrifying for you. Oh, Kathy, darling, I'm so sorry. What's happened since? You said you were involved in a case.'

Wiping her tears, she said, 'Ian has caught the two men, and when their case comes to court I will have to appear.'

'Oh, darling, I am sorry. That will be an ordeal for you.'

'I'm certainly not looking forward to it, but at least they won't be able to put another woman through such an ordeal. I want to be there when they are sentenced. That way I'll at least see justice done.' Getting to her feet, she said, 'I am so sorry you had to come home to such news after what you've been through.'

He rose from his seat and took her into his arms. 'Mine was nothing in comparison. Now come on, let's get back to the others and try to put this behind us.'

'And now I'm worried new about Maisie,' she said as they walked back to the living room. 'I just hope she hasn't done anything stupid.'

Maisie Bates was sitting in an interview room with Ian and his colleague. A WPC was standing by the door. Maisie looked round the stark space and said to Ian, 'Not exactly like home, is it?'

'No, it's where we interview criminals. Let me assure you that this is a serious business. It's not a game, Maisie. You may be in real trouble, and unless you are honest with me I'll be unable to help you.'

She felt the panic rise within her. The severity of Ian's expression only added to her fears. He was very much on duty and she felt the force of his position as he looked at her.

'What do you want to know?'

'Tell me about your association with Sonny Nolan.'

Her heart sank. 'I buy some of my clothes there.'

Ian waited. 'And?' Seeing her hesitation, he lost his patience. 'For goodness' sake, girl, you were his runner! Stop messing me about – I'm trying to keep you out of prison, for God's sake!'

'Prison?' Her eyes nearly popped out of her head with shock. 'What do you mean, prison?'

'Sonny Nolan is a racketeer, you know that. I want to know what you delivered and to whom, on his behalf.'

'You want names?' She was horrified at the thought of getting these people into trouble.

'Yes, I want names and details. Here.' He pushed a pen and paper towards her. 'Write them down.'

Now she was terrified, remembering how Sonny warned her off him and his shop. 'If Sonny Nolan knows I've done this, he'll kill me!'

'If you do as I say, he'll soon be in custody and you'll have nothing to worry about, but if you refuse, it will be you, Maisie, who will be sitting in a cell after I charge you with handling stolen goods.' He sat back. 'Your choice.'

Seeing the determination in his face, she started to write.

When she'd finished, Ian picked up the list. Reading through it, he said, 'You've missed out a name here.'

'I have?'

'Yes. Bert Smart. You went to his house one night, didn't you? Don't lie to me, Maisie, because I know you did.'

'Yes! I only went once. I met that man Jack Winters there and he threatened me. He wanted to drag me upstairs, but Mr Smart stopped him.'

'What did you take there?'

'I don't know what it was; it was a parcel, tied up with string.'

'Was it different from the others you delivered?'

'Yes it was. The others were coupons of some kind, usually in an envelope. Sonny said I was only to hand the parcel over to Mr Smart himself.'

'Which you did?'

'Yes, and when I saw Sonny later I told him about Jack and said I'd never go there again. But a couple of days ago, Jack grabbed me by the throat in Canal Walk and took all my money.' She looked furious. 'After he left me I went to Sonny's shop and told him what had happened. He said I was lucky that was all he did.'

'Did he say anything else?'

'Yes. I mentioned seeing Jack at Mr Smart's when I delivered the parcel. He said I was to forget I'd ever been there.'

'Yes, I bet he did.'

Maisie was now really worried. 'Are you going to arrest me, Ian?'

'Not for the moment.' He gazed at the young woman in puzzlement. 'Why on earth did you get tied up in all this?'

'I wanted to earn enough money to buy the beautiful dresses that Sonny Nolan had. They were exquisite and I wanted them.'

'All this for vanity. How could you have been so stupid?'

'I wanted to look nice. For heaven's sake, this war is awful and I'm young. Gracious, everyone is on a fiddle of some kind. I wanted to look nice when I went dancing, that's all! That's not a crime, is it?'

'Of course not, and I can understand that, but the way you chose to get those dresses *is* a crime, and one that will have consequences.'

'What sort of consequences?' she asked.

'That we'll have to wait and see. But the fact that you've helped us with our inquiries will encourage the judge to see you in a better light, and the fact that you are a silly woman without a sensible thought in your head may also help.'

'You don't like me very much, do you?'

Ian laughed. 'It's not a case of liking or disliking you, Maisie. I just want to shake some sense into you. Don't you think your family has been through enough? What with Kathy's rape, and Jimmy being injured?'

She gave him a calculating look. 'Yes, the fact that he came home upset your plans, didn't it, Ian?'

Ian's voice was cold. 'You should also try to learn to think before you open your mouth. That would save you getting into more trouble.' He rose to his feet. 'You need to write down all you've told me in a statement. This detective will stay with you, then I'll find a car and send you home.'

He was filled with anger as he walked down the corridor to his office. That troublesome girl, he fumed to himself. Self-centred, wilful – and bright, but without any morals at all. She uses people for her own benefit and doesn't blink an eye. But one day, if she isn't careful, she'll be made to pay for it and that will come as a terrible shock to her.

When eventually Maisie returned home, she was surrounded by her family and Jimmy, all asking questions at the same time. She covered her ears and yelled at them.

'Shut up! I can't hear myself think.'

It was Wilf who spoke. 'All right, Maisie, what's this all about? And I don't want you telling me lies.'

She knew there would be no point in doing so; everything would soon be out in the open now the police were involved. 'I've been working for Sonny Nolan, making deliveries for him. It seems he was dealing in illegal goods.'

Kathy stormed at her. 'What do you mean – *seems?* You knew damned well he was a dodgy bloke, yet you still went ahead. When *are* you going to learn any kind of sense?'

Jimmy intervened. 'I'm sure she had a good reason, Kathy.'

She glared at him. 'Then let's ask her. Well, Maisie, speak up!'

Maisie was defiant. 'He paid me good money and it helped me pay for the smart dresses he got from London. I also bought extra clothing coupons from him, if you want the truth.'

'A very noble reason to put yourself in this position, I must say!'

Wilf's anger knew no bounds. 'How dare you stand there and tell us you willingly broke the law? Haven't I always taught you that honesty is the best policy and to live by the rules – haven't I?'

This was too much for his daughter. 'Don't you stand there, Dad, and preach to me about what's right and what's wrong, not when you've been continually unfaithful to my mother!'

'Maisie! How could you?' Kathy looked at her sister with horror.

'Well, it's the truth! He's been bedding that Betty Langdon for ages, as well you know.'

Kathy looked across at her mother, who was sitting tight-lipped and silent.

Wilf, ashen with shock, looked at his wife. 'Annie,' he began.

'Shut up Wilf!' she said. 'Thank you, Maisie. I hope you're proud of yourself!'

Maisie, now her temper tantrum was over, looked shamefaced. 'I'm sorry, Mum. I didn't really mean that to slip out, but I couldn't bear him being so sanctimonious. I didn't mean to tell you about it.'

'Oh, I've known about it almost from the beginning, but I chose to shut my eyes to it, hoping it would blow over. Now, thanks to you and your petulance, I have to deal with it! I don't think I'll ever forgive you.' She walked into the kitchen and closed the door.

'You rotten little cow!' snapped Kathy. 'You don't give a damn about anyone but yourself, do you?'

Maisie burst into tears. Jimmy walked over to her and put an arm round her. She turned and clung to him.

'You're not cross with me as well, are you?'

'I think you have been very foolish and now unkind to your mother. Why on earth do you behave like this?' He looked over her shoulder at Kathy, who just glared at him and went into the kitchen to comfort her mother.

Annie was standing by the window, looking out to the small back garden.

Kathy stood behind her and enfolded her in her arms. 'Oh, Mum, I'm so sorry.'

Patting Kathy's hand, Annie said, 'It's all right, love. As I said, I've known about your father and Betty for a long time.'

'What are you going to do about it?'

'To be honest I don't know, and at this moment I don't even want to think about it.'

'Fancy a walk?' suggested Kathy. 'Perhaps a breath of fresh air will do us both good.'

'Yes, let's get out of the house for a while.'

'I'll get our coats,' said Kathy, 'and we'll go out the back way.'

'Mum and I are going out,' she announced as she collected their coats. To Jimmy she said, 'I'm sorry that your day has been spoilt, Jimmy, but my mother needs me.' And she left the room.

Wilf took his coat from behind the door and turned to Jimmy. 'Want to come to the pub for a drink, son? I need one right now.'

Jimmy looked at Maisie and seeing her despair said, 'No, I'll stay for a while, then go home. Another time, Mr Bates.'

When they were alone, Jimmy looked sternly at Maisie. 'You did a terrible thing to your mother tonight, Maisie. How could you be so cruel?'

'I didn't mean to. It only came out because Dad was preaching at me.'

'Do you realise that you may well have put their marriage in jeopardy?'

'I didn't do that. My father did that when he climbed into that other woman's bed!'

He looked at the beautiful girl staring so defiantly at him. 'Maybe, but you haven't helped and you must take some responsibility for that. You cannot go through life without any regard for other people's feelings. It just won't do.'

'I do think of others. I think of you.' She flung her arms around his neck. 'I worried about you when you were away... I cried for you when I knew you were injured.' She caressed his face. 'I'm not entirely selfish.'

She gazed into his eyes. 'I would die for you if I had to.'

Jimmy looked into her eyes, now brimming with tears. 'Oh, Maisie, I don't know what I'm going to do about you, I really don't.'

'Kiss me' she said, and lifted her mouth to his.

## CHAPTER TWENTY-SEVEN

Kathy and Annie strolled along the Esplanade – fortunately lit by a full moon – arms entwined, collars up, and scarves tied to keep out the chill. They were both lost in their own thoughts. Kathy was livid with her sister and even more annoyed with Jimmy, at the way he'd comforted the wayward Maisie. What the girl needed was a good slap! All Kathy's sympathies were with her mother. Maisie had brought her trouble on herself but her poor mother didn't deserve to have her marital problems thrown in her face like that. It was unforgivable.

Their steps had taken them to the pier and Kathy suggested they go to a restaurant there and have a coffee. 'Come on, Mum, it will warm us up.'

As they opened the door, the feeling of

warmth was very welcome. Several tables were occupied and the atmosphere was certainly more pleasant than the one they had left behind.

As the waitress served them, Kathy sat back and said, 'Well, this is better.' Then she told her mother, briefly, about her conversation with Jimmy.

Annie looked fondly at her daughter. 'You're a good girl. I don't know what I'd do without you.'

'You'd manage just fine,' Kathy told her. 'I don't know any woman who is stronger than you are. You've managed the household during difficult times. We have never come home but there was a decent meal on the table. Then there's your work in the WVS.' She caught hold of her hand. 'You were a tower of strength to me when I was raped ... and you still are. You knew about Dad and you kept it to yourself. That took guts, Mum.'

'Oh, I don't know about that, Kathy love. I didn't really want to face up to the facts. I hoped your dad would get over this madness. Men are such daft creatures. Throw a bit of temptation their way, and believe me, it takes a real man to resist.'

'I could kill him! For God's sake, he's old enough to know better.'

'His age was the problem, I would think,' Annie suggested. 'Betty Langdon is much younger, she's pretty, and I'm sure it fed his ego to think he was desirable to her.'

'I can't believe you're sitting here making excuses for him,' Kathy said, anger flashing in her eyes.

'I'm not; I'm just trying to understand.'

'Well, don't be so bloody understanding! You are the wronged person in all of this. He and Maisie are alike. Both selfish and self-centred. Neither has given any consideration to the consequences of their actions.'

'Ah well, Maisie will soon have to face hers. She's been found out. Perhaps it will teach her a lesson. After all, she won't listen to any of us.'

'Dad too has had a lesson. Have you thought what you're going to do about him?'

'I married him for better or worse, Kathy. However, he's not going to get away unscathed, I can tell you. Oh, no. I'll have him crawling on his hands and knees for a long time!' She started laughing. 'Revenge can be enjoyed, you know.'

Kathy joined in the laughter. 'You'll be able to get all those jobs done around the house he's been putting off. He won't want to miss the opportunity to get back into your good books.'

'Or my bed! I intend to put up the camp bed for him. God, it's uncomfortable!'

The two women laughed until the tears ran down their cheeks and their sides ached.

'Oh, Mum, do stop! My stomach hurts.'

'Not as much as your father's back will after a few nights.' And they both started laughing again.

Eventually the two women walked home. As they arrived at the back door, Annie said, 'Now wipe that smile off your face. We are about to start round one!'

They found Maisie alone, sitting by the fire, reading a magazine. Looking up, she told them, 'Dad has gone down to the pub and Jimmy's gone home.'

'Was he all right?' asked Kathy. 'Let's face it, his first visit was not quite what we had planned. I hope he wasn't too upset?'

'He was fine. He said he'd be in touch,' said Maisie, nonchalantly turning the pages.

Kathy wondered how her sister could sit there, so unconcerned, as if nothing at all had happened, showing not a bit of remorse for the havoc she'd created. She wanted to shake her until her teeth rattled, but in deference to her mother she remained silent.

'Kathy,' said Annie, 'will you come and give me a hand? Bring a torch; I need to get something from under the stairs in the hall.'

The two of them extricated the camp bed from the mishmash of stuff stowed away in the glory hole and carried it between them to the foot of the stairs.

'Where are you going with that?' Maisie asked, coming into the hall.

'Mind your own business!' Kathy snapped, and proceeded to climb the stairs behind her mother.

Wilf Bates was filled with trepidation as he put the key in the lock on his return from the pub. Maisie with her big mouth had certainly put the cat among the pigeons, and he wondered how Annie was going to react. He knew he had no choice but to face her.

Both the girls had gone to bed without exchanging another word with each other and Annie was sitting by the fire, listening to the wireless. When Wilf entered the living room, she looked up and stared at him, waiting to see what he was going to say.

Playing for time, he took off his coat and hat, hanging them up behind the door.

'It's very cold tonight,' he said. There was no response from his wife.

Sitting down opposite her, he said, 'Look, Annie, love, I can't tell you how sorry I am about Betty. I don't know what came over me.'

Calmly, she said, 'That's all right, Wilf. You made your choice. Best go and pack your clothes and move in with her permanently, then we'll all know where we stand. There'll be no more need for pretence.'

Shocked to the core, he said, 'Move in with her? Whatever do you mean?'

'Inasmuch as you seem to like sharing her bed rather than mine, it's best you go – and take your dirty washing with you. I've put it in a pile on the bed.'

'You've got it all wrong, Annie. I don't want to go and live with her.'

'I don't suppose her husband will think much of the idea either, but when he comes home you'll just have to tell him what's been going on and hope he's as understanding as I am!'

'Christ, Annie! Are you out of your mind?'

'Please don't swear, Wilf, especially on a Sunday, and especially when I'm being so accommodating. No, you run along, back to your blonde.'

'But I don't want to go to her! I want to stay with you. You are my wife, this is my home, you and the girls are my family.'

Annie's anger rose. 'True, but you were able to forget that fact every time you climbed into bed with Betty Langdon!'

Wilf was panicking now. 'Please let me stay, Annie, love. I know I did wrong and I'm sorry. If I could turn back the clock, I would. Don't turf me out!'

'Give me one good reason why I should let you stay,' she demanded.

'Because I love you and the girls.'

She was scathing in her reply. 'You don't know what real love is. If you did, we wouldn't be having this conversation.'

Wilf was desolate. 'Annie, I beg you, on bended knee if you want, please let me stay. I'll do anything, anything at all, if only you'll forgive me.'

'Forgive you?' With a withering look, she said, 'I'm not at all sure I'll ever be able to do that. I'll certainly never trust you again.'

'You have my word, on the girls' lives, I'll never be so stupid again.'

'How dare you use the girls to swear by! Not only were you unfaithful to me, but you were unfaithful to them as well. You put everything in jeopardy for a bit of sex on the side! Well, I just hope it was worth it!'

'Nothing is worth losing my family for! I just couldn't believe a young woman would want me, that's all. It was madness on my part.'

'Had you fallen in love with another woman, I would find it easier to understand. That can happen to anyone. But you! You were a middle-aged man tempted by a bit of skirt, and you ought to have known better.'

She paused for what seemed to Wilf an interminable time, and then she said, 'Very well, I will give you a second chance, for the sake of the girls. Frankly, I'm not sure that I, personally, want you around at all.'

'Oh, thank you, Annie. I give you my word

you'll never regret it.'

She just raised an eyebrow and didn't reply.

'Would you like a hot drink before we go to bed?' he asked.

'No thanks. I'm too tired; it's been a traumatic day one way and another.'

'Well, let's hope a good night's sleep will help us all,' he said, and they went up the stairs together.

On the landing, in an alcove beneath a window, was the camp bed, all made up with clean bedlinen and ready for use.

'What's that?' Wilf asked.

'That's where you'll be sleeping from now on. Your clothes are still in my room, but please knock on the door first, if you need anything. Goodnight.'

Wilf was left standing opposite the door, which had been closed firmly in his face. Stunned, he sat on the edge of the camp bed, shaking his head in disbelief. If he was honest, it was what he deserved, he conceded. In fact he was lucky to still be in the house! Never had he seen Annie like this. So in control – so adamant – so sure of herself; he knew he was going to have to work hard to regain her respect and trust. The days of illicit sex were over. He would ask to be put on different ARP duties, because his paramour was not going to like it now that, after returning to her bed, he was once again going to end their relationship. He couldn't possibly work with her any more.

In the master bedroom, Annie Bates moved over into the middle of the bed and stretched out. How marvellous to have all this space to herself. No more being disturbed by Wilf's snoring, no more having to haul the bedding back to her side when her husband had rolled over and taken it with him. As for sex, it hadn't been that exciting, and at this moment she couldn't bear to let him touch her. In time, she'd allow him to share the room again, but not for a while. Oh no, not for quite a while. She snuggled down and was soon in a sound sleep.

On the landing, in the camp bed, Wilf tossed and turned, cursing the thin mattress which was already making his back ache, wondering just how long he was going to have to suffer such purgatory.

Jimmy Greene was lying on his bed, propped up with pillows, going over the dramas that had unfolded earlier that day. He couldn't get his head round the fact that his Kathy had been raped and not told him! He'd wanted to question her further about it, but she'd obviously been too upset. Disgusting pictures flashed through his mind as he contemplated what the two men had done to her. How hard had she fought, he wondered, and then was filled with guilt at such doubts. With two drunken men what chance did she have? Then there was the detective. Was this the fellow that Maisie had hinted Kathy was seeing during his absence? If so, what was the nature of their relationship? Was it more than just friends?

He'd been shocked to discover Wilf's infidelity. Wilf Bates, solid citizen, married man, partaking in extramarital sex? The way that Maisie had spat out that accusation was dreadful! So cruel and unfeeling. His heart went out to poor Annie, a woman for whom he had the greatest respect ... and then there was Maisie herself.

What was he to make of this wild child? She was in deep trouble and he was certain she didn't really understand the seriousness of her situation. She was selfish, self-centred, destructive and wilful. All these things. But, as far as he was concerned, she was different. She truly loved him. Loved him with a passion that was all-consuming. When she told him she would die for him, she meant every word and he believed her. Then when they were alone and she'd told him to kiss her ... he had done so. There wasn't any point in asking himself why. He'd done it because he'd wanted to. There was something about the girl that stirred him. Even four years ago, there had been a chemistry between them. Then it had been easy to dismiss as a schoolgirl crush, but now it was far more. And he knew it was dangerous.

Whereas he was apprehensive about it, Maisie revelled in it. When he'd kissed her, she'd looked into his eyes and laughed triumphantly.

'I knew you wanted me, Jimmy darling. I always knew it, even before you did. We belong together, you and me. We make sparks happen between us. Oh, I'm so happy,' and she smothered him with more kisses, until he held her away from him.

'There's been enough trouble in this house for one day,' he told her. 'I'm going home before this gets out of hand.'

'You silly, wonderful man,' she said as she walked to the door with him. 'It's already out of hand. I want you, and, although you won't yet admit it, you want me. I can wait.'

'Good night, Maisie,' he said as he left. Even after she closed the door, he could hear her humming with pleasure.

## CHAPTER TWENTY-EIGHT

In the Bates household, there was a feeling of an uneasy truce. Wilf was being very careful not to upset his wife any further and Maisie, although not apologising for her outburst, tried to be helpful, which was totally foreign to her nature and was treated with cool indifference by her mother.

Kathy was feeling nauseous. Realising her fears were now all but confirmed, she made an appointment to see her doctor. When she'd made the appointment, she rang Ian Harvey and asked him if he would go with her to explain her predicament.

'I don't think I can face this alone,' she told him.

'You don't have to, Kathy. I'll be there to hold your hand.' And he was.

The doctor confirmed her pregnancy as Ian sat beside her in the surgery. The detective took Kathy's hand in his and spoke to the doctor.

'You realise the situation, sir. No one can expect Kathy to carry this child.'

The doctor nodded sympathetically.

'I do understand,' he said. 'I'll make arrangements for Kathy to be admitted to the hospital for a termination as soon as possible. If you wait a moment, I'll call them now.' After a quick discussion on the telephone, he had arranged a bed for her, three days hence.

'Thank you,' Kathy said. 'I just want this over with.'

She and Ian walked back through the park, holding hands. They stopped and sat on a bench beneath a tree – now devoid of leaves – and chatted.

'When will you tell your fiancé about this?' Ian asked.

'Tonight. We're going out for a meal. I've not mentioned the fact that I might be pregnant.' With a wry smile she added, 'Poor Jimmy, he's finding it hard enough to deal with the fact that I was raped. Goodness knows how he'll take this news.'

'If he loves you, Kathy, he'll support you.'

She became thoughtful, and then said slowly, 'I got the feeling that he thinks I should have managed to escape from those men, that perhaps I didn't put up much of a fight.'

Ian was horrified. 'Didn't you tell him that we were able to recognise the perpetrators by the deep scratches on their faces?'

'To be honest, I've hardly discussed it with him at all.'

'So he has no idea what you went through?'

'No. Frankly I found it impossible to tell him. I haven't told anyone ... not even you. I want to forget about it, not recall every filthy detail!'

He wanted to take her into his arms and comfort her, but instead he asked, 'Will he take you to the hospital and stay with you?'

'I don't want him there. It's going to be bad enough as it is, without my having to worry about how he's coping with it. He makes me feel guilty.'

'Very well then, I shall come with you. You are *not* going alone!'

'Would you? I should be so grateful if you would. You make me feel so secure, Ian.'

This time he did hold her. Pulling her close to him, he said, 'Oh, Kathy, Kathy, if I could have saved you from going through all this I would. But you're like your mother, you have her spirit. You'll get through it, you'll see.'

'Then afterwards,' she said, 'there'll be the court case. I'm not looking forward to that, having to describe what happened for all and sundry to hear.'

'I've thought of that,' Ian said. 'I'm trying to get the case heard in a closed court. The public won't be allowed in.'

'Can you do that?'

He stroked her hair. 'I can try.'

'It would be wonderful if you could. I suppose that Maisie will have to appear in an open court when her case comes up?'

'Yes, I'm afraid so.'

With an anxious frown she said, 'I wonder what will happen to her?'

'Don't you worry your head about your sister, Kathy. Maisie will always cope with what life throws at her and, believe me, she'll always come up smelling of roses! You worry about yourself.' He looked at his watch. 'I'll walk you home, then I have to get back to the station. I've a lot of paperwork to get through. I probably won't see you for the next two days, but I'll pick you up and take you to the hospital. I promise.'

When Kathy walked into the living room, Annie was in uniform ready to go on duty. She took one look at her daughter and asked, 'What's wrong?'

'I'm pregnant, Mum.'

'Oh, love,' said Annie, enfolding her. 'I was afraid you might be.'

'You guessed?'

'I've had two children. I recognised the signs. So, what happens now?'

Removing her coat Kathy told her. 'In three days' time I go into hospital for a termination. Ian is coming with me.'

'And Jimmy?'

'I'll tell him this evening, but please don't tell Dad or Maisie. I couldn't face that at the moment. Now go along or you'll be late. I'm fine, honestly.'

Jimmy Greene was in a particularly good mood that evening. The physiotherapy he was having was helping him a great deal, and he was without any serious pain. Soon he hoped to do away with his crutches and use a stick until his injury was completely healed. The only thing that marred his euphoria was the fact that eventually he might be returned to his company. However, he would meet that problem when it arose. Tonight he was going to ask Kathy to marry him before he could be sent away. It would be a night to celebrate.

He collected her in a taxi and took her to the Belmont Hotel in Portswood Road.

'The food is supposed to be good here, considering there's a war on,' he told her, as they settled at a table.

They chose from the menu and ordered some wine, then Jimmy began. 'I may soon be able to get rid of my crutches,' he said. 'The physio is really pleased with my progress.'

'That's wonderful,' Kathy said, delighted for him.

He beamed at her. 'I'm beginning to feel normal again, thank God! I feel that now I can really start planning for the future, and that's what I want to talk to you about, darling.'

Kathy's heart sank. She had planned to tell Jimmy her news at the end of the evening, wanting him to enjoy their time together before she dropped her bombshell, but she couldn't possibly let him start making plans without knowing what was before her.

'I have something I need to tell you first, before we start to discuss the future.'

'You're looking dead serious, darling. Whatever is it?'

'I'm pregnant.'

His mouth fell open. 'You're what?'

'I was at the doctor's this morning and he confirmed it.'

Jimmy was speechless. He just sat and stared at her.

'I'm going into hospital in three days' time to have a termination.'

'Oh, my God!'

'Is that all you can say?' she asked, glaring over the table at him.

'I'm just so shocked. I had this evening all planned. I wanted to talk about our getting married ... and now you tell me this.'

Kathy, whose nerves were at breaking point, lost her composure. 'Well, I am *so* sorry I spoilt your plans, but this wasn't something I wanted to have happen to me, I can assure you!' She stared into his eyes. 'You have no idea, have you? I was brutally raped by two drunks, and I am now carrying a child fathered by one of them. How do you think I feel?' She threw down her napkin and ran out of the restaurant, almost blinded by tears.

Jimmy hurriedly paid the bill and followed as quickly as he could manage on his crutches. Outside he looked left and right, but Kathy was nowhere to be seen.

Ian Harvey had been kept busy for the past few days. The missing weapon from the bank raid had been discovered in the mud along the Esplanade by two teenagers who had been trying to fish at low tide. Ballistics had matched the gun with the bullet taken from the wounded guard and to Ian's delight there were fingerprints on the barrel which matched those of Bert Smart. In his panic to get rid of the weapon, the villain must have removed his gloves to enable him to throw it further away. The case was watertight now, along with the statements from Jack Winters and Maisie Bates. Both men had been before the court and charged and were now awaiting trial.

Sonny Nolan too had been arrested and charged with handling stolen goods and being in possession of an offensive weapon. The bullet that Ian had found on the premises was further vital evidence which helped to tie the racketeer in with Bert Smart. That and Jack's statement, followed by Maisie's which documented the delivery of the weapon, made his involvement a certainty.

Maisie was called back to the station, where Ian told her that if she appeared for the prosecution, it would help the police and her.

'After all,' Ian said, 'you were unaware of the contents of the parcel you delivered, and the judge will take your evidence into consideration when he comes to your dealings as a runner for Sonny Nolan.'

'Do you think I'll go to prison?'

'If you're lucky, you'll get away with a fine and be put on probation. You will have a criminal record, of course. That means if you do anything illegal in the future, the court will throw the book at you.'

'Well, I'm not going to be that stupid, am I?'

Ian sat studying her for a moment. 'I would hope not. I'm hoping that you've learned your lesson. But I don't think you realise the seriousness of having a criminal record.'

'What do you mean?'

'Do your employers yet know about your predicament and the impending court case?'

'Of course not! Do you think I'm crazy?'

'There is a possibility that when they do, and believe me, it will be in the local paper, they may dispense with your services, and finding another job could be a problem. Not many employers will consider anyone with a criminal record.'

Maisie cursed beneath her breath. Then, looking at Ian, she arrogantly proclaimed, 'Then I'd better get married. My husband can keep me!'

'Really?' He tried to hide a smile. 'Do you have anyone in mind?'

'Oh, yes. I certainly do. Can I go now?'

Gathering his papers together, he said, 'Yes, Maisie, and for goodness' sake keep your nose clean, for all our sakes.'

As she walked through the main thoroughfare of Southampton, Maisie's mind was working out her plan of action. If she lost her job, she would have no income, and if what Ian said was true, finding another job was going to be difficult. Yes, marriage was the answer ... as soon as possible if she had her way!

As she reached her front door, she saw Jimmy Greene approaching, now walking with one stick.

'Well, look at you!' she exclaimed.

He waved the stick in the air, grinning widely. 'Great, isn't it?'

'Indeed it is. Come inside and I'll make us a cup of tea to celebrate.' She settled Jimmy in a chair, raked the embers and made up the fire. 'Won't be a minute,' she called from the kitchen.

'What time will Kathy be home?' he asked.

'Not until late. She's working.' She came in carrying a tray with a teapot and two cups. The brown kettle on the fire was beginning to whistle. After warming the pot, she put in two spoonfuls of tea and poured the water on it.

'This may be a bit weak,' she told him, 'but until Mum gets our ration next week, we're a bit low.'

'That's fine,' said Jimmy. 'How's Kathy?'

Maisie looked puzzled. 'Haven't you seen

her lately?'

Pursing his lips he said, 'We fell out the other night when I took her out to dinner, and when I called the day after she wouldn't talk to me.'

This was great news as far as Maisie was concerned. 'Why are you wasting time with her, Jimmy darling? Things have changed since you went away. People change too. To be honest, I'm not at all sure that Kathy wants to settle down with you.'

'What are you getting at?'

'She's been through a great deal. Getting raped was a dreadful ordeal for her, and then of course there's Ian Harvey,' she said deviously.

'What about Harvey?'

Sipping her tea, she said, 'I was with them when they met at the Guildhall, and they became friends. It was all above board,' she hastened to add. 'He knew she was engaged, but of course when Kathy was raped, he handled the case. He was so supportive. I don't think she would have got through it without him, you know.' She sat back in her chair and smiled.

'Are you trying to tell me that now they are more than friends?'

'Oh, don't misunderstand me, Jimmy. I don't mean they've slept together, but it's fairly obvious that the man is in love with her!'

'She's pregnant, did you know?'

Maisie choked on her tea.

'Obviously you didn't. She told me just after we'd ordered our meal. That's what we had the row about.'

'Who is the father?' Maisie asked.

'One of the rapists, of course – at least that's what she said.' A frown furrowed his brow. 'Why did you ask that?'

'I really don't know. I'm sure she's telling you the truth.'

'She's going into hospital tomorrow to have it terminated. That's why I came round today. I was less than sympathetic, which was unforgivable. That was why Kathy blew her top.'

'The fact that she's going to have an abortion proves the fatherhood. She couldn't do that otherwise, could she? I could do with a bit of support myself,' Maisie continued. 'I've just come back from the police station. I'm going to be a witness for the prosecution in the case about the bank raid and I'm really scared.'

'Scared of what, being in court?'

She nodded. 'These men are really hard nuts. What if they send someone after me? After all, my testimony will help to send them down.'

'Oh dear, Maisie Bates, your middle name is trouble!'

'I can't seem to help the way I am. I want

different things from life. I want to live a little. Is that so bad?'

'No, of course not, it's the way you go about it that is, you silly girl.'

In a trembling voice she asked, 'Jimmy, would you please give me a cuddle?'

'Come here, you daft thing.'

She snuggled into his arms. 'I need someone like you to take care of me.' She buried her head in his chest with a satisfied smile on her face.

## CHAPTER TWENTY-NINE

On the morning that Kathy was due at the hospital, she stayed in bed as Maisie dressed for work. Before leaving the room, Maisie sat on Kathy's bed. 'Jimmy told me about you going into hospital today,' she said. 'I hope it all goes well.' She gave Kathy a quick hug and left the room.

Kathy threw back the bed covers and ran a bath. She had already packed a small bag the previous evening as the doctor had told her she would probably be kept in overnight. Once she was dressed, she went down to the kitchen, where Annie was waiting with a cup of tea for her.

'You all right, love?' her mother asked.

'Not really, Mum, if I'm honest. I'm carrying a new life, yet I'm about to end it. That doesn't make me feel great. The baby is innocent in all this.'

'And so were you, don't forget that, Kathy. Ask yourself, if you went through with the pregnancy, how would you feel about the child? It would be a constant reminder of what happened ... and when it was old enough to ask about the father, what would you say then?'

'Don't you think I've been through all this in my mind? I *couldn't* bring the baby up, I just couldn't.'

'And no one would expect you to. Once this is over, you can put it all behind you. Well, until the case comes to court, and then you can really move on.' She sipped her tea slowly. 'Jimmy will come round about it all, you'll see. When he called, he looked really concerned when I told him you wouldn't see him. I'm sure he's sorry.'

'It's too late, Mum. I needed his support then. If he really loved me he would have showed more understanding.'

'Men are funny creatures, love. A woman is stronger in adversity every time.'

'Ian isn't like that. He's been a rock to me.'

'Yes, I know, but then he's different from most. Maybe his job gives him a better understanding.'

As she spoke, there was a knock at the door.

'That'll be him now,' said Annie. 'I'll go and let him in while you put on your coat.'

'How's Kathy holding up?' were his first words as Annie opened the door.

'She's naturally upset,' she told him as she followed him down the hall.

'Hello, Kathy. All ready?'

'As I'll ever be. Shall we go?'

Annie walked to the door with them and gave her daughter a hug. 'I'll see you tomorrow. I've taken the day off.'

'Thanks, Mum,' said Kathy and kissed her cheek.

'I'll be there until she comes round,' Ian assured Annie. 'Don't you worry, everything will be fine.'

Ian parked the car in the hospital grounds and carried Kathy's case in one hand and gripped hers with the other. He waited until she was undressed and settled in the ward, then he sat by her bed and handed her some magazines.

'Take these. Time hangs when you're in here,' he said. 'I'll sit in the waiting room when they take you to the theatre and I'll be here when you wake up.'

Kathy suddenly leaned forward and clung to him.

He held her, trying to soothe her worries with words of comfort, until she let go of him. 'All right now?' he asked.

'Yes, thanks. I just needed a hug.'

Trying to lighten her mood, he chuckled and said, 'Believe me, I was more than happy to oblige. Any time in the future you feel the same, promise you won't hold back!'

She started to laugh quietly. 'Oh, Ian, what would I do without you?'

'Well, consider this, young lady. You only have to say the word and you will never need to be without me.'

Although he was still smiling, she knew he meant it.

'When this is all over, I'll give your offer serious consideration,' she told him.

'That makes me a very happy man, Kathy.'

At that moment a nurse came along to prepare her for surgery. Ian kissed her tenderly on the mouth and said, 'I'll see you very soon.'

Whilst Kathy was going through yet another of life's dramas, Maisie was suffering one of her own. She had almost reached the staff entrance of Tyrell & Green's when a rough-looking character grabbed her by the arm, pushed her up against the wall and threatened her.

'You had better be careful what you says in court about Mr Smart, or he'll do for you, missy. You never delivered no parcel to him from Sonny Nolan, you was never there, understand?'

‘I understand,’ she said, her legs trembling.

‘Be a pity to spoil that pretty face of yours, wouldn’t it?’

She was speechless with fear and just nodded.

‘Don’t you forget!’ he said and walked away.

Maisie was violently sick. There was no way she could go to work and behave normally; she was shaking from head to foot. She staggered across the road to Watts Park and found a seat. She took out a cigarette and lit it with trembling fingers. What was she to do? If she lied and didn’t give her evidence, as she had just promised, the judge would throw the book at her when her case came up and she would probably go to prison. Well, no way was she going to prison for a man like Smart! But how could she save herself without putting herself in mortal danger? Who could she turn to? Not the police, they couldn’t protect her all the time. She needed to think.

When Kathy came round from the anaesthetic, she slowly opened her eyes, wondering where she was.

‘Hello, Kathy.’ She felt her hand being squeezed and looked into the eyes of Ian Harvey. ‘I told you I would be here.’

Tears welled in her eyes and trickled down her cheeks.

'Now then, darling, it's all over,' he said and gently wiped her face. 'There's nothing to cry about, not any more.' And he kissed her hand and then her lips. 'I'm going to take care of you.'

'Thank you,' she said and closed her eyes.

Ian watched her steady breathing with a feeling of relief. No operation was without its dangers and to hear her voice was all the reward he needed. He sat, holding her hand, watching her sleep.

The barman at the Solent Social Club answered the telephone, then putting his hand over the mouthpiece called to one of his customers. 'Leo, there's a girl on the blower for you. She won't give me her name.'

Leo Banks ambled over to the bar. 'Hello?' He listened for a minute and asked, 'Where are you?' Then, after a few seconds, he said, 'Wait there until I come.' And he walked out of the club.

Twenty minutes later, he entered Watts Park, and in the distance saw a figure sitting on a park bench. He walked over and sat beside the girl.

'Now, what's this all about?'

'Thanks for coming,' said Maisie. 'I didn't know who else to call.' She told him the whole story about her being a runner for Sonny Nolan, about delivering the parcel to Bert Smart and how she'd been threatened that morning.

Leo listened carefully. 'You've got yourself in a right mess, girlie. Bert Smart doesn't make idle threats.'

'But I don't want to go to prison!' she cried. 'The police told me if I helped them, I would probably get probation. I don't want to go inside.'

Frowning, he said, 'No, you wouldn't like it, believe me. What makes you think I can help?'

'To be honest I'm not sure you can, but there was no one else to ask. And when I met you, the people around you seemed scared of you and that must mean you have some sort of power.'

He chuckled. 'You're not scared of me though, are you?'

'No, but I wouldn't like to upset you!'

That amused the villain and he burst out laughing. 'I like your spirit, girlie. I liked it when you came to the club, but you go where angels fear to tread and that can be dangerous, as you've found out.'

'Can you help me?' she pleaded.

He studied her and said, 'You know, you do remind me of my daughter. She had the same stubborn streak as you.'

'Does she live with you?'

'No, she's dead. Killed in a bar room brawl.'

'Oh, I'm so sorry,' said Maisie. 'I wouldn't

have asked if I'd known.'

'That's all right. It was a long time ago, but because of her, I *will* help you.'

The relief on Maisie's face was very apparent. 'Oh, thank you so much. What will you do?'

'You don't need to know, but I want you to give me your word you'll keep out of trouble from now on.'

'Believe me, I will. I've already been told, if I do get probation and don't keep my nose clean, they'll throw the book at me.' She gazed at Leo. 'I've been very stupid, but I know when to stop.'

The man got to his feet. 'This is the last time I want to see you, understand? This one time, I'll get you out of trouble, and after that you're on your own! Don't you dare let me down!'

Maisie stood up and hugged the man. 'Thank you, oh, thank you. I won't let you down. I promise.'

'If you do, you'll be sorry. Do I make myself clear?'

'Very. I told you, I wouldn't like to upset you.'

'No, you certainly would not! Now go home, and when it comes the time to give your evidence, you do so. There will be no more threats. You can count on that!' And he walked away.

Maisie slumped back on the bench, her

heart racing. She had no idea what the big man would do on her behalf but she suspected it would be violent. There was an air of menace about him ... and today, she *had* been frightened of him.

As Leo Banks walked back to the club, he muttered angrily to himself, 'Why do these bloody kids take so many chances?' If his daughter had done as he'd asked of her she would still be alive, he brooded, and now this stupid girl had got herself mixed up with the wrong crowd too, but he admired her spirit. The fact she had contacted him was a brave decision, although she probably didn't know anything about his background or she'd have run a mile. Still, however unknowingly, she had spoken to the one person who could do something about her predicament.

He disliked Bert Smart intensely. He was a chancer and had at times tried to move in on Leo's territory. It had caused several confrontations in the past, but Smart had come to realise that he, Leo Banks, was not a man to be crossed and had backed off. Leo and his men would make one call on Smart's gang. That's all it would take. Without their leader, the men that were left would be too scared of the consequences to defy him and he would send a message to the man himself. If Smart was sent down for some considerable time, the gang would soon dwindle. There was no one strong enough to lead them once he was out of the picture, which would suit Leo just fine.

That evening, Leo Banks went mob-handed to Bert Smart's house and confronted the remaining members of the gang.

They burst into the house, breaking down the door, then proceeded to beat the men sitting in the kitchen. It was absolute carnage, with blood spattered everywhere. He left in no doubt that they had all understood his warning.

The following day, Ian Harvey collected Kathy from the hospital and took her home. Annie was waiting with the obligatory pot of tea – and a mother's love.

Kathy, looking pale and wan, sat on the settee and let the sympathy wash over her like a comforting blanket. But as she sat there, she was filled with guilt at taking the life of this unborn child. Would she ever be able to come to terms with doing so? But what was the alternative? Would she have ever been able to love the child? It would have always been a reminder of the day it was conceived. What if she had grown to hate it? How tragic for an innocent child to have been robbed of a mother's love and with a rapist for a father. Yes, she was sore and uncomfortable, but the mental agony of her condition, if she was really honest, had been removed. She would have to learn to put all this behind her. She still had to face her time in court, but if the men pleaded guilty, she might not have to appear to give evidence at all and that would be a godsend. Her only problem now was Jimmy.

Ian sat beside her and handed her her tea. 'Here, drink this, it will do you good. Now you must take care the next few days and rest as the doctor said.'

'I don't know how to thank you,' she told him.

But he stopped her. 'Enough of that. You just get well.' He rose. 'I must get back to the station. I'll pop round in a day or two and see how you are, if that's all right?'

'Of course it is. And thank you.'

He leaned forward and kissed her, then, giving Annie a hug, he left.

'That man is worth his weight in gold,' said Annie quietly as she sat beside the fire.

'Yes, I know.'

'I've made some soup. Would you like some?'

'That's just what I need ... and thanks, Mum, for being here today.'

'Where else would I be? I'll get the soup plates.'

Kathy put her feet up on the settee, snuggled down and sighed. Why was it that she suddenly felt like a child, she wondered?

It didn't matter how grown up you were, when you were poorly, the only place to be was at home and cosseted by your mother. She dearly hoped that one day she *would* have a child to love and cosset, one that was born of love with a man she wanted to spend her days with. She was engaged to Jimmy and they were supposed to be getting married, but was he the man she wanted to father her children? She wasn't at all sure that he was.

## CHAPTER THIRTY

Maisie made her way home after her meeting with Leo Banks. She would tell them at work tomorrow she'd been unwell, which wasn't a total lie. As she walked she wondered if her sister would be back from the hospital. Last night, when Kathy didn't return, Annie had explained why to her, not knowing that Jimmy had already told her. But she had been surprised when Annie said that Ian and not Jimmy had gone to the hospital with Kathy.

'Don't you find that a bit odd, Mum?' she had said. 'After all, Jimmy is engaged to Kathy, not Ian.'

'It was Kathy's own choice,' Annie

snapped. And the subject was closed.

When Maisie let herself into the house, she found Kathy curled up on the settee under a blanket with her mother pottering in the kitchen.

'How are you feeling?' she asked her sister.

'Not too bad. Why aren't you at work?'

'I didn't feel very well, so I sat in the park for a while, then decided to come home.'

'What's wrong with you?'

With a shrug Maisie said, 'I don't know really. I just came over a bit queer. It's worn off now but I thought I'd call it a day.'

A knock on the front door stopped any further conversation.

'Get that for me, Maisie,' called Annie from the kitchen. 'It's probably the milk-man; ask him for two pints, will you?'

It was not the milkman, Maisie discovered when she opened the door. It was Jimmy Greene, holding a large bunch of flowers.

'Maisie! I didn't expect to find you at home.'

She smiled warmly at him. 'Then this is your lucky day!'

He ignored her remark, asking anxiously, 'Is Kathy back from the hospital?'

The smile faded. 'Yes. You'd better come in.' She stood aside to let him pass.

Kathy was taken aback when Jimmy walked into the room. He crossed over to her and knelt beside her. Kissing her cheek, he asked,

'How are you, darling?'

'I'm all right. Well, a bit uncomfortable, of course, but fine. What on earth are you doing here?'

He pulled a chair over and sat down. 'I was worried about you, knowing what you were having to go through. If only you had let me talk to you when I called last time, I would have offered to take you to the hospital.'

'It's all right, Ian went with her,' Maisie volunteered.

'Maisie!' called her mother from the kitchen. 'Come and give me a hand, will you?' When her daughter reluctantly appeared, Annie grabbed her arm. 'Have you no sense at all? Can't you see that Jimmy wants to talk to Kathy without you hanging around stirring up trouble?'

'I only told the truth!'

With a knowing look Annie said, 'You were stirring. Now you keep out of it. Those two have a lot to discuss and they need privacy. Here, peel these potatoes for later.' She handed Maisie a knife. 'And keep your nose out of what doesn't concern you!'

Jimmy Greene was definitely displeased to hear that Ian Harvey had taken Kathy to the hospital. This man seemed always to be around! 'How did Ian come to take you to the South Hants?' he enquired.

'Because I asked him to,' Kathy told him. 'After our last conversation I couldn't imagine you would want to be there and frankly I didn't want you with me, not at that time.'

He looked contrite. 'I'm sorry about my reaction to your news. It was unforgivable, but it was as much of a shock to me as it must have been to you.'

'You just have no idea what I've been through. Perhaps that's understandable as you were away at the time, but Ian was here, and he helped me through it.'

'Do we still have a future together, Kathy?'

'Oh, Jimmy, your timing is dreadful! I've just had an abortion, for God's sake! How do you expect me to be able to think about the future at the moment?'

He was at a loss. He knew he'd been clumsy, but he wasn't sure how long he'd be home and he wanted to plan for the future before the army sent him away again. He got to his feet and put the chair back.

'I can see you are weary. I'll leave you to rest.' Stooping down beside her, he held her hand. 'I just want you to know that, more than anything, I want us to have a life together. But more than that, I want you to get better, *then* we'll talk again. All right?'

Kathy nodded her agreement. 'I'm sorry, Jimmy.'

'I just want you to be happy. I'll call again in a couple of days.'

Maisie heard him walking down the

hallway and rushed through the living room. 'I'll just see Jimmy off the premises,' she said.

'I'm sure he knows the way by now.'

Kathy's sarcasm wasn't lost on her sister, who chose to ignore it. She caught Jimmy as he was about to close the door. 'How about meeting me for a drink later?' she quickly asked. Before he could answer she said, 'I'll be at the Duke of Wellington in Bugle Street at seven o'clock!' She closed the door.

'I just caught him,' she said as she walked through the living room.

'Of course you did, you nearly broke your neck rushing down the hallway!' retorted Kathy.

'I was just being polite.'

'Will you two stop!' Annie said. 'I don't want to hear you bickering. Maisie, make yourself useful and go to the greengrocer. He said he would be getting some oranges in about now.' She went to a drawer in the dresser and handed her daughter four ration books and some money. 'Here. We are allowed one for each person ... and don't eat yours on the way home!'

'Do you want anything, Kathy?'

'Will you get me a packet of twenty Craven A? I'm almost out of cigarettes. Pass me my bag and I'll give you the money.'

Both Annie and Kathy breathed a sigh of relief when Maisie had gone. 'That girl drives me round the bend sometimes,' Annie said. 'She was always in trouble, even as a small child; goodness knows what she'll be like when she has to go to court. I only hope she doesn't try to be clever when she's in the witness box.'

'She'll be too scared, Mum. It isn't something you look forward to. I'm dreading the thought of going.'

'Well, let's hope you won't have to appear, love.'

Letting out a deep sigh, Kathy said, 'It's just as well we don't know what's ahead of us, isn't it?'

Looking at her daughter with affection, Annie tried to comfort her. 'I know that your life looks a bit grim at the moment, but after Christmas when your case comes up, you'll be able to start afresh.'

'Jimmy wants us to get married and I think he's got the idea of bringing it forward so we can do it before he's sent back to his company.'

'Has he said as much?'

'Not in so many words, because I've stopped him talking about it, but I'm sure that's what he has in mind.'

'Is that what you really want, Kathy?'

Running her fingers through her hair, she said, 'To be honest, I don't know.'

'Well, I've always thought that when in doubt, don't,' Annie advised. 'Marriage is for life, or should be. With the wrong man, it's a life sentence. Better to be an old maid.'

Kathy chuckled. 'I've never thought of being one of those, I must confess. I want a home and children even after all this, but I'm not sure I'm ready for it yet.'

'Then don't for heaven's sake make any plans. You've got plenty of time ahead of you.'

Kathy pondered this advice and declared, 'You're absolutely right. I must tell Jimmy I won't be rushed into marriage; we'll wait until he's discharged. After all, this war can't go on for ever!'

Having finally come to a decision, Kathy settled more comfortably and read the magazines that Ian had bought her.

Maisie, having queued for ages to get her four oranges and then Kathy's cigarettes, strolled around window-shopping. Now that her contact with Sonny Nolan had been broken, she had no spare clothing coupons to buy new clothes, but as her wardrobe was now well stocked with her previous buys, it wasn't too disappointing. But hats didn't require coupons, so she wandered into Plummer's and spent time trying on every hat on the stands, preening in the mirrors one way and another, and ended up buying a smart brown felt model to wear that evening for her date with Jimmy. She was certain he would show up, as she hadn't given him the chance to refuse and she was sure he wouldn't want her sitting in the bar alone.

Walking home she was filled with the joy of anticipation at the thought of being with the man she so desired. Things were obviously not going well with Kathy and him, which suited her very well. She could comfort him and worm her way into his affection.

Maisie entered the saloon bar of the Duke of Wellington just after seven o'clock. She didn't want to be there early and sit alone. Apart from the locals, there were several British soldiers and some GIs there. It wasn't the done thing for a decent girl to enter a bar alone. Looking around, she saw Jimmy sitting by a table and walked over to him.

'Hello. I'm so pleased to see you.'

'You didn't give me much choice, did you?' he said.

She laughed. 'Now don't tell me you can't do with a bit of cheering up, and you know I always do that!'

'You are outrageous! What would you like to drink?'

'I'll have a gin and tonic, please.'

When he returned with the drinks he asked, 'Well, young lady, what's this all about? Why did you ask me to meet you?'

She gazed at him, eyes shining with mischief, and said, 'I need to see you, be near you – see you smile. Make sure you're getting better. After all, I came to see you in hospital – your welfare is my concern. Isn't that reason enough?'

'You are up to no good, Maisie Bates!'

'Well, darling Jimmy ... is that an offer? After all, I've been saving myself for you. Waiting in the wings, so to speak, until you get your priorities right!'

He started to laugh. 'Oh, Maisie, you really are a case.'

'There you are! I made you laugh. That alone must have been worth the drink you bought for me.'

'I used to laugh at your letters. They did cheer me up – they were certainly a welcome relief.'

'There you are then; I was doing my bit for the war effort.' She placed a hand on his knee. 'I felt close to you when I was writing. When you were away, I worried about you and I missed you so much, you have no idea.'

He gazed steadily at her. 'I don't understand this devotion to me that you have, Maisie. To be honest it is a puzzle to me.'

'It's no mystery. I've been telling you for ages, I love you with every fibre of my body. I always have and I always will.' There was no jollity about her now, no pretence.

'What am I supposed to do about that?'

'Love me, just once. If it is the only time we ever have together, I will always have that night to remember.'

'You're serious, aren't you?'

'I have never been more serious in my life. Please, Jimmy, do this one thing for me. I'll never ask you for another.'

He sat staring at her for a very long time, thinking about the conversation with Kathy, feeling more than a little aggrieved that Ian Harvey had once again been at the forefront of his relationship with his fiancée. He felt rejected. He took Maisie by the hand and said, 'Come with me.'

## CHAPTER THIRTY-ONE

Jimmy and Maisie walked into the Dolphin Hotel and up to the reception desk. 'I'd like a double room for one night for my wife and me,' Jimmy said.

'Yes, sir. Would you sign the register please?' Whilst Jimmy did so, the receptionist took a key from a rack and handed it to him. 'Do you require a porter to carry your luggage?'

'No, thanks. My wife is only here for a few

hours so we are travelling light.'

'Of course, sir,' she said knowingly. 'The lift is over there, your room is on the second floor.'

As the lift door closed, Maisie snuggled in to Jimmy. 'Mrs Greene. I do like the sound of that.' Gazing up at him, she added, 'You could get used to the idea, you know. I'd make you a good wife.'

'You never give up, do you?'

She just laughed.

The room was elegant, with its draped windows and matching bed covers. They turned out the overhead light, leaving the bedside table lights on, giving the room a more intimate glow. Maisie took off her coat and hat, throwing them on to a nearby easy chair; then, turning to Jimmy, she undid his battledress jacket and removed it.

'That's better,' she said, as she undid his tie. Then, putting her arms round his neck, she kissed him slowly and passionately.

As he returned her kisses, Jimmy undid the buttons down the front of her dress and slipped his hand inside to gently caress her breast.

Maisie was in heaven. Here she was in the arms of the man she'd lusted after and loved since she was fifteen. She'd fantasised about this man for so long – had pictured being in his arms, being kissed by him – and now it was a reality.

They stripped themselves of their clothes and lay on the bed together, exploring each other's bodies, kissing, fondling, drowning in their need for each other, without embarrassment.

'Oh, Maisie, Maisie, Maisie,' Jimmy moaned as he buried his head between her full breasts, 'you are so dangerous to know.'

Running her fingers through his hair she said, 'Tell me you have always wanted me. Tell me!'

'I've always wanted you,' he said in a voice husky with desire.

She was triumphant. 'I knew it! Kiss me, Jimmy, and then show me how much.'

He rained kisses on her lips, her neck, her breasts, ran his tongue down over the mound of her stomach, and then her womanhood, making her writhe with ecstasy.

'Oh, my God,' she cried, 'I never knew it could be like this. Please don't stop.'

He sat astride her. 'Stop? Are you crazy? I couldn't stop now if I wanted to and I certainly don't want to.' He slowly entered her and smiled to himself as she moaned, murmuring words of love. Demanding even more from him.

'You are an insatiable little minx,' he cried as he rode her. 'My God, I haven't known a woman like you. You're wonderful!'

'How many have there been before me?'

With a chuckle he said, 'A few.'

They eventually lay entwined together, satisfied, Maisie gently caressing her lover, kissing him softly, bathing in a glow of happiness.

'Did I make you happy?' she asked.

'You made me very happy,' he answered, kissing the top of her head and stroking her blonde hair. 'But then I'm not your first man, am I, Maisie? You've done this before, that's obvious.'

Ignoring this, she said, 'We are going to stay all night, aren't we?'

'If we did, what would your mother say? Wouldn't she be worried?'

'No,' said Maisie. 'I told her I would be staying at a friend's house.'

He looked at her with some surprise. 'You were taking a lot for granted. How could you be sure I would fall in with your plans?'

She smiled lovingly at him. 'How could you possibly refuse me? I knew deep down you wanted me, I just hoped it was enough ... and you see, I was right.'

He started to laugh. 'Oh, Maisie, you are incredible. Life would certainly not be dull with you around.'

She snuggled closer. 'You could always find out just how much fun we could have. I told you we spark together, we belong ... when are you going to see that?'

'I am engaged to your sister. This changes nothing.'

'If you really loved her, you wouldn't be here with me. There has always been a chemistry between us, if only you would have admitted to it. Kathy could never love you as much as I do.'

'You don't get it, do you? You asked me for one night and this is it. I still am in love with Kathy and we will get married when I'm demobbed.'

She was livid. 'How could you have made love to me as you did, and still love my sister?'

'Sex and love for a man don't necessarily have to go together, Maisie. In your case you have been throwing yourself at me for years, and now you're a grown woman, sexy, needy, wanting me so much that you never gave a thought to betraying Kathy. And here we are!'

Her eyes narrowed as she looked at him. 'You didn't care about betraying her either, so don't make me out to be the only sinner here.'

'Kathy and I are at odds with each other right now, but we'll sort things out. If you feel badly about it, you can leave.'

She gave a wicked chuckle. 'Don't be ridiculous, the night isn't over yet. I might as well be hung for a sheep as a lamb,' and she climbed on top of him.

Christmas Day was cold and crisp. The Bates

family were sitting round the table eating breakfast together, planning the day ahead.

'Dinner will be ready after the pub shuts,' said Annie. 'You girls can help me prepare the vegetables. We'll put the turkey in the oven, the pudding in the steamer, and then we can all go down to the pub for a drink.'

'Turkey, Mum. How lovely,' Kathy said enthusiastically.

'The butcher and I are pals,' Annie said. 'His wife and I work together in the WVS and that helps a great deal. Is Jimmy meeting us at the pub?'

Maisie pricked up her ears and listened.

'Yes,' said Kathy. 'He thanked you for the invite, and he's looking forward to it.'

'What's Ian doing over the holiday?' Annie asked.

'He's spending it at home with his parents.'

'You've seen him lately then?' Maisie enquired.

'We had a meeting with the solicitors handling the rape case. They are waiting to see if the two men are going to plead guilty or not. It comes to court in three weeks' time. I'll be glad when it's over.'

'Well, we don't need to dwell on it today,' said Annie firmly. 'After breakfast we'll open our presents before we do the veg.'

At noon, the family walked to the local pub just along the road. The bar was decorated extravagantly with paper chains and paper lanterns. Along the shelves behind the bar, holly and mistletoe lay among the bottles. Tom the landlord was wearing a Santa hat. He greeted every customer warmly, and carols were playing on the wireless in the background, which added to the festive spirit.

As they settled at a table with their drinks, Annie looked round at her family and smiled with satisfaction. Wilf and she had survived his affair with Betty Langdon; Kathy was now fit after her abortion and seemed to be coping with life, although she and Jimmy had yet to name a day to wed. And Maisie ... she wondered about her younger daughter. Something about her had changed in the past weeks. She didn't seem so happy-go-lucky. Yes, she still went dancing and met her friends for various outings, but it was as if a light had gone out in her character somehow. Annie would catch her watching her sister every now and again, and she wondered why. Shrugging off these thoughts, she joined in with the singing in the bar.

Maisie was on edge waiting for Jimmy Greene to arrive. After their night of passion, he'd not treated her any differently when he called to see Kathy, or take her out. It was as if nothing had happened between them at all. She wondered how he could do it. It had broken her heart to think he could have taken their time together so lightly when to her it had been so important. She walked to the bar and bought herself another gin and tonic.

Wilf saw her do so, and turned to Annie. 'Maisie is knocking them back a bit, isn't she?'

'It's Christmas, Wilf, that's all. She's just enjoying the atmosphere here.'

At that moment, Jimmy walked into the bar. He saw where the family were sitting and crossed over to ask what they were drinking before going over to the counter.

Maisie sidled up to him. 'Hello, you gorgeous man. Happy Christmas!'

'And to you, Maisie. I'm in the chair. What are you drinking?'

'Gin and tonic, please. I'll help you carry the glasses over to the table if you like?'

She sat back and watched him hand round the drinks, then sit beside Kathy, kiss her and put his arm round her shoulders. It was as if someone had plunged a knife into her heart, it hurt so much. Jimmy had made it very clear to her that he still intended to marry her sister, but deep down she still held on to the thought that she could win him over.

Two hours later, it was a merry crowd who poured out of the local, everyone going off in different directions to enjoy their Christmas fare. Wilf took Maisie by the arm as she was a bit unsteady on her feet.

'What you need, girl, is some food inside you,' he told her.

Waving an arm in the air she cried, 'Merry Christmas, Dad! What a great morning that was, wasn't it?'

'You're drunk!' he snapped.

She giggled. 'Do you know, I do believe I am. How perfectly splendid!'

'I'll get your mother to make you some coffee when we get home.'

'Oh, Daddy dear, don't be such an old fuddy-duddy. Let's dance. Come on, let's you and me show these others how it's done.'

'Will you behave yourself!' And with some difficulty he kept control of her until they reached the house, when Annie insisted she sit and drink a cup of strong coffee.

'Kathy and I will see to the dinner. You are more than useless right now.'

'Sorry, Mum.' Maisie slurred her words as she took the cup.

In the kitchen Annie muttered angrily to Kathy, 'I don't know what's got into her today, I really don't!'

'She just got carried away with the Christmas spirit, that's all.'

'In more ways than one!' snapped Annie.

Eventually everyone sat down at the table. To her delight Maisie found herself seated next to Jimmy. 'I had a great time in the pub. Did you have a great time in the pub too?' she asked, still in an inebriated state.

He grinned with amusement. 'Not as great as you did, I think.'

'I love Christmas,' she continued, and had started to say something else when her father spoke.

'Maisie! Shut up! Eat your food.'

She looked at Jimmy and pulled a face just like a naughty child, and started giggling. Then under the table she moved her leg against his, pressed it slightly and gazed lovingly at him.

The conversation during the meal went from one subject to another with ease and some merriment, planning what they would do when the war was over. How things would be so much better.

'Imagine no rationing!' exclaimed Annie. 'I can't wait to wear a decent pair of stockings and to be able to go into the butcher's and buy a joint of meat of my choice. And how I long for bread made with white flour instead of the National Loaf, which is like cardboard!'

'I want the end to utility clothes,' said Kathy. 'I want collars, cuffs and pleats back, not skimped seams.'

'I'll settle for a bottle of Scotch,' Wilf volunteered. 'An occasional glass from under the counter is enough to ruin the soul of a man.'

'I just want to leave the army and get back into civvy life,' Jimmy stated. 'That would be enough for me to start with.' He smiled across the table at his fiancée. 'Then perhaps I can at last get Kathy to marry me.'

'I might run away with the milkman instead,' she teased.

'Or a detective!' Maisie chipped in.

Jimmy stared hard at her. 'Don't start,' he warned, but Maisie, still in an alcoholic haze, was beyond caring.

Lolling back in her chair she looked at Kathy through glazed eyes. 'Why don't you come clean? You're leading Jimmy on, that's all. You're in love with Ian Harvey and he with you. Why don't you admit it once and for all?'

'Why don't you mind your own business!' Kathy retorted.

'No, I'm not going to. Why should I? I love Jimmy with all my heart and have always done so. Can you say the same, Kathy? Well, can you?'

Jimmy intervened. 'Maisie, you've said enough. It's Christmas Day, after all. Don't spoil it for everyone.'

'Yes, Christmas, goodwill to all men and all that bosh, well let's have a bit of good will here!' She was seething now. 'Stop leading Jimmy on, Kathy! He will have to go back to his company when he's better – are you going to send him away believing a lie? Well, *are* you?'

No one spoke. The air was filled with tension.

Jimmy looked at Kathy, waiting for her answer. She said nothing.

Maisie was triumphant. 'Don't feel too guilty, sister dear. Jimmy's not quite the innocent in all of this, otherwise he wouldn't have slept with *me!*'

'He what?' Kathy demanded.

'A couple of weeks ago, so if you do marry him don't go to the Dolphin Hotel because Mr and Mrs Greene have already stayed there!'

There was uproar around the table. Everyone spoke at once.

'Maisie, whatever are you saying?' Annie was aghast.

'How dare you sit there and say that?' Wilf thundered.

'Because it's true! Ask Jimmy!'

Kathy stared across the table at her fiancé. 'Is this true or is Maisie just stirring up trouble again?'

Jimmy Greene remained calm. 'Yes, it's true. Now you answer Maisie's question as honestly. Are you in love with Ian Harvey?'

Everyone stopped shouting to listen to her response.

It was immediate. 'Yes, I am.' Taking off her engagement ring, she held it out. 'I'm really sorry.'

With a sardonic rise of his eyebrows he said, 'I'm sorry too.' Pushing his chair back he got to his feet. 'Thank you, Mr and Mrs Bates, for a lovely lunch. I'm sorry your day has ended like this after you've gone to so much trouble, but now I think I should leave.'

Maisie started to get up, but Wilf pushed her back into her chair. 'You stay put, my girl. You've made enough trouble for one day.' And he walked down the hall with Jimmy Greene.

Opening the door he said, 'How could you have done such a thing! Hasn't Kathy been through enough without having to learn that you took her sister – my daughter – to bed?'

Jimmy Greene's cheeks flushed but he said, 'It seems as if Kathy doesn't want me anyway. I'm sorry to have spoiled your day, Mr Bates.' And he walked out of the house.

Wilf walked slowly back to the living room and sat down. 'Well, I really don't know what to say.'

Kathy glared at her sister. 'Are you satisfied now?'

'Yes!' she said defiantly.

'You really have no morals at all, do you? You slept with my fiancé and didn't give a damn.'

'That's right. You've been playing footsie with Ian long enough; I can't see there is much difference.'

'Ian and I were just friends. I never shared his bed.'

With a sly grin Maisie said, 'But I bet you would have liked to.'

Annie had had enough. 'Just shut up! You might be my daughter, Maisie, but I am ashamed of you. You set out to trap that lad; I've watched you try your tricks on him for years. You were trespassing. He belonged to someone else.'

'You wouldn't have thought so the other night.'

Annie slapped her hard across the face. 'You're nothing but a trollop!'

The slap and her mother's accusation seemed to sober Maisie.

Her arrogant air disappeared. 'I just happened to be in love with him. Is that a sin?'

'But he wasn't free, Maisie, and that's what makes it so wrong.'

'And you went to bed with him!' Wilf cried.

Annie shot him a look that was filled with danger and he shut up, remembering his own indiscretion.

'Well, it's all water under the bridge now, Mum,' said Kathy. 'I suppose it was going to happen eventually, breaking my engagement, I mean.' She looked at her sister with an icy stare. 'As for you, don't you come to me when you are in trouble ever again. As far as I'm concerned, from now on I don't have a sister. You have destroyed that bond for ever.' She rose from the table, collected the dirty dishes and walked out of the room.

## CHAPTER THIRTY-TWO

Boxing Day in the Bates household was very strange. The Christmas spirit had disappeared with Maisie's outburst at the dinner table. The repercussions had taken the joy out of the festivities altogether. Kathy was subdued and Maisie was suffering from a giant-sized hangover and being ignored by the rest of the family. She made herself a cup of tea, took an aspirin and returned to her bed. Kathy had eaten hardly any breakfast and gone for a walk, leaving her parents to talk over the events together.

'Although I think Maisie behaved disgracefully,' Annie remarked, 'she actually brought things out in the open. Kathy didn't want to marry Jimmy because she's fallen for Ian, and, although I'm fond of Jimmy, Ian is the man for her, in my opinion.'

'Well, he was here when she needed someone and Jimmy wasn't,' said Wilf.

'No, it's more than that. Ian is older and

more a man of the world. His work will have made him into that. He saw Kathy after she'd been raped and knew what she'd suffered and, what's more, understood her anguish. Jimmy didn't, and I don't blame the lad for that.'

'I'm not at all sure I agree with you,' argued Wilf. 'Young Jimmy has been on the battlefield. He knows what suffering is.'

'Ah, yes, but this was his woman and sex was involved. That makes it different. Men are funny about that.'

Wilf thought it safer to keep out of such conversations. He didn't want to talk about sex with his wife in case his affair was brought up. 'Well, what's done is done. Do you think Kathy will go and see Ian now she is a free woman?'

'I've no idea. We'll just have to wait and see.'

Coincidentally, Kathy Bates was asking herself the same question. She had told Ian she would think about his offer, but she was reticent about going to him. She knew she wanted to be with him, but after everything that had happened she was confused. Was she ready for another serious relationship yet? She still had to face the court case before she could think about any future.

She was sorry to have broken her engagement to Jimmy the way she did, but she had been shocked to discover he had actually taken Maisie to a hotel and spent the night with her. Had anyone asked her about such a possibility she would have bet her life savings that he would be faithful to her. The revelation had shaken her to the core. He didn't even look guilty when he confessed to them all that it was true! As for Maisie ... what could she think? She knew her sister's failings, but never, never, did she imagine she would betray her in such a way. It was unforgivable.

Ian had spent Christmas Day with his parents and a few relations. It had been a happy time, but throughout the day he'd thought of Kathy, wondering how things were between her and Jimmy Greene. Now she was seeing more of him would she decide to marry him after all? He, no doubt, would join her family for the festivities. Would they plan to marry before he returned to his company? The very thought drove him to distraction. He loved this brave woman with all his heart and he was going to lose her to another man.

Later that day, Maisie, feeling somewhat recovered, dressed and came downstairs. She made herself a sandwich and a cup of tea and told her parents she was going out. She walked purposefully to Jimmy Greene's house and knocked on the door. His mother opened it, to Maisie's disappointment.

'Can I speak to Jimmy, please?'

'He's not here, Maisie. He went out this morning early and I don't know when he'll be back. Can I give him a message?'

'No, it's all right, thanks,' she replied and walked away.

Where was he, she wondered? She so wanted to see him. After all, he was free now. Kathy, having returned his ring, had given her a clear field and she was determined to continue their newfound relationship. She had no doubt that he would want that too, because hadn't they had a wonderful time together? They belonged to each other; now, surely, he could see that. She'd just have to wait, that's all. There was a bitter winter chill in the air, so, reluctantly, she returned home.

Jimmy Greene was sitting in a pub, slowly getting drunk. The future he'd looked forward to so much had gone up in smoke. Kathy was in love with another man! He ordered another pint. He sat remembering the many times he'd looked at her picture to help him through the hard times when he was fighting in France.

He had been a fool to take Maisie to the Dolphin Hotel. He should have realised she wouldn't be able to stop herself from crowing about it to her sister. If it hadn't come out yesterday, it would have done at a later date. Then Maisie had forced Kathy's hand, which infuriated him. Given time, he felt he could have won her over. Yes, that Ian bloke had been a rock to her during her traumatic days, but he and Kathy had a great relationship, built up over the four years they had courted, which he felt could have been rekindled had he been given more time with her ... and now it was too late.

Maybe if he could talk to her and get things sorted out, they might still stand a chance. He would give her a couple of days to cool down and then call on her. If they could go somewhere and talk things out together, fences could be mended. Yes, that's what he would do, he decided. He downed the remains of his glass and walked home.

Having found out what shift Kathy was working, two days later, Jimmy was waiting outside the factory. He scanned the crowd of people as they swarmed out, making way for others coming in to start their shift. He almost missed her, but just caught sight of her walking along the road with her friend. He ran and caught up with her.

'Hello, Kathy. Can I have a word?'

'Jimmy! You took me by surprise.' Looking at her friend, she said, 'I'll see you tomorrow,' and turned back to Jimmy. 'I'm glad you came. I need to talk to you.'

He was delighted. 'Shall we go for a drink somewhere quiet, then?'

'I'm not exactly dressed to socialise. Does it matter?'

'Of course not. Come on, we'll go to the pub round the corner.'

They sat with two halves of bitter and Kathy spoke first. 'I just wanted to say how sorry I was that Christmas Day turned into a nightmare.'

'Yes, it certainly did. Look, darling, I hope you can forgive me for sleeping with Maisie. It was a moment of madness and it didn't mean anything. It doesn't mean that I don't still love you and I still want you to be my wife.'

She just stared at him. 'How can you sit there and say that it ... didn't mean anything? Is that supposed to make me feel better?'

'Well, no...'

'No indeed! For your information it doesn't! Not only did you sleep with another woman, you slept with my own sister!'

'I know, I know, but if you could find it in your heart to forgive me, it will never happen again, we can get over this. Start afresh. I'm still in love you, Kathy!'

She took a sip of her beer and looked at Jimmy Greene. But she knew that he was different now from the man she'd loved for years. That man would never have betrayed her. 'Ah, well, that's the difference, you see. I'll always have a place in my heart for you, Jimmy, but I am no longer in love with you. If I'm honest, I fell in love with Ian a long time ago, but I didn't realise it until just lately.'

'In other words, Maisie and I didn't make a difference.'

'Oh, believe me, it made a difference! My mother may have two daughters but I do not have a sister! Not any longer. I will never be able to forgive her. You can have her for all I care and good luck to the two of you!'

'But I don't want her.'

'Then you'll break her heart – and maybe that will be her punishment.'

'Oh, Kathy! After all we've planned together.'

'Yes, and that's sad,' she said, 'but better to make a break now than after we were married.'

'I suppose you've seen Ian Harvey and told him you're now free?'

'No, as a matter of fact I haven't. I have a court case coming up and I can't even begin to think of anything else.' She stood up. 'I hope we'll always be friends, Jimmy, but that's all we'll ever be.' She leaned forward and kissed him softly. 'Goodbye. Take care of yourself.'

Jimmy watched her walk out of the bar, knowing their future together was over. And it was all his fault.

The following week, Ian got in touch with Kathy to discuss the forthcoming trial. He suggested meeting over a drink instead of at the station. He thought it would be less formal and easier on Kathy. Although he longed to see her, he dreaded hearing that she'd set the date for her wedding.

For her part, Kathy was equally nervous. At this stage she didn't want Ian to know she'd broken her engagement as she didn't want to be under any further pressure. All she could think about was having to face the men who had raped her in a courtroom. It was giving her nightmares.

When she walked into the lounge bar of the Polygon Hotel, she saw Ian sitting with his back to her. She could feel her heart pounding and longed to touch the neatly cut dark hair and gently caress his neck, but she took a deep breath and walked up to the seat beside him.

'Hello, Ian.'

He stood up and kissed her on the cheek. 'Kathy, how lovely to see you. Sit down and I'll get you a drink.'

She removed the glove on her right hand but kept the other on, thus hiding the fact that she was no longer wearing Jimmy's ring.

On his return, Ian talked about the forthcoming trial. What would happen if she was called to the witness box; trying to reassure her that her solicitor would guide her through the examination.

'It won't be easy for you, Kathy, and you will be cross-examined. All you do is try to remain calm and answer the questions put to you. If they plead guilty, you will be spared this ordeal, but as yet we don't know the situation, I'm afraid.'

'I'm dreading it,' she confessed.

Ian longed to hold her to reassure her. 'You'll do just fine. Afterwards, you'll be able to put it behind you and get on with your life.' He waited to see if she was going to tell him of her future plans, but she didn't.

'How's your family?' he asked.

'Fine. Mum's still doing her WVS work as well as queuing for anything that's going, cooking delicious meals out of nothing. Dad has been growing vegetables to help out.'

'And Jimmy?' He couldn't help it, he had to ask.

'Waiting to see when he'll be signed off to return to his regiment.'

She hadn't mentioned wedding plans and Ian was not going to ask. It would seem that it wasn't imminent or she would have done so, he felt.

They eventually parted company.

'I'll see you on the day of the trial,' he told her. 'Until then try not to worry too much. I'll be there to hold your hand if needed.'

He smiled at her, trying to give her some confidence.

'Thanks. I'm sure I'll need it.' She kissed him on the cheek and walked away. Much as she had longed to cling to him to feel the safety of his embrace, she knew she couldn't let her feelings show, not until all this was over. Then she would be able to think more clearly.

## CHAPTER THIRTY-THREE

The day that Kathy Bates had dreaded was fast approaching, when she would have to face the trial of the two men who had raped her. She had meetings with the solicitor who was appearing for the prosecution.

'I'm waiting to hear if the men have decided to plead guilty,' he said. 'If they do, you will not have to appear in the witness box.'

'What are the chances of that happening?' Ian asked, who was there giving moral support to Kathy.

'Hard to say. If they do plead guilty, it may make a difference to the sentence the judge hands down.'

'You mean they will get to spend less time in jail?' Kathy was appalled at the idea.

'Not by much,' the man told her, 'but when you are facing years inside – and they will do that – a few years off makes a great deal of difference.' He looked at her sympathetically. 'To you, that will seem very unfair, but believe me, they will go down for a considerable time. The notes about your injuries will make sure of that.' He hesitated, then tentatively said, 'Of course, if you allowed me to bring in the termination, their sentence would be much longer. We could truthfully say the trauma of it all had had a profound and continuing effect on you.'

Kathy paled. 'No, no! I couldn't bear that. I don't want that information brought up if it's possible to keep it out of the public domain.'

'I fully understand,' he told her, placing a hand on her shoulder. 'This is going to be an ordeal for you whichever way it goes. I need to let you know that the press will be there.'

Kathy covered her face with her hands. 'Oh, my God!' she murmured.

Ian put an arm around her. 'It will be a seven-day wonder, Kathy. People forget what they read very quickly.'

'I wish I could do the same,' she said. 'This is bringing it all back to me.'

He turned her face to his. 'When this is all over, you'll feel free of all this trauma.'

She didn't answer, just buried her face in his chest.

Maisie too was having to face up to her day in court. She would appear a week after Kathy. Not that the girls discussed this with one another. Since the debacle at Christmas, they spoke to each other only when it was unavoidable, which made living together as a family very uncomfortable. Both Annie and Wilf were finding the strained atmosphere hard to cope with.

'How long is this going to go on for?' Wilf asked his wife one evening when they were sitting together.

Annie shrugged. 'Until Kathy leaves home, I would think. According to her, she and Ian have been so busy with the trial that as yet they haven't spoken of the future. I just pray, when it's all over, we'll have a wedding to plan, if things work out as I hope.'

'Have you seen or heard anything of young Jimmy Greene?' he asked.

'I saw his mother the other day and she said he was soon being returned to his company. He's just waiting to be passed as fit.'

'Has Maisie seen him at all?'

'I've no idea – and I don't ask.'

It so happened that Maisie had bumped into Jimmy as she was leaving work the previous evening and had begged him to meet her tonight. He had reluctantly agreed and she was on her way now to see him. They had arranged to meet outside the bombed remains of Holy Rood Church.

Maisie was tense with nerves as she saw him waiting, but she smiled brightly. 'Hello, Jimmy! My word – no walking stick?'

He smiled back. 'No, at last I can walk under my own steam.'

'That's wonderful. I'm thrilled for you. Can we go somewhere to talk?'

'All right. Where do you suggest?'

'How about the Dolphin Hotel? We're only a few steps away.'

They walked into the entrance of the hotel where they had spent the night together. Then they had been happy; tonight the atmosphere between them was quite different.

Once they were seated with their drinks, Jimmy came straight to the point.

'What did you want to see me about?'

'I haven't seen you for ages, and I couldn't bear it any longer. I thought that now you are no longer engaged to my sister, you would have wanted to be with me. But you haven't been in touch. Why?'

He studied her closely. 'Why would you think that I would?'

She laid a hand on his arm. 'How can you say that after the wonderful night we spent together in this very hotel?'

He sipped his drink and said, 'But that's

all it was, one night. I thought I made that perfectly clear. And that's what you asked for – one night of love. That was it, Maisie.'

There was a steeliness in his tone which sent Maisie's heart plummeting. 'But now you are free we can spend many more nights together.'

He looked at her with amusement. 'A tumble with you, dear Maisie, would be lovely, but I'll be going away again soon and I think it best that we just get on with our lives.'

She was distraught. 'But I want to be part of your life. You want me, you know you do – you told me as much!'

'That was then, Maisie, and I did want you at the time, but I have no plans to make you a permanent feature,' he said cruelly. 'I loved Kathy, not you. I was deeply hurt when she broke our engagement. All my plans, the ones I dreamed about when I was in France, were all with her. Why can't you understand?'

'Yes, I *do* understand that, but things have changed! Oh, Jimmy, my love for you is far deeper than Kathy's ever was and I still feel the same, can't you see that?'

'Dear Maisie, that breaks my heart, but sadly, I don't feel the same. I'm not in love with you.'

'But you could be!' she pleaded. 'I made you happy that night, I make you laugh, you said life would never be dull with me. Don't you see what a wonderful time we could have together?'

He took both her hands in his: 'I don't deserve such devotion because I can't return it. I am *so* sorry.'

Tears welled in her eyes. 'Does this mean goodbye? Please tell me it doesn't.'

'You'll find someone else in time. Someone who loves you with the same depth of feeling as you have.'

'I don't want anyone else!' she cried.

'There's nothing more to say. Come along,' he said, getting to his feet. 'I'll take you home.'

Maisie walked beside Jimmy, blinded by tears, so desolate that she couldn't speak.

When they arrived at her house, Jimmy said, 'You have to grow up, Maisie. It's time you realised that the world doesn't turn around you and what you want. There are others to consider.'

'You didn't consider Kathy when you made love to me!'

'You're right, and although we enjoyed each other, I do regret letting your sister down. She didn't deserve that. Even if she hadn't fallen in love with Ian Harvey, she would never have forgiven me for betraying her.'

'Well, she certainly hasn't forgiven me; she only speaks to me when she has to!'

'She will one day, you'll see, but it will take time.'

She grabbed the front of his battledress. 'Please, Jimmy, don't turn your back on me. Don't throw my love for you back in my face. I couldn't bear it!'

Leaning forward, he kissed her forehead. 'Goodbye, Maisie. Take care of yourself.'

As he walked away she screamed after him. 'Come back, please come back!' But he kept walking.

Maisie fumbled as she tried to put her key in the lock. When eventually she did, she ran through the house, through the living room and up the stairs, sobbing her heart out.

'Bloody hell!' exclaimed Wilf to his wife, 'Whatever is wrong with her now?'

'Best not to ask,' Annie said. 'If she wants us to know, she'll tell us.'

Kathy Bates sat outside the courtroom with Ian, waiting for the trial to begin. Her hands were shaking. The men had elected to plead guilty in the end, so Kathy was being spared the witness box, but she insisted she wanted to sit in the courtroom and watch them being sent down.

'At least I can see justice done on my behalf,' she told Ian.

As he was a witness, Ian had to wait to be called, so Kathy, accompanied by her parents, left the detective and found seats inside. She gripped her mother's hand as the two men were brought up from the cells to stand in the dock.

Kathy stared hard at them, but to her they were strangers, standing to attention in their army uniforms. She found the whole thing quite surreal. However, as the day progressed and the prosecutor brought forth his witnesses, Kathy had to relive the whole episode.

The doctor was called and described her injuries, which made Annie cry out when she heard them. When Ian told about matching the bite marks on the victim to one of the defendants, it was too much for her. She had to leave the court.

As the soldiers gave their evidence, Kathy paled when the one with the deep voice spoke. In her mind she once again heard the filth he uttered as he used her, and she felt sick.

'Do you want to leave, love?' asked Wilf anxiously.

'No, Dad. I'm staying until they're sentenced.'

It was three days before her moment came. She sat up straight and dignified as the judge gave his decision. Most of what he said was a blur to her; she was only interested in the number of years they would spend behind bars. She did hear the judge say that they were both lucky not to be facing a charge of murder. He sent each of them down for ten years.

Outside, Ian was jubilant. He picked Kathy up in his arms and swung her round, kissing her as he put her down. 'You saw justice delivered today, Kathy. Those bastards have paid the price for what they did to you.'

'It wouldn't have happened if you hadn't found them,' she told him, blushing at his kiss.

'I would have spent every day of my life looking if I'd had to,' he declared. 'Come on, this calls for a celebration.' And he took them to the Polygon Hotel.

As Kathy and her parents joined him in drinking champagne, Annie said, 'Thank God that's over. You'll be able to get on with your life now, love,' and she hugged her daughter.

Although happy with the verdict, Kathy wasn't feeling jubilant. Hearing the second man's deep, rasping voice had brought back every detail of that horrendous night and her hands trembled as she held her glass. She wanted to crawl into a corner and hide.

Ian noticed and silently signalled to the others, who changed the subject and decided to take her home. Once there, she said she felt exhausted and went straight to bed.

'It'll take time,' said Ian, as he was about to leave, 'but she'll be fine eventually.'

Maisie, who had been very subdued since her encounter with Jimmy Greene, came home from work that evening and found a much happier atmosphere in the house. She surmised that the court case was over.

'What was the verdict?' she asked her father.

'They got ten years each,' he told her.

'How's Kathy?'

'She's exhausted and has gone to bed. Make sure you don't disturb her when you go up,' said her mother.

Maisie went upstairs and, walking into the bedroom she shared with her sister, found Kathy awake. 'I'm glad it's all over for you,' she said. 'It couldn't have been easy to sit and listen to it all.'

Kathy was floored by this unexpected sympathy and understanding. 'No, it wasn't easy at all.' She paused, then said, 'I hope your case goes well next week too.'

'Thanks,' Maisie said and went to the bathroom.

In the cells of Lewes Prison, Bert Smart was pacing the small space, muttering angrily, reliving the conversation he'd had during visiting hours last week when one of his men had come to see him.

'Where the hell have you been?' demanded Smart. 'You haven't been near me.'

The man looked shifty. 'We had a visit from Leo Banks, guv.'

'What the devil did he want?'

'He caused fucking chaos. His men gave us all a good thrashing, warned us off that girl. And he said, you behave and leave her alone or he'd do for you.'

'What's she got to do with him?'

'Beats me, guv.' He looked sheepish. 'I've got more bad news, I'm afraid.'

'Well, spit it out!'

'All the others have buggered off, mostly to the Smoke. I'm the only one left.'

'Are you saying they were more afraid of Banks than of me? Is that what you're saying?'

'Well, you're in here, ain't ya? He's on the outside and you know what a hard bastard he is. Yes, they were bloody terrified!'

Smart cursed loudly. 'It's that bloody stupid Jack Winters' fault. If he'd done his job right we would have been away with that money and Banks wouldn't be on my back. I'll find out where Winters is sent and I'll get word to someone inside the same gaff and I'll do for him! No one lets me down and gets away with it.' He glared at the man opposite and said, 'You come and see me after the trial and tell me where he is.'

'All right, guv, I will.'

And now, pacing up and down, Bert was still filled with anger and the lust for revenge. One day, when he was again, a free man, he would settle with Banks too. No matter how long it took. That bloody girl's evidence was going to send him away for a considerable time and there was nothing he could do about it!

## CHAPTER THIRTY-FOUR

The day of Maisie's court case arrived. She sat nervously waiting to be called into court. Her long-suffering parents were with her, trying to calm her nerves.

The solicitor for the prosecution talked over her evidence with her.

'You will be cross-examined severely,' he informed her. 'Try to keep calm. Answer their questions clearly and truthfully. Whatever you do, don't lose your temper!'

It was a long day and Maisie wasn't called. She walked home, a nervous wreck. As she clung to her father's arm she said, 'I don't think I can do this, Dad.'

'You don't have any choice, love. They will have you up for contempt of court if you refuse and you don't want that.'

The following day as she sat waiting, she saw Jack Winters walking down the corridor, escorted by two policemen. He spotted

Maisie and leered at her.

'I paid you back, you bitch! I hope they send you down.'

He was hustled away, but seeing him only made Maisie worse. She sat shaking from head to foot. Then, to her great surprise, she looked up and saw Ian and Kathy walking towards her. Jumping to her feet she flew into her sister's arms.

'Kathy, I'm so scared!'

'Now come on, this isn't like you. Where's that spirit, that bloody-mindedness we know so well?'

Annie and Wilf came over. 'What are you two doing here?' Wilf asked.

'I rang the office to see how things were going and they told me Maisie was likely to be called today. Kathy wanted to be here with her, so we came together. I may be called too, so I'm told.'

Maisie looked at her sister. 'You still wanted to come after what I did to you?'

'Looking out for you seems to be a habit,' Kathy said. 'Now come on, pull yourself together! How you give your evidence will help when it comes to you being charged. You've got to put on a good show. You know you can – you're the best actress I know!'

Maisie began to laugh. 'It is *so* good to see you. I'll do my very best, I promise.'

As Jack Winters walked towards the witness

box, he heard murmurs coming from the dock where Bert Smart, the men who were with him on the raid and Sonny Nolan were sitting. Winters didn't glance once in their direction, but kept his eyes on whoever was questioning him.

He told the whole story about the planning of the raid and how he'd messed it up, and named names. There was little the solicitor for the defence could do and eventually Winters was dismissed and sat in the court, handcuffed between the two officers of the law.

Then Maisie was called. She walked to the witness box, head held high.

The prosecutor questioned her first.

'You worked as a runner for Sonny Nolan, is that right?'

'Yes, sir.'

'What did that entail, please tell the court.'

'Mr Nolan would give me envelopes to deliver to different addresses.'

'Did you know what was in those envelopes?'

'Not always, but I did see him putting clothing coupons and petrol coupons into some of them.'

'Did he give you a parcel to deliver to Mr Smart on one occasion?'

Taking a deep breath to calm herself, she answered, 'Yes, he did.'

'Did you know the contents of the parcel?'

'No, I did not!' Her voice rang out. 'I was told by Mr Nolan that I was to make sure I only handed it over to Mr Smart himself.'

'And did you do this?'

'Yes, sir, I did, and I told Mr Nolan I wouldn't go there again.'

'Why was that, Miss Bates?'

She pointed to Jack Winters and declared, 'Because that man tried to molest me. He tried to drag me upstairs, but Mr Smart stopped him.'

'Were you acquainted with this man?'

'I met him at a dance and he walked me home. He tried to get fresh with me and I kneed him then ran away. He was livid and one night we met again at the Guildhall and he caused a scene, but then he was chucked out. At Mr Smart's house he said I was unfinished business.' She glared at Winters and thought, Tit for tat, mate.

'Why did you become involved with Mr Nolan?'

'Well, sir, he sold beautiful dresses but some were expensive, more than I could afford. When he offered me the job and said he'd pay me, I took it to save money so I could buy the dresses.' She smiled and added, 'I like to look nice, you see.'

'Surely when you did this you knew you were handling black market goods?'

'To be honest, sir, I didn't give it much thought.'

'When did you stop working for Mr Nolan?'

'Just after the robbery attempt on the bank, that man Winters caught me going to the shop in the Ditches. He threatened me and robbed me of all my money. When I got to the shop and told Mr Nolan what had happened and reminded him I had met Jack Winters at Mr Smart's place when I delivered the parcel for him, he told me to forget Mr Smart and the parcel and that I had ever been there. Then he told me never to go to the shop again.'

'Didn't you wonder why?'

'Not really. I was fed up with it all anyway. It was too dangerous. Some of his clients were a bit dodgy.'

'Thank you, Miss Bates.' The solicitor sat down.

Maisie waited with bated breath, knowing she was now going to be cross-examined.

'Miss Bates,' the defence started. 'Are you really trying to make us believe that you were only in this black market scam just to pay for a few dresses?'

'It's the truth, sir.'

'Well, I don't believe it for one moment. I think you were well aware of what was going on, that you worked alongside Mr Nolan knowing full well what you were doing and taking advantage of the opportunity to make a packet of money, like all racketeers.'

'You can believe what you like, sir, but I only made a few pounds. I had to save for weeks to pay for a dress. Twelve pounds over three weeks isn't my idea of making a packet of money.'

There was the sound of chuckles around the courtroom.

'I think you're lying about not knowing the contents of the parcel you delivered to Mr Smart. I think you were in on the whole plan to rob the bank!'

'I was not!' cried Maisie. 'How could you even think such a thing?'

'Why not? You delivered clothing and petrol coupons, knowing that was against the law. What's the difference?'

'There's a great deal of difference! Everyone is on the fiddle in a small way during these hard times. I bet you've got one on the go if the truth were known.' Annie hid her head in her hands in despair. 'But robbing a bank, now that's real villainy, and I'm not into anything like that!'

The solicitor continued to try to trap Maisie until the judge told him to move on, and Maisie was told to sit down.

The trial dragged on for two more days. Ian was called to testify that he had found the bullet at Sonny Nolan's shop which matched the gun used at the robbery. The guard who'd been shot gave his evidence and eventually Smart and Nolan and the other men changed their pleas to guilty as the evidence against them was overwhelming. Then the court awaited the verdict.

Bert Smart was sent down for seven years, his men for five. Sonny Nolan got a three-year sentence, as did Jack Winters. Maisie was called to appear a week later to face her charges.

Having heard the others sentenced, Maisie was in a terrible state. She asked Ian what he thought would happen to her.

'It's impossible to say. It all depends on the judge and how he views your case. The fact that you helped the police will be some advantage, of course, but other than that you'll have to wait and see.'

'I've been such a fool,' she cried. 'I thought it was a bit of fun, and I must confess I found it exciting.'

'Oh, Maisie!' said Kathy in exasperation. 'Will you never learn?'

'Believe me, I *have* learned. Jimmy said it was time I grew up, and now I have!'

But life wasn't as simple as that, as Maisie learned when she appeared in court and stood in the dock, listening to the ruling of the judge.

'You are a foolish young woman,' he said. 'Through your own vanity, you chose to ignore the law of the land, and although you were helpful to the police during their inquiries you cannot be allowed to walk away without punishment. I hope you realise that I could send you to prison.'

Maisie's legs gave way and she was held up by the two women warders standing beside her.

'However, because your evidence assisted the police, I shall take that into consideration. I am placing you on probation for nine months, but if you appear in this court again, I shall punish you severely.'

Maisie burst into tears.

Outside the courtroom, Annie cried and clung to her younger daughter. Wilf lit a cigarette to calm his nerves, and Kathy was comforted by Ian.

Wiping a tear away, Kathy said, 'When he said he could send her to prison, I thought she'd had it. My heart was pounding so much I thought I was going to pass out!'

'She was a lucky girl,' Ian said. 'That particular judge is very hard on sentencing.' He smiled at her. 'Now perhaps we can all get back to some kind of normality.'

Kathy removed her gloves to find a handkerchief in her handbag, and Ian saw that she wasn't wearing a ring. He led her aside, then took hold of her hand. 'Does this mean that you're no longer engaged?'

'Yes,' she said quietly. 'I broke it off on Christmas Day. It seems that Jimmy and

Maisie spent a night together at the Dolphin Hotel.'

'So that's what she meant when she said she was surprised to see you after what she did to you. Well, I'm not surprised you broke your engagement.'

'That wasn't the only reason,' she said quietly, gazing up at him.

There was something in her expression that made Ian catch his breath for a moment. 'And what was the other reason?' he asked.

'Maisie was drunk and she accused me of not loving Jimmy because I was in love with you. Jimmy asked me if that was the truth.'

Ian took Kathy's hands in his. 'And what was your answer?' he asked softly.

'I told him it was, that it was you I loved.'

'Kathy darling, you have no idea just how long I've waited to hear you say those words.' He took her into his arms and kissed her.

Wilf nudged Annie. 'Well, it looks as if those two are sorted,' he said with great satisfaction.

Ian eventually released Kathy and they walked over to the others.

'Mr Bates,' said Ian, 'will you let me marry Kathy?'

With a broad grin, Wilf pumped Ian by the hand. 'Indeed I will, son. Congratulations!'

'I haven't asked her yet,' Ian said.

'Well, what are you waiting for?' demanded Wilf.

Ian took Kathy's hand and said, 'Kathy Bates, will you make me the happiest man on earth and be my wife?'

'Oh, yes, I will.' And she flung her arms round his neck and kissed him soundly.

Annie and Maisie rushed forward to embrace them both. Afterwards, they all went across to the Polygon Hotel to celebrate with champagne.

Maisie held up her glass and said quietly to her sister, 'I'm very happy for you both. Ian is the right man for you.'

'Thanks, Maisie. I hope one day you'll find someone and be just as happy.'

## CHAPTER THIRTY-FIVE

On 6 May the news that everyone had prayed for came over the wireless. The war was finally over! There were massive celebrations all over the nation. Street parties took place. Women raided their meagre rations to make food for the celebrations. Trestle tables were set out; bunting flew over every building and across narrow streets. Bands played, troops marched and pubs were bursting with customers.

At the Civic Centre, crowds danced and sang. Strangers kissed one another, old differences were forgotten and spirits were high. The Bates family were among the hundreds gathered at the town centre.

Ian picked Kathy up, kissed her and spun her round. 'We'll be married in peacetime after all. Isn't that wonderful?'

Wilf and Annie were dancing and Maisie was jiving with a GI. It was a night filled with memories to last a lifetime.

July was a month of further celebrations for the Bateses as Ian and Kathy were to be married at St Michael's Church. Kathy was to wear a wedding dress loaned to her by her friend Joyce.

'I want you to wear it,' Joyce said. 'Your wedding day is so special and I want you to feel wonderful as you walk down the aisle.'

Kathy was thrilled, as the dress had been bought before the days of utility wear and was luxurious. The bridal headdress and veil they purchased from Tyrell & Green's. The headdress was shaped like a tiara and made of pearls with diamante which sparkled in the light.

Maisie was to be the only bridesmaid, wearing a dress made from an evening gown they had found at Annie's WVS shop. The pale blue suited Maisie's blonde colouring perfectly.

Annie had splurged her coupons on a frock and matching coat in a deeper blue, with a smart straw hat and accessories in cream. Wilf had his one good suit cleaned for the occasion.

As he said, 'It's as good as new because I've hardly worn it. I will buy a new trilby, though.'

The sun shone on the morning of the wedding. The ladies of the house were getting dressed in their finery, ready for the great occasion: Annie calm on the outside but inwardly nervous, Maisie fussing about her hair, and the bride deliriously happy and being assisted by her good friend Joyce, whose husband was home at last.

Kathy stood up and faced her friend. 'What do I look like?' she asked nervously.

'Absolutely beautiful! Your dad will be bursting with pride as he walks you down the aisle on his arm.'

Annie swept into the room. She was talking as she came through the door until she saw her daughter and stopped mid-sentence. 'Oh, Kathy love, you look stunning. I could cry.'

'For God's sake don't do that, Mum, or we'll all start,' Kathy begged.

'I came to tell you the first car is here, so Maisie, Joyce and I will be off. I'll see you in church.' She kissed Kathy and said, 'Be happy, darling. You've chosen the right man for that.' And she left, leaving a scent of lavender in her wake.

There was a tap on the door and Wilf came in. 'You look amazing,' he said proudly. 'Shall we go downstairs? The car will be here any minute.'

As they stepped out of the front door to go to the vehicle, the street was lined with well-wishers, all cheering and calling out their good wishes. Pedestrians waved as the beribboned car started to move away.

'Everyone loves a bride,' said Wilf as he waved back. 'I feel like the bloody king sitting here and you, my girl, look fit to be the queen.'

At the church, the sound of the wedding march began as the bride arrived and was led down the aisle. Waiting nervously, Ian stood in the front pew with Tim Taylor, his best man. They both turned to look at the bride.

'You are one lucky devil,' Tim said with a grin as they stepped out to meet her.

The reception at the Court Royal Hotel was a happy affair, with Tim giving a hilarious speech, telling the guests of the days when he and Ian trained together, and the strange things that happened to them during their early days spent on the beat.

'Now, of course, he's older and wiser. He's

a marvellous detective, but more, he's a man of integrity. I was honoured today to stand by him as his best man. He will make a fine husband for his lovely bride – but if he fails in any way, Kathy, report him to me and I will see he gets sent down to serve his punishment.'

He sat down to great applause. Ian rose to his feet and, looking round the room, thanked everyone for coming to share the happiest day of his life. Taking Kathy's hand in his he said, 'I am a very lucky man to have found this lady and I will spend the rest of my life looking after her and making her happy. A night in the cells will not be necessary, thank you, Tim. I have already taken on a life sentence, one that I will serve willingly.' He thanked both their parents and those who had generously given wedding presents, before sitting down beside his bride.

'I love you, Mrs Harvey,' he said as he kissed her.

'I love you too. A policeman's lot isn't that bad, is it?'

He laughed delightedly. 'No, indeed, it really isn't.'

Later in the day, the guests gathered outside as the newlyweds drove off in a taxi to catch a ferry to the Channel Islands, where they were to spend their honeymoon.

As they walked up the gangway, Ian turned to his bride and asked, 'Are you a good sailor, darling?'

'I don't know. I guess we'll soon find out.'

'I hope you are, because I would hate to think I've wasted money on a cabin!' he teased.

'What a terrible thing to say!'

'There is one other thing I'm worried about,' he admitted.

'Whatever is that?'

'How the hell am I going to carry you over the threshold of a cabin? Have you seen how narrow the doorways are?'

Kathy started laughing until the tears rolled down her cheeks. 'You are such a fool!'

He too was laughing. 'Oh, Kathy darling, we are going to have such a good time together. Come on, let's go to the bar and celebrate.'

Taking hold of his hand, Kathy Harvey went with him, certain that this would be the first of many celebrations in their years together.

Back at the reception, the gaiety continued, but a short time later Annie found Maisie sitting alone, smoking a cigarette and deep in thought. Sitting beside her daughter, Annie removed her hat.

'That's better. What's up, love?'

'I was thinking about Jimmy Greene,' she said. 'You know, Mum, I really did love him. It wasn't a crush; it was much more than that.'

'He took advantage of those feelings, though, didn't he?'

'Not really. If I'm honest, I threw myself at him, but although I think he was fond of me in a funny way, it was always Kathy he loved. He told me so.'

'So in the end neither of you got what you wanted, did you?'

She shook her head slowly. 'No, we both missed out.'

'You know, Maisie, I believe in fate. Although it was dreadful, Kathy being raped brought her and Ian together and he was the right man for her. You being in court and on probation has taught you a lesson, and your father discovered he couldn't play fast and loose and keep his family. We've all been through the mill to bring us to this point in time.' She stroked Maisie's hair. 'There's someone out there for you, darling, you just have to be patient.'

'It won't be Jimmy Greene though, will it?'

'No, it won't. He wasn't the one for you.'

Maisie threw away her cigarette. Getting to her feet, she found her spirit. 'In which case, I'd better start searching for him now. That could be fun!'

'Oh, Maisie,' Annie exclaimed, 'I don't

think you'll ever change, and – surprisingly – that makes me really happy!'

The two women returned to the reception and an uncertain but hopeful future, having learned that life has a habit of sorting itself out.

The publishers hope that this book has given you enjoyable reading. Large Print Books are especially designed to be as easy to see and hold as possible. If you wish a complete list of our books please ask at your local library or write directly to:

**Magna Large Print Books**
Magna House, Long Preston,
Skipton, North Yorkshire.
BD23 4ND